HER LAST SUMMER

NINA MANNING

Boldwood

First published in Great Britain in 2024 by Boldwood Books Ltd.

Copyright © Nina Manning, 2024

Cover Design by Head Design Ltd

Cover Photography: Adobe Stock

The moral right of Nina Manning to be identified as the author of this work has been asserted in accordance with the Copyright, Designs and Patents Act 1988.

A CIP catalogue record for this book is available from the British Library.

Paperback ISBN 978-1-80426-588-8

Large Print ISBN 978-1-80426-589-5

Hardback ISBN 978-1-80426-590-1

Ebook ISBN 978-1-80426-587-1

Kindle ISBN 978-1-80426-586-4

Audio CD ISBN 978-1-80426-595-6

MP3 CD ISBN 978-1-80426-594-9

Digital audio download ISBN 978-1-80426-592-5

Boldwood Books Ltd
23 Bowerdean Street
London SW6 3TN
www.boldwoodbooks.com

In loving memory of Mark Parker. You are gold.

PROLOGUE

The water is so cold it takes my breath away. And then in the place of my breath, is an image. An image of him as he watches me struggle.

I'm not ready. I'm never going to be ready.

Voices are echoing around me; I'm hitting ripples of waves but I'm not sure if they're trying to embrace me. I am gasping for air now, breathing in and out no longer comes naturally. I'm bobbing up and down, the waves carrying me. The horizon appears and disappears, and she is there, but I cannot reach her. Time was deceptive. I felt I could hide behind it, but it's fluid, never stopping to allow me to come to terms with anything, to seek repentance. I had vowed I would never get back into the water, but of course, this was always going to be the outcome. I never really had a choice.

My focus begins to get hazier, and the memories start to pound at me, hitting me hard with every pelt of wave. Voices are louder but I can't speak, I can't shout, I can't ask for help. Just like it was all those years ago, I feel helpless, powerless to what is happening to me.

Hands on me, under my arms, I am being lifted and pulled. I land in a RIB boat, faces staring at me, talking to me, asking, telling, 'You will be okay, Rey, we've got you now. You're safe.'

But they don't know, they don't understand, that keeping me in the water was the only way to keep me safe.

1

NOW

The air was so thick and dense, the room so hazy I could barely make out the body in front of me. But I knew they were naked, and because the sun was coming up, I knew I stayed the night. The bong that the man was sucking on was filling the air around me with plumes of smoke and I half closed my eyes so that he was completely gone, and the smoke became clouds, and I was in the middle of them, floating. I was wrapped up in their fluffiness and I felt warm and protected. Like the way he made me feel last night. But the night gave way to morning as it always does, and I wanted to move to find my way home, but to do that would also bring with it reality. There was some slow trance music playing low and the smoke was clearing. He was making his way over to me on the bed. He put his arm across me and kissed me. He tasted of last night's alcohol and tobacco.

But I was not the girl I had allowed myself to be last night, I was someone else. I was everyone. Yet I was no one. I shuddered at his touch but not in the wanting way I did last night. I kissed him back then I sat up. I heard his soft voice coaxing me back to bed, but I needed to be gone. I needed to get up and prepare myself for whomever I would be today. I don't know who I am, yet everyone knows who I am.

I asked if I could borrow his hat and scarf to hide my face as I prepared to leave his house. He nodded and told me he would call me later. But I already knew I would not answer and he like everyone else would go on to tell their tale of their experience with the actor Rey Levine, how she was cold and non-committal. How she was wild one minute and shut off the next. I thought about these things, but I did nothing to change them. I didn't ask anyone for help because I didn't know if there was anything wrong with me. I thought everyone felt this torn-up version of themselves unless they were drinking or taking drugs. Or if they were acting. Then they could be anyone. But I couldn't act and be drunk perpetually, so I was left with this fragmented empty shell that I was forced to inhabit most of the time. It was what it was. It was all I knew. And it was now.

I left the man's house before dawn. He was not a stranger. I knew *of* him. He's in the 'industry' and if you're in the industry you're all a little messed up and so we just use one another. That is what I told myself. But I knew my demons, where they came from and how they grew and grew and became so entwined inside me that I couldn't wake up for even one day and think that I was a capable, loving, person who in turn deserved to be loved.

There was a dark shadow that followed me wherever I went. I could never escape. It was forcing me to remember, but when I tried to reach for the memories, I hit something hard and solid and could never reach them.

Outside in the street, people were milling around everywhere because every day is market day in Camden, and it was summer. There was a mist in the air and the sun was creeping into the sky, etching the edges of the grey a hazy yellow and I knew it would be a good day. I knew I needed to feel grateful for what I had, for what I had become, but I could not forget. She was everywhere; in the wind, in the rain, in my dreams and nightmares. Some days I could feel content enough to believe she was just in my imagination and that I only ever had one younger sister, not two. But then I felt her all over again. And I knew she was real. I lived each day with the memory of Corsica and the night Franny left us. I knew I did something terrible, something wrong. I knew this was all my fault – somehow in many ways and not just one. It was often like a reel playing on repeat. And when I saw it and felt it all over again, I thought about what I could have done to have made it better. And I wouldn't have done what I did. That one terrible act, a rash decision of a desperate teenager. I was older and supposedly wiser. But I lost her. Forever. I was only left with fragments of memories of who she was, that I must cobble together each day to remind me she was once real. She did exist. It was her face that greeted me every morning and said goodnight to me every evening. I woke up in a stranger's bed sometimes because I didn't want to keep being reminded, I didn't want her to haunt me. Yet when I tried to forget her, like last night – and I was able to forget her – I woke up the next morning laden with guilt. I apologised profusely to her – silently in my head. I'm sorry. I just needed a night without you. And then she was back, begging me not to go, telling me to stay. And every single time, I went. And every single time she was not there when I returned.

2

NOW

The phone ringing through a hazy half-dream stirred me and I rose, too quickly, making me light-headed. I grappled on the bedside table and found the phone, but I ended up nudging it, so it fell to the floor with a heavy clump on the reconditioned floorboards. The ones I'd had done six years ago when my career was just flourishing, when I was an actor that everyone was beginning to recognise and I could no longer leave my house without sensing that someone was watching me, or even secretly filming me with their camera phone. These last few years have been quieter. I could say it was my decision, but things spiralled. She, Franny, eventually got the better of me. It was inevitable; I have been hiding from the pain since I was almost seventeen. The last film I had been in, I behaved so badly on *and* off set that the job offers dried up afterwards. The work I was offered beyond that, I had considered beneath me, when in hindsight, I should have taken the roles. I had overthought it. I presumed I was being punished for my behaviour and I let myself slip into a downward spiral of negativity. The job offers were the sort of things I had done before and would have served me well, given me back that scrap of reputation that I needed and so badly craved.

I knew that the call would be from my agent. She was, after all, the only person who called me at ridiculous hours of the morning – aside from my mother, but it was even too early for a call from her. She usually reserved the voice-to-voice until she was well and truly lubricated. Gin being her drink of choice. She would begin around 10 a.m. meaning that by midday I was on her mind, either as someone to lay into because all the emotions from the past were high and intense. It had been a few weeks since I had heard from Mum. I was due a call.

By the time I found my phone, it had rung off. It had been my agent. It was just after 9 a.m. I had been asleep for a mere few hours, having collapsed into my bed after completing the walk of shame. Sylvie would be leaving me a message as I lay there, telling me that I needed to get up, start exercising, and maybe think about my career, maybe post something on Instagram. Show people that I am still alive, that I have a fire burning within me. I could almost hear her voice anyway without the need to dial into the voicemail. *Rey, I assure you, the work will come back in. You're not a failed actor, nor an out-of-work actor. This is simply a quiet period.*

A quiet period that had lasted nearly two years were the words she would never say to me. But I felt them, in the same way, I felt the expanse of time that stretched between the last job I did and now. I thought about that last gig, the three-part drama series. A thriller. I played the sister of the killer who had known what he was doing all along and chose to protect him. Before that, there had been a small part in *Dragons*, a film that did well in the UK and worldwide and gave me recognition. Before those, other films, mainly British. I had landed my first job at twenty-two. It had been nine years of solid acting then... nothing.

I got out of bed, pulled on a hoody over my vest top, stepped into the kitchen, flicked on the kettle, and squeezed cat food from a pouch into Freckle's bowl.

I put the radio on, leaving it tuned into BBC 6, and went about searching for food for myself. I had skipped dinner last night and opted instead for a line of white powder up my nostril, an amuse-bouche to the array of drinks which had followed and were the catalyst to falling into the arms of... I don't remember his name. I knew he was working on a TV drama, and I think at one point I may have begged him for a role.

I am lucky that I purchased this basement flat early on in my career or I would be, quite frankly, screwed. Freckle had come into my life four years ago, a present to myself after a particularly messy breakup. Not the only messy breakup, just one that had managed to mess with my already pickled brain. Despite being a basement flat, it is massive, and the kitchen/diner front room gets a good amount of light from the huge window. And I often take myself upstairs to the small patio area I had embellished with some potted plants that, despite not knowing anything about gardening, I have managed to keep alive for several years. It is quite the little oasis. I made a coffee and took myself up there, settled myself on the reclining chair, and contemplated the day ahead.

I heard my phone ringing again and I ignored it, choosing instead to close my eyes and soak up the mid-morning sun. It was early June and it had rained solidly for three days. Now it was bright and warm, and it was giving me life. London, especially Camden in the summer, was all I ever needed to survive, to get me through another year, despite the background noise in my mind. The constant chatter, the constant what-ifs and regrets. The face of my sister. So small. So precious.

The phone rang again. I put my coffee down and walked back down the small flight of steps to the back door that leads into my flat and headed for my bedroom. Someone who calls three times in a row must have something important to say and if it is my agent again, then maybe, just maybe, it is finally a job. God knows I had waited long enough and God knows I needed the money more than ever. My bank balance, which had looked healthy a few months ago, was dwindling, and I didn't like the measly figure that showed up whenever I logged onto Internet banking. The phone cut off just before I reached it and when I checked, Sylvie's name was there again. My agent needed to speak with me. I called her back immediately and she answered, almost breathlessly and my heart began to soar a little at the prospect of this being the beginning of something and then I stopped myself. It could be a meet and greet, a few measly thousand; it could be another talk show offer. I knew by now not to get my hopes up.

'Sylvie,' I said when I heard her pick up.

'Rey.' There was excitement brewing in her voice, I could hear it even as she uttered that one syllable. 'I have news.'

I took a sharp breath in and waited.

'I have a job. An actual job. A film.'

I let out a breath. 'Thank fuck,' I muttered not necessarily to Sylvie. The relief, if it was a perfume, would be palpable and would have spread across my bedroom by now.

'The film already has quite a buzz around it. They're already talking about awards.' Sylvie paused for reaction.

'Okay.' I allowed a flutter of excitement to bubble up inside me.

'The production company is Expanse. You've never worked with them before. They had someone who had started working with them already, but she's pulled out, so they asked for you. And...' Sylvie took a deep breath. 'They spoke about the last film, the breakdown.' Sylvie said the word as though she had just gritted her teeth. I hated the way she referred to it as that, especially in that tone. I went a bit off the rails, delayed grief, shock, whatever you want to call it. A breakdown didn't sound right, it felt ancient, like something that I heard my parents discussing about people they knew. A breakdown to me was a middle-aged man, once confident and powerful moping around in their dressing gown, drinking their best brandy in the middle of the day and shouting across the lawn at the postman, a mass of unshaven and unkempt hair. That was not me. I had upset some people, said some things I should not have said, not to their faces at least. And I drank. And I smoked and I took drugs. The drinking and drugs was much less than it once was, I was still doing a little but at least I was more focused now. I still thought of Franny every day, she was still ever present, but I was not staring into the abyss any more. And I believed Sylvie that the work would come back in. I had always believed her. And now it was. But why were they questioning the past for goodness' sake?

'And I assured them,' Sylvie continued, 'that it was a family matter and you have sought help, you have been working very hard on your...' She paused to think of an appropriate word, then plumped for 'Yourself. Which you have!' she added. 'You've been very quiet.'

'That's because I haven't had any work.'

'I know, which is why I am here now, telling you that you have. I just want to know you're okay and up for it?'

I paused for a moment. I didn't want to rush in with a high-pitched 'I am!' which would sound unconvincing.

'I'm fine, Sylvie. Really, I am.'

I heard her sigh with relief, and I congratulated myself on my mini performance. Had it escaped her mind that she was managing an actor?

'Okay. Well, one more thing, and this should cheer you up, they have already confirmed Dexter Rice to play the lead male.'

There was more silence from me. Dexter Rice. To say I had dreamt about working with Dexter once or twice would be an understatement. I had already worked with a few of the great

British actors, but Dexter was a young breakthrough star, had already bagged several blockbusters under his belt, and was now by all accounts making the very stylish and highly recommended move for someone in his privileged position – to a lower-budget indie film. This was everything I wanted to hear and more.

'But I haven't auditioned?' I suddenly added.

'I know. I know. But I am confident that the part is already yours. They have specifically asked for you, Rey. They loved your performance in *Cry Baby*, they know you are the one for this part. Of course, you'll go along for a read-through, but I am almost 100 per cent sure this is yours. It was in their tone of voice. I was on a three-way conference call, Rey! Two of them were in LA. That never happens. Like ever.' Sylvie's tone was increasing. I could imagine her sitting in her home office, the door firmly closed, blocking out her husband and three sons. This was the only time she ever got to herself when she was working, sitting at her desk and to be able to deliver such high-class news was what made the job worthwhile to Sylvie. She was in her little world in that room, moving and shaking and changing people's lives and the face of British and worldwide cinema from a small office in a four-storey terraced house in Richmond upon Thames. It amazed me and I was in awe, despite being out of work for almost two years. I wasn't her only client of course, and as she had assured me so many times, my time would come. And she was right. It had.

'And this is the beginning of it again, Rey, I promise you, once you have this film under your belt you are well and truly back in the game. There is no doubt about it. Okay. Now, we have some work to do to make sure you get this role. I suggest coffee, at our usual haunt on Monday. I'll bring the script.'

I blew out a breath 'My God, Sylvie, I can't believe this is happening, it's been so long. Like so long. I've forgotten what to do.' I laughed.

'And that's why I'm here, listen I need to get out and see you, get away from all the savages I live with. We'll go through everything and prep you good and proper.'

'Thank you, Sylvie. I know it's been a long time coming and I am truly grateful, I just honestly thought people were going to demonise me for those things I said and the way I was around that time. I just want to move on and for everyone to move on with me.'

'And they will, sweetheart. And I am sorry it's taken so long. It's the way of the business though. Fits and spurts. But we're on an up now so let's keep riding that wave and keep you on the screen for a good while to come.'

'I can't wait to see the script. What's the basic concept?'

There is rustling of paper from her end, and I imagined her putting her glasses on and nosing through the document in hand. 'It's a sort of family saga, set in the eighties, a drama with a bit of a romance. A woman returns to the Highlands for her estranged father's funeral only to discover a whole host of things have been going on in which he was involved and which she now finds herself drawn into, so ends up staying for an extended period. You're a closed character at first, you're not happy to be there. Dexter plays a local fisherman who was scorned by your father and so takes an instant dislike to you but later that relationship does blossom into something more. That, I am afraid, is all I know. But due to the location, it proves to be an absolute cracker in terms of cinematography, and because you're technically estranged, you only need a very soft accent, if at all, you've been in London for the last decade and so lost it. Or chose to give it up.'

'Brilliant, I love it. It sounds exactly what I need to get my teeth into.' Suddenly images of Dexter and me in a clinch were all I could see. And not just on screen. I shook them away. This was not about me, or my needs and desires, this was about getting Rey Levine back out there as an esteemed actor, ready to receive all the awards.

'Anything else I need to tell you...' Sylvie's voice was strained; I imagined her pouring over her notes. 'Potentially a slight accent, happy to spend time in Scotland,' Sylvie sang out the requirements more to herself than to me. 'Oh, and a strong swimmer. There will be some sea swimming required for the shoot. I hope it's not too cold up there for you.' Sylvie laughed.

The whole world froze.

This is all your fault.

I grappled for something to lean on, but there was nothing close by. I fell towards the window sill and leant my weight against it, suddenly I felt heavier than I thought I could ever be. My stomach felt as if it had fallen right through me, I imagined it as an empty cavernous space. My mouth was dry and I began looking around for a drink. Usually there was one next to my bed but today an empty glass sat in its place. I had a sudden recollection of drinking the water from the night before last before I fell into bed this morning, my head a fuzzy mess as though my brain had been hacked out and replaced by cotton candy.

'Swimming?' I heard myself say eventually. 'Will they not get a stunt double for that?' I laughed and tried to make it sound real, but it was pathetic even to my own ears.

'Oh, I wouldn't think so, it will be you they want to film in the water. Nothing stunt-like, but...' She paused to read again. 'It does say here "would need to be a strong enough swimmer to do several metres in the ocean". That's not a problem, is it? I should have asked, sorry; I presumed everyone can swim.'

'I...' I tried to speak but my mouth had well and truly dried and my throat began to feel scratchy. I was probably going to come down with something. Too many late nights. Too many bad substances. Images began to swell through my mind, and I tried hard to use the same techniques, to mentally push past them the way I had so many times before when they had reared up so quickly and fiercely. But already I could feel the darkness pulling its veil over me. Images came at me one after another. I could barely make out who or what they were. I finally found myself back in the moment with Sylvie. How could this have happened? Why would they want me to swim? How can I tell her that I can't do it?

'Rey?' Sylvie's voice pierced through my thoughts, dragging me back to the horrible realisation that I was being asked to do something I didn't, no... couldn't do.

'Swimming's not an issue, is it? Like I say, I forgot to ask and I just presumed...'

I breathed in deeply and silently let out the air. 'Not a problem, Sylvie. None at all,' I lied without any more thought. I could already see my career drifting away from me and I couldn't let that happen. I needed to hold onto whatever opportunities came my way. I would deal with the swimming thing. Of course, I could. Maybe they could find a double if they really wanted me.

'Great.' She sounded relieved. She could probably see her well-earned commission disappearing before her eyes. I'd had her worried there for a moment and she had sensed me stalling. I couldn't let Sylvie or anyone else down any more. Acting was what I was born to do and I had fucked up too much already. This could perhaps be my last chance. My absolute fucking comeback movie.

'So I'll see you Monday then? About 10 a.m.?' Sylvie said.

'Perfect, can't wait. I'll see you then.'

I hung up the phone and collapsed onto my bed, still clutching the mobile in my hand. I was shaking, my insides whirling like a tumble dryer.

I pulled my phone close to my face and began searching for the stories, the ones that I had read a thousand times already. I had saved them all on my phone, just a hit on a link, and I was in. Thrust back to my early days as an actor, when the press had set upon me like a pack of wild animals, dredging up any story and unable to believe their luck as they feasted on the tragedy of a little girl lost in Corsica; the same little girl who was my little sister.

The Levine family were holidaying in Corsica when the youngest daughter, Franny went missing. She has never been seen since.

I recollected the tired and panicked face of my aunt and how the police were there until the early hours. It had all been such a whirlwind. She was there one minute and gone the next.

Eventually, I sat up and took a long deep breath and took myself over to my mirror in the bedroom where I shook my head at my reflection. What did I do to deserve this? Two solid years of no work and then the opportunity of a lifetime comes along, and I must swim to do the job.

I thought about how long it had been. Fourteen years since I had even dipped a toe in the water, a swimming pool, or the sea. I even hopped over puddles in the street as they seemed to elicit the same fear in me as greater pools of water. And all because of her. Because of my little sister, Franny.

I took myself back up to the terrace to sit on the bench, the sun was once again warm on my face, but I felt cold all over. I needed that job. Damn it, I wanted that job.

I knew I was terrified of ever having to get back into the water and that was what I should be most scared of. As soon as Sylvie mentioned what I needed to do, I felt the familiar fear that I had been trying to hide from for years – that the water now scared me. But as I scratched past that fear, I could sense something else, something that was disturbing me even more. It was murky, it was dangerous, it was lurking in the darkness and it was coming to get me.

3

NOW

Monday couldn't have come quick enough. I had spent the weekend trying to distract myself enough not to have a total meltdown but also trying to find a solution to the problem. There was just no way that I could accept the job when I had to swim. I was going to put it to Sylvie today that this was what needed to happen: I would consider walking into the water, and then they would need to get a body double to cover any actual shots of me in the water. If Sylvie was right and they wanted me as much as they said they did then surely there would be some wriggle room.

Sylvie was already seated in a booth in our favourite cafe when I arrived on time. Her laptop was out in front of her, surrounded by piles of paperwork; one bundle I recognised as a script and my heart began to beat so fiercely I was sure that was what alerted Sylvie to my arrival and not the clicking of my heels on the floor.

Sylvie rose and kissed me, slipping back into her chair and straight into agent mode.

'Now, the script has arrived, so I need you to get familiar with it ASAP. There is already a lot of hype around this film; the locals have already started to kick up a fuss, some good, some bad. The good being our lovely Dexter, the bad being they feel the exposure to the area could be too much, the film company will ruin the untouched natural beauty, blah blah. I get it, I get it!' Sylvie threw her hands up. 'But, my darling,' both hands landed on mine, 'the buzz doesn't end there, there will be so much hype about you returning to the screen and my God I am so excited for you. This is exactly what we needed and more, and you've not even read it yet. But as I said, I think Expanse wants to go through the formalities, see you read, but they've pretty much made their mind up. Just please go there and blow them away.' Sylvie paused for air. 'Do you need a drink? Let's get you a drink.'

She raised her hand to a passing waiter and then looked at me for my order.

'Oh, latte. Large.'

The waiter nodded and walked away.

'You look amazing, by the way.' Sylvie rummaged through her piles of paper without glancing at me. This woman was permanently in overdrive mode.

'Now this, I believe, is yours.' Sylvie picked up the whopping great script and handed it to me. 'They had it specially delivered over the weekend. They've highlighted some of the parts they feel would be good for you to focus on for the read-through.'

Sylvie leaned forward, her chest resting on the table, her chin almost touching the surface.

'This is it, my girl. This is what you've been waiting for. The big rebrand, the great comeback.' Her voice was low and slow. 'Now, I sense some hesitation, which is perfectly understandable. You have been out of the game for a while, things change, and the industry has changed again, even in such a short space of time, believe me, I struggle sometimes to keep up. But I have your back all the way, I'm your agent, that's my job. So, do you want to tell me what's eating you or do I presume we have a deal? Because once they hear you read, they will want to hire you for this job. So, Rey, this is your chance. Tell me now. Are you in or are you out?'

'Of course I'm in!' I said in such a way that I even convinced myself. The words I had planned to say to Sylvie that would see me backing out of the swimming scenes were quickly swallowed down. Because I couldn't say no or come across as wishy-washy. Sylvie was laying herself out on the line for me, I had to show that I was willing and ready in every way.

'Thank the Lord!' Sylvie sang. 'Because honestly, Rey, if you had have ducked out of this one after so long off the screen, I would have not been happy,' she said sternly. Then she grabbed my hand. 'But you've made me so happy!' Her voice was a complete contrast, happy and sing-song-like.

'Well, I'm happy that you're happy!' I raised my eyebrows and tried not to think about the virtual impossibility, which was me, getting into the sea after so many years.

Later on when I left the café, I was feeling a mixture of emotions, but underneath all of them was pure terror. I had put myself in an impossible situation. And there was no way out of it except lose the job.

I walked the long way back to my flat, taking in anything around me, conversations between strangers, birds in trees, trucks rushing past, trying to distract myself, unsuccessfully. I found myself outside my local leisure centre. I hadn't stepped inside a gymnasium or health club ever. Not since I had been a child.

Funds were still tight until filming began so it would be unwise to take up a private gym membership.

I walked through the double glass doors into a badly lit foyer, the echoes of small children screaming through the corridors and in the cafe to my left sent electric shocks through my body.

'Can I help you?' a young girl in a tight green polo shirt with the logo of the centre embroidered on the chest was looking at me, expectantly.

'I...' I looked past her, to see if I could see the information I was looking for. 'I'd like to become a member.'

* * *

Fifteen minutes later I had filled out a form and a direct debit mandate and a plastic card was handed to me.

'Looking forward to seeing you soon,' the girl called after me. I wondered if she was on commission with all the happy vibes she was putting out.

'No, I do not want to see you soon,' I muttered to myself as I left the club. It was obvious that the young woman was itching to get back to her colleague to tell them she had just signed up Rey Levine. She had done a double take when she saw my name on the application form. I was already wondering if it was a bad idea to use a public space to get myself back into the water. Even thinking those words made my stomach lurch. Private gyms were a waste of money in my opinion, when all I wanted to do was swim. Even though, ironically, the last thing I wanted to do was swim. I wasn't prepared to part with almost a hundred a month to do a few laps. This was the best way; I could go in early when no one was around. I would wear a cap and goggles, and no one would recognise me. I had managed to some degree to effortlessly sink into the fabric of Camden life, a melting pot of cultures, a heterogeneous collection of men and women who filled the streets and cafes. Where I lived in Camden, everyone looked famous whether they were or not.

I had done what I needed to do. Now I just had to prepare for the read-through and cross my fingers.

* * *

'Oh my days, Rey. They loved you. I mean, really loved you.'

The call from Sylvie that I had been equally hoping for and dreading came a day after the reading. I hadn't expected to hear back so soon. I was relieved the wait was over, but now the real work had begun.

'I'll send you all the dates through, but the schedule is broken down throughout the year and is already behind because of the dropout. It was Shaya Falks by the way.'

'I had my suspicions,' I said, but I had been googling like a mad thing and scouring her social media and I had asked around a bit. I bet Shaya Falks would have no problems getting into the sea. But the rumours were she was pregnant and the schedule would have been too gruelling for her. But what about me? It was not just gruelling – it was clearly not even going to be possible, and I was just coasting along with it all right now. I didn't feel anything over the fact that I had taken Shaya's place, because she was never going to be the one for this job if she was growing a human. It was always meant to be me, and I had already convinced myself that she would not have done nearly half as good a job as I intended to do. I had to focus on what was good about this and not about the one thing that was terrifying me and could potentially ruin me and my career.

'The idea is to get up the Highlands asap, get as many sea shots done before the water turns too cold. Not that it's going to be that warm anyway my love.' Sylvie laughed almost demonically, and I shuddered, wishing I could laugh along, wishing that the bitterly cold northern sea was my only problem. 'Then get you back up in the autumn for the land shots.'

'Thank you, Sylvie. You're the best.' I ended the call knowing I was truly grateful but also knowing that I was completely and utterly terrified.

Yet that wasn't always the case. I *had* loved the sea; I would run to it as though it had been calling me. It was my safe place, yet I feared it the way one feared something which was stronger and more forceful than them. It enveloped me within its waves, yet it could harm me at any time. It was that dichotomy which I experienced each time I was in or near the ocean.

My mind jolted as a darker force tried to punctuate my thoughts. My head felt hollow, as though I were floating. Terror gripped me like a vice, and I felt paralysed. The darkness was coming for me. I knew it was related to the sea, yet it was at the same time unrelated. This inexplicable fear that was not just about getting into the water began when I took the job. It was something far more terrible.

The sea was one thing I thought I could never live without. Until one day, I could.

You should never have been in the water.

The words come at me. Words from my mother. I thought I was such a good girl. Always doing what was asked of me.

You should never have been in the water.

The night I went into the water was the night I never saw Franny again.

4

CORSICA, JUNE 2008

'What a jolly spot.' Mum tried to stand still but I could see her swaying. She had started drinking on the plane and as Dad was the designated driver when we landed, she hadn't stopped until we reached the villa.

'It isn't jolly, Flic, it is...' Dad paused to think of the word: 'resplendent.'

Mum walked past Dad and grabbed his shoulder, more to keep herself upright, I was sure.

'Of course, Digby. You're right. The way the sun is hitting the terracotta roof, it seems to be sending an array of colours across the ground.'

'Terracotta is dull, Flic; it does not reflect light.' He shrugged my mum's hand off his shoulder and carried on walking towards the front entrance. Travelling was not my dad's best pastime, but he liked the destination. I felt the same familiar grind in my gut at the words my dad used, he had stopped using his nicest words for our mother a long time ago. I wondered how she felt when these verbal blows came at her. Was she numb to them now? I wanted to sidle up to her and say, 'Hey, how does it feel?' I too knew the absence of my father's attention. How he used to save all the good words up for me, which would spill out of him like a waterfall, and I would be waiting at the bottom, ready to be drenched with loving phrases and compliments. But I was older now. I had opinions, I voiced how I felt about most things. I saw the way my father flinched when I spoke. Did he feel threatened by me? I wondered. I wasn't the innocent little girl I once was. Did I scare him with my knowledge and wisdom of the world? Those books that he kept in his library, that he thought would only be for him, had passed through my hands in record speed. I was the very living, breathing Roald Dahl's Matilda. 'I've created a monster,' I once heard him joke as I recited some facts about the history of Greece when we travelled there with some of his oldest friends. They had laughed whole-heartedly, not understanding that there was perhaps real meaning behind his words. He had glanced at me with both longing and concern. At sixteen, I was almost an adult in their eyes. I was no longer the little girl. Dad had retreated from me when he saw me grow into a woman. He wasn't sure how to deal with women, it seemed.

The sun scorched my skin where I stood, I felt sweat pooling in my lower back. Mum would be looking for a drink as soon as we got into the villa, I could already imagine a crystal glass, gin or something similar over rocks of ice so cold the glass was wet with condensation on the outside.

But as I waited outside in the relentless heat, my body became rigid, not wanting to move towards the front door. A family holiday was supposed to be a happy event, one to remember forever. But already, I knew this was not going to be so.

My two younger sisters, Scarlett and Frances, or Franny as she was known to us, ran ahead, but just before they did, Dad placed a firm hand on Franny's shoulder. I saw the way he pressed his thumb into her shoulder blade a little, a little physical warning to take it easy. To not run too quickly. Or maybe he was trying to hold her back from growing up too soon, the way he had tried to do with both Scarlett and me. Franny too would grow, but for now she was small, she was young. And she was his favourite now. She was the one he wanted to spend time with. Scarlett was tall and looked as though she could be a teenager, but she was only twelve and a very young twelve at that, but she had started to develop breasts and was increasingly embarrassed about it. She still acted like a little girl and quite often was happy to be treated like one. Always torn between wanting to be older like me and fuelled with envy at the attention her younger sister got. I never envied her middle-child status. Franny was six and as fierce as a lioness. We were all blonde and blue-eyed, and lean. When we were all much younger and Franny just a baby, I remember how people would stop and look at us, as though we were an artefact in a museum. They would study us, as though they couldn't believe we were quite real. I often looked at them for far too long, trying to see right into their eyes, into their souls, so they would see into mine. Wondering what their lives were like, their homes, their relationships with one another. *Were they like me?* I wanted to ask them. The words would form in my mouth, teeter on the edge of my lips, then Mum would grab at my arm and pull me away, a small laugh to hide her embarrassment.

'Come on, Rey, keep up, girl. Come and see your cousins, it's been over a year. They will be dying to see you,' Dad called over his shoulder but didn't stop to help me carry my backpack or the heavy suitcase that I was struggling to get across the paving stones that led up to the villa.

My cousins who had lost their father three years ago. I had no idea how I was supposed to greet them, what I was supposed to say to them. I knew I would not receive any guidance from my parents. My foot slipped out of my flip-flop and heat seared my skin.

I tugged at my suitcase, over the stones which were all a little uneven, so the wheel kept on catching.

Mum's head moved slightly as though she were checking on me, but then she wobbled on ahead and into the open arms of Dad's sister, Vanessa, at the front door. I watched the way Vanessa held my mum briefly and then looked her up and down, assessing her condition, already ready to step in and take charge when she was needed. Which she would be. But it was my aunt who needed taking care of. She was the one who had lost her husband and this was the first time we had all been here together in three years.

Aunt Vanessa clocked me and came running to assist me. I felt a swell of relief, and also happiness. I craved the affection and attention she gave me. She had always been there for me, even when my uncle Rob passed from his unexpected heart attack. He was only fifty. No one saw that coming. He was a man of great stature, and power, ranked highly in the police force. I was never sure what rank exactly, but my father always seemed a little intimidated by him. But not me. I only felt at ease and calm with Uncle Rob. Especially here in Corsica. Corsica had been our time, mine and Uncle Rob's. Of course, he shared himself with everyone, but when you had him all to yourself it was as though you were the only two people on the planet.

Vanessa had been distraught and in mourning ever since he had died. No one would ever replace the man who had been the love of her life. No one could ever replace the man who made me feel so safe and protected.

'Rey, darling, let me help you with that.' Vanessa threw one slim, tanned, athletic arm around me and kissed me fiercely on the cheek, the Chanel No. 5 she habitually wore, clung to my already clammy skin.

'Welcome to Corsica, my darling girl. I hope you've been paying attention in French lessons this year; I want to hear you rolling your tongue.' Vanessa laughed and I looked at her inquisitively. I hadn't seen her in almost six months since she'd been in London on a business trip, and she had seemed sullen then. But this Vanessa was shinier. Sunnier. Maybe it was simply the weather, but already I had a feeling that had begun to spread through me. Something was different. I could sense it in her. She had brought whatever change had occurred outside with her to greet me and I could feel it as though it were a living thing.

'It's so nice to see you.' I spoke into her ear just before she released me.

'And you too dear. You know you're my favourite niece.' She smiled and took the handle I had been using to drag the case and lifted it easily to her slim waistline and marched ahead with it. I did a little horse-like skip and caught up with her.

'Well don't tell the other two,' I quipped, continuing our tradition of greeting, this little charade had been running for a good few years now, even Uncle Rob had played along when he'd been alive. I felt a surge of panic in my gut rise up to my chest. He wasn't here. This holiday was not going to be the same.

'I tell them all the time.' She winked. 'Now, I've put you in the back room, away from all the raucous. You know how things get when we've had a shandy or two.' She was referring to them as a collective, but we both knew it was my mother she meant. She stopped at the doorway and propped the suitcase up. I looked at the sweat beads lined up along her brow.

'That way, you can get your beauty sleep can't you?' She stroked my cheek with the back of her hand and gazed at me. I knew I was more than a niece to Aunt Vanessa; I was like the daughter she never had. Vanessa had two sons, my cousins, Faren and Cormac. They all lived in Dublin now, to be closer to Uncle Rob's family and came out to this villa two or three times a year. Except Vanessa had barely been out here the last few years, since Rob died. And certainly not with all of the family. That was why this was such a special occasion. We were all together again after so long. We would all dance around the absence of Uncle Rob. My father too tight-lipped and British to say anything that would bear any real meaning and maybe mark the occasion with some sort of joy; my mother too drunk and careless with her words, undoubtedly already geared to say the wrong thing. My sisters too young, too silly and into themselves to even notice his absence; and the cousins, the cousins who had lost their father at such a tender age, well, I had yet to see what effect that would have on them and this holiday. I wondered if Vanessa was ready to begin to celebrate life again and if being here on this trip was as much about that as soaking up the south of France sun and practising our French.

'And I have put all your favourite dollies in there, the ones you loved to play with all of those years ago. My God, I could never stop you. Every time I asked you where you'd been you would tell me playing with the dollies. Do you remember?' There was an urgency in Aunt Vanessa's voice. The image of the dolls appeared in my mind; a sickly feeling stirred in my gut.

I touched my aunt's arm. She had become so skinny since Uncle Rob died. She was desperate for things to be normal, for us all to follow the narrative, and show the world that we were all just one big happy family. Except we were all alone out here.

Completely unobserved.

'Yes, Aunt Vanessa, I remember,' I said and I saw her face soften a little.

At the door Vanessa's French housekeeper for many years was waiting to greet us.

'Jolie!' Dad was chorusing. 'It's so good to see you.' He made a show of kissing her then promptly dropped his bags at her feet.

Jolie gave Mum a quick hug and then moved over to me.

'My goodness, you grow so quickly. How did this happen?' We

kissed our hellos and Jolie looked me up and down. 'It has been too long.'

'Jolie.' I held onto her hands long after our kisses.

I took the suitcase from Vanessa; I was now able to manoeuvre it across the marble floor of the villa.

The cousins were called and arrived promptly to greet us, in an awkward gangly manner. Faren was fourteen, Cormac would be turning seventeen soon. He had grown tall and muscular like his dad had been. Having their three female cousins come to stay for a fortnight was far too embarrassing for them. I spared them any further blushes.

'All right?' I said simply.

'How are ya?' they said, I noted a hint of an Irish accent which hadn't been there before, seeing as they had only moved there after their father's death.

We were all congregated in the large hallway, Mum clinging onto her nephews a little too hard, when a man appeared in the doorway that led into the drawing rooms.

'Hello.' He spoke softly in a British accent. He was tall, lean and his skin a golden brown, wearing only a white T-shirt and faded blue shorts. He looked about Vanessa's age, in his early fifties, and instantly I knew. This was what was different about my aunt and it was this man. I didn't even need him to introduce himself or for Vanessa to say anything to know they were an item, that he was the reason she was back in her villa, looking and sounding a little bit like her old self.

'Everyone, this is Wallace.' Vanessa was suddenly at his side. Her arm had slipped behind his back and his arm rested on her shoulder. She looked perfectly cosy there, tucked up under his armpit. 'Wallace and I have been spending time together recently, so I asked him to join us on this trip. I hope you'll all make him feel welcome.'

'Oh, Vanessa dear, this is wonderful.' Mum clapped her hands together, releasing the cousins, who saw their opportunity to edge away.

The room felt too warm and too packed.

'Sis, you kept this very quiet.' Dad's voice was low and monotone. I felt my body stiffen at his tone, it held a warning, and I sensed Vanessa heard it too. But she seemed to bat it off. He approached Wallace and held his hand out. 'Digby.'

Wallace reciprocated and the two men shook hands firmly for a few seconds.

'Good to finally meet Vanessa's big brother. I have heard so much about you.'

I watched the interaction with intent, and I became entranced with Wallace's eyes. They were a bright blue, almost like the French sky and ocean itself. He had locked eyes with my dad and wasn't going to look away first. Dad did not match Wallace's enthusiasm, but he did look away first. My father who stood at almost six feet, suddenly seemed so much smaller standing next to Wallace.

'I think this calls for a drink. Where's Jolie?' Dad looked around, unable, it seemed to look at Wallace again.

'Oh, leave Jolie, you know what she's like, she'll want to have all the luggage upstairs, come, I'm perfectly capable of making a round of drinks.' Vanessa walked into the drawing room, and we all followed. The room was often used at the main congregating area even though there was also a formal sitting room. I looked out the French doors, which led onto a patio and the pool. There was a mini bar in the corner and Vanessa went straight up to it.

'What are we all having, après spritzers?'

'Oh yes, sounds wonderful. Let me help.' Mum squeezed herself behind the bar and Vanessa did her best to work around the extra body as if it wasn't an inconvenience. The cousins flopped on beanbags, followed shyly by my sisters.

Franny began to perform in her innocent way, not even knowing she was entertaining and both cousins were silently impressed with her, I could tell. She was a doll and could hold someone in the palm of her hand without even trying. I didn't want to see that side of her fade to nothing. Like I knew it would. Because it had happened to me, and I had seen it happen to Scarlett.

Suddenly the cousins were laughing loudly and pointing at Scarlett. She had flopped on the beanbag and was pretending to slide off. It was something she had been doing of late. Attention seeking, our mother called it, and on this occasion, I had to agree with her. Being a middle child was proving difficult for Scarlett. She had changed so much since Franny had been born. Now she resorted to this tomfoolery for attention. And it had worked. I watched her get herself up from the floor, a peaky colour in her cheeks, grinning at her audience.

'It's dark and stifling in here, Vanessa, let's get some of that Mediterranean breeze flowing through.' Dad walked over to the terraced doors and began fiddling with the catch. 'Let me see my beautiful family – have you seen how beautiful they have got, Ness? It's been so long; you must have missed them,' Dad said and I was suddenly hot and desperate for the doors to be open. That left me and Wallace standing next to one another. He looked down at me, a tight-lipped smile forming.

'Rey is it?' he asked quietly.

I nodded, unable to speak or acknowledge this man who had stepped into my uncle's shoes, so suddenly and without warning.

'Bet you're glad to be back in Corsica. After all this time.' The pause between the two sentences made me feel uneasy. The way he referred to that passage of time between Uncle Rob dying and him standing next to me made it seem as though it was nothing and that him being here was always going to happen and there was nothing any one of us could have done to prevent it.

I looked up at him and felt myself grimace. My skin suddenly felt cold and prickly, despite the searing heat in the room –I could hear Wallace's breath, loud and disturbing next to me. I could smell something that was part deodorant or aftershave, part sweat and my stomach began to feel hollow. I had been terribly sad when my uncle Rob had passed, but I had never missed him as much as I did right then. I wished for him to return promptly, for things to feel as they did. For him to make me feel safe. At least when Uncle Rob had been here, I had two adults, him and my aunt Vanessa who were like parents to me. They made me feel whole and that was all that mattered. I watched Vanessa behind the bar with my mum, being as accommodating and patient with her as she always was, as Mum tried to be helpful, but I could see she was spilling liquids and laughing to cover up her mess. Then Vanessa looked over, and flashed a huge smile, which I thought was for me, then I felt Wallace's body shift and turned to see his face light up. The smile was for him. Why was she smiling at him, couldn't she see this was not the man for her? Couldn't she smell him from there?

It was then I felt as though I were having an out-of-body experi-ence as a pounding in my ears began and then grew louder and louder. My body convulsed. I could hear Dad still struggling with the doors, muttering expletives, and rattling at the frames, Mum's forced loud laughter from behind the bar, and the whining voice of Scarlett as one of the cousins goaded her. My armpits sprinkled with sweat. I looked at Franny, sitting sweetly and quietly. Calm and unaffected.

It was all out of my control. This holiday was going to turn into a nightmare. Suddenly an overwhelming desire to charge at one of them, any of them overtook me so fiercely, that I just had to run. I hurried from the drawing room and into the hallway where we had all been gathered moments earlier, when everything had been fine, when there wasn't a man pretending to be my uncle waiting in the doorway, ready to ruin my life.

I headed straight to my room, but with a conflicting notion, I was seeking solace and safety although I wasn't sure I would find it there. When I got into my room, my case was already there next to the bed, delivered by Jolie. And just as Vanessa had promised, there on the shelf in the far corner of the room were six dolls. Soft bodies with malleable arms and legs, all different sizes. All dressed in pretty frocks, with braids in their hair. My stomach twisted at the sight of them. Yet at the same time, I felt a familiar ache for them, a sort of sorry feeling. I walked over to the shelf and stripped them naked, then I began manipulating their little bodies into positions. By the time I had finished it looked like a doll orgy. I left them where they were, limbs entwined with one another but when I returned to my room later that night the dolls had been relieved of their positions and laid out just as they had been, dressed again, all lined up neatly next to one another. No one would mention it, and I would not say anything about how they always somehow magically ended up back that way.

5

NOW

I glanced through my phone and there I was. A photo of me snapped about a year ago, in Soho when I was shopping with the girls. I was thankful that I looked good. It was one of those shots, where they had caught me off guard and I didn't look haggard. I was wrapped up in a scarf, my hair neatly dyed a dark brown, one of the many shades and styles of hair I was experimenting with during that time when I was doing everything and anything to escape myself, what was going on inside. I was wearing sunglasses and I had just turned around and bang, they snapped me. My mouth was half open as though I was saying something. But overall I looked good. I had forgotten about this photo. I zoomed in and held the shot between my fingers as I observed my skin and hair, appreciating how good I looked considering I had been abusing my body with all sorts of alcohol and chemicals most nights.

Rey Levine to star with Dexter Rice in Highland saga.

I liked the sound of that headline. These were stories I didn't mind. It was good publicity. I should post a link to it on my social media, though. I was sure my followers would go up as they always did whenever I got a new job and it had been some time.

The front door opened and there was a scuffling of shoes and a loud, 'Hello!'

'In here!' I shouted from the sofa in the open kitchen-diner.

'I can't believe you got the job, you lucky bitch.' My best friend, Tammy arrived in front of me, her arms outstretched, yet laden with brown paper bags stuffed to the top with what looked like gourmet delights. She promptly placed them on the dining table and fell on top of me. She smelled of cigarettes and her Versace perfume, an undertone of something coconut – perhaps her expensive facial products.

She kissed me all over my head and both cheeks and I laughed and pushed her away. She propped herself up next to me on the sofa and flicked her dark hair to one side. It always managed to stay where it was for a while after she had done that. I wasn't sure whether it was a product she used or maybe it was just natural, but it looked annoyingly good all the time.

Her nose was pierced with a gold ring which elevated her to a status of cool that was way beyond anything I hoped to reach, even in this small world we called show business. Tammy had bagged a BAFTA award for her role in a series about a girl in the eighties who was born as the wrong gender and battled against her family, the medics and the state for a sex change. She wasn't just my friend; she was someone whom I aspired to be.

'Dexter Rice? I mean, hello!' her voice sang out around the room.

'I know. What can I tell you,' I said picking my phone back up where it had flipped out of my hand after Tammy jumped me. Tammy walked over to the table and began removing delicious looking dips, breads and cheeses.

'He's a total shagger you know.'

I presumed Tammy was still talking about Dexter Rice.

'Is he now, and how would you know?' I asked with intent because Tammy had been in the industry longer than me. She hadn't just lost two years of her life to unemployment; Tammy Murray was still grafting away. She had just finished a comedy series in America where she had been living for the last eight months.

Tammy was now rifling through her handbag and began applying a bright red lipstick.

'I said, how do you know?' I said louder and with more intent.

She clicked the lid on the lipstick and dropped it in her handbag. 'Duh, I lived in LA, it was common knowledge.'

'Right. But you weren't ever witness to these countless shags?'

'Ergh, no, it wasn't like that, I wasn't into orgies, Rey.' Tammy squealed.

'That was not what I was implying. I'm saying you can't just go spouting stuff about people if you don't know the truth. Especially in this industry. God, Tammy, don't you know how damaging that can be?' My heart was pounding hard. I wasn't sure where the outburst had come from.

Tammy raised an eyebrow at me. 'Are you nervous about the shoot?'

I didn't need to think too long to answer that question. I was nervous beyond anything I had ever felt before, but telling Tammy was futile. Trying to explain my fear of water to her would simply open a portal to a world I had closed a long time ago. Tammy knew that my sister had gone missing in France, but I had not expanded on it any more than that for a good reason. There was only one other person who knew what happened that day in France. So although I knew I would never have to reveal to anyone what had happened, I still wasn't able to let go. As much as I didn't want to get back into the water, I was also hoping that by some miracle it could be the thing to cure me of this burden of guilt.

'A little,' I lied. 'I guess I'm feeling a bit rusty, that's all.'

'It's like riding a bike,' Tammy quipped. 'Besides, you are a natural. That's why you're so good at it, that's why you're still working.'

'Just about,' I spat, and Tammy looked at me, she dropped her shoulders and her head tilted to one side.

'Listen, everyone has at least one bloody breakdown in their life. It was quite spectacular the way you did it, actually. Very rock and roll I thought. Don't—' she pointed at me '—be ashamed of who you are. What happened is part of you. Just own it, yeah? Besides, you're back now and you have Dexter Rice by your side. Has he like texted you or anything yet?'

'No, why would he have texted me?'

''Cos you so fine and he be lucky to git you!' Tammy ripped into a southern American accent she had been using for her recent role.

'That's cute. But I need to focus on nailing this job, not—'

'Nailing Dexter Rice!' Tammy exploded into laughter. But images of Dexter and I began forming in my mind until I was staring hard at the wall, soaking up everything my imagination was throwing at me.

'Hello?' Tammy's voice pulled me back into the room.

'Well, that wasn't quite what I was going to say, but sure. Must not try to nail Dexter Rice,' I said like a mantra, hoping that I could handle my own objectives. I needed this film to represent me as an actor again, not someone who slept with their co-star.

Tammy looked at me for a moment and then her eyes widened. Then the accent was back.

'Oh, you in trouble, girl.' And we both exploded into hysterics.

My phone let out a ping, an alert for a news report. I looked back down at my phone. It was hard-wired to show me celebrity news and gossip over anything else due to the algorithms. And I was used to seeing the occasional papped photo of me like the one I had just seen this morning. This was all good press. Sometimes, there were posts or a little piece about what I was wearing or who I had been spotted out with. It was all cute and harmless. I had once been the epitome of a British actress, living in London, keeping myself out of social media enough so I didn't piss anyone off. Until I wasn't. But just then, in front of me was an image so familiar that it hurt my chest to look at it. I must have omitted a sound of some sort, as Tammy glanced around.

'Everything okay?' Tammy turned back to what she was doing.

'Erm...' My left hand was partly covering my mouth when Tammy looked around again and this time, she abandoned the goodies and flopped down next to me.

'What is it, Rey? Let me see.'

Tammy held her hand out and I passed her the phone, but I still wanted to see so I leaned over her as she stared at the photo that accompanied the news story. The headline read:

Missing sister Rey Levine's biggest role to date.

I felt my stomach churn. The photo that accompanied it was the photo taken on *that* evening. Of my father, with all three of his girls. Hours later, everyone would be searching for Franny, and no one would be able to find her.

I read the sub-heading moved onto the text that accompanied it.

A family holiday ended in tragedy.

Actor Rey Levine was just sixteen years old when her sister went missing on what was to become their last summer away as a family. Levine was thought to be away from the family holiday property on the evening when Franny Levine, just six years old at the time, was allegedly taken from the villa. Despite an extensive search and a case that lasted almost three years, Franny was never found. It was known that Levine had left the villa that evening with her elder cousin to attend an unlicensed party on the beach...

Tammy sucked in a breath and shook her head. I stopped reading at that point. I just couldn't go on.

I couldn't move.

The gut wrench of guilt.

Waves licking my arms.

This is all your fault...

The wretched darkness that was threatening to engulf me.

I sucked in air as though I had been underwater.

'This is sick. I mean, where did they even get this stuff from?' Tammy spat.

Journos would go to the depths of depravity to collect the info to get a story, but this was easy fodder to them. It was all out there at their fingertips. But even as we both stared at the screen, I was wondering the same as Tammy. But not where they got the info from, but who would have given them such a detailed account.

I thought of all the people who had been on that final trip. I spoke so rarely to any of them, and others I had never seen or heard from again. Including Wallace and my aunt Vanessa. I received little communication from my father.

'This will blow over,' Tammy told me. 'Again,' she added with an eye roll, and I wanted to believe her but although I heard her words, they wouldn't stick. Because reading this news story, all I could think was that it was there for a reason. The fabric of the past that I believed was tightly woven was still being picked at the stiches, and maybe, just maybe, it was all finally going to come apart, revealing everything that we were and were not as a family.

Later that night when my phone rang, I was already in bed, getting an early night, bracing myself for my first swim in the morning. I didn't need to think too hard about who it might be. It was almost as though she had her own ringtone in my head.

I hesitated to pick up it up as I always did. A flurry of emotions worked their way through my body, starting with immediate guilt for even considering not answering, to frustration, anger and finally sadness. The last emotion was always the one that accompanied me as I picked up.

'Mum.' I breathed out the word.

'Rey,' she battled back. Then she let out a sigh, a prelude to whatever was coming next. I knew she would want to talk about the headlines, but she would want me to mention it first. 'Is it raining there? It's raining here.' She asked absently now. I noticed she had become a lot more so in her ways recently. Absent. She sounded tired. And when she wasn't tired, she usually sounded ratty. It had been too long for her; I knew time was now taking its toll.

I looked towards the window; the blinds were partly closed. 'No rain here, Mum.'

'Honestly, I don't know why I moved here sometimes, south of France in the middle of summer and not a scrap of sun all day.'

Could never coming home really constitute moving somewhere? It was the narrative that Mum used no matter who she was talking to. Even her own family, who was so aware of what had happened, of what staying in France had meant to her. How she had abandoned the rest of us for her mission. Her desire to be near to the last location that her daughter had been seen.

'Well, it's not raining here, Mum.'

'I know, I check all the weather reports.'

I imaged my mum sitting in her two-bed apartment in Corsica, overlooking the sea, with nothing much to do all day except buy groceries for one and check her phone for the news and weather.

'Have you thought about coming home? You know, the annex is still there.'

Mum spat out a laugh. 'I don't need to live in my ex-husband's garden.'

I wanted to say the 'ex' part wasn't entirely true. You needed a divorce for that.

I had been trying to convince my mother to come home for years, that her mission was futile. That she should be moving on with her life and not holding onto this notion that her youngest daughter was just going to walk into the local village one day and everything would return to normal. I thought about the odds of that happening and I saw Franny as the young woman she would be now.

I took a moment before I spoke again. This time I almost whispered the words. 'It's been fifteen years, Mum.' There was a hint of desperation in my voice, not just to point out how long it had been, but maybe that time might have healed a little. That I wouldn't ever have to hear those words again. That this was my fault.

She sighed again and I could imagine her turning her head away even though I wasn't in the same room as her.

'Time, time, time,' she muttered. 'It's all you ever talk about. I want to be here, Rey, has that ever occurred to any of you?'

I thought about Mum, the socialite when I was a child, every dinner party, every soirée took it out of her. I knew she was never in her natural habitat then, that she forced herself to be the woman that my dad needed her to be, but the place she was in now, as beautiful as it was, she was alone except for the ever-present memories of a life that had once been, living in limbo, forever suspended in a holiday that never came to an end. I often thought of her like the characters from *Dungeons & Dragons*, a show I had heard of but was too young to have seen it. The characters were trapped inside a game and couldn't get out. I felt this about Mum. She had created some sort of endurance test, yet she had everything she needed to set herself free.

'I suppose you've seen the news story,' I said, cringing as the words left my mouth. I didn't want to talk about this now, not ever.

'Well of course I've seen it, Rey. The whole of the town is talking about it. This is all because of you, you know.'

'What?' There it was again. The blame.

'Flaunting yourself. You just can't help it can you, you always had to be the centre of attention. You always were a little—' Suddenly, my mother's voice faded away. I was not sure what that final word was going to be, but I could guess.

Another voice came on the line.

'Hello. Rey?'

It took me a moment to try and place the voice, the soft tone. The French accent.

'Jolie?' I spoke.

'Yes, Rey, it is me. I am here with your mother.'

'So I see. Hello, how are you?' It had been so long since I'd heard Jolie's voice, my gut ached with nostalgia, and I felt a sadness welling up through me.

'I am good, thank you, Rey. Your mother, she is a little, shall we say, puffed up.'

I knew she meant riled up or something to that effect.

'What are you doing there?' I asked and then wondered if that had come across as rude.

Jolie cleared her throat and went quiet; I heard a muffled sound and the breathlessness in her voice as she spoke.

'I am just walking to another room, Rey.'

I waited a moment and Jolie began talking again, clearly this time.

'That is better, I wanted to leave the room, so your mother could not overhear our conversation. She is with the television now.'

'Okay,' I said inquisitively.

'I bumped into your mother in the town a few months ago. She had been unwell.'

'Oh.' I felt a stirring in the pit of my stomach, this was not going to be good news, I knew.

'Yes, she had been unwell for some time, and so she went to the doctors, and she was sent for tests.'

My mouth was dry. For everything that I thought of my mother, I did not wish death upon her.

'She has a dementia.'

I wanted to correct Jolie's grammar, but I stayed silent and let the reality of her words sink in. My mind was already awash with questions. Like how could she have dementia? She wasn't even sixty years old.

'When I saw her in town a few months ago, we got talking about the past.' Jolie cleared her throat, and I wondered what part of the past they had discussed. 'Your mother ask me if I am working and I was not, so she asked if I would come to work with her at her flat. I ask her if she need a housekeeper and she told me she need a carer.'

'Okay,' I said, as a way of asking her to continue.

'She has declined quite rapidly I am afraid and I had thought she had contacted you all to tell you but today when I see her reading the news on her tablet, I ask and she say she had not told you, so forgive me for interrupting your phone call but I thought that you should know. Her health is in decline. She is saying things, some things that do not make sense.'

'Like what?' I interjected.

'Oh,' Jolie sounded caught off guard, 'so many strange things, she is forgetful, and clumsy, but I suppose the one thing that stands out the most is talking about Franny.'

I waited another beat for Jolie to continue. 'She says that Franny is better off where she is.'

I held my breath, not wanting to reveal any emotion to Jolie. It had been such a long time since I had seen or spoken to her. I had been sixteen the last time I saw her, on the cusp of adulthood, but still really just a child. Now we were two adults talking as though we had only spoken last week. It was too much for me to comprehend on top of the news of my mother's illness.

'I guess people say all sorts with this kind of illness,' I said eventually.

'I agree. I haven't paid any particular attention to anything she has said. It is very sad for me actually.'

'I understand, Jolie. I appreciate you taking on the role for her at this stage, and after everything we all went through. It must be very difficult.'

'So you are not to worry. I will take care of her the way I took care of all of you for so many years,' Jolie said in an earnest way. She would never try and brag about how she dedicated her summers to just being there for all of us and never complaining once.

'That is mighty good of you, Jolie. I presume you have agreed some sort of remuneration already, I mean before she began to deteriorate.'

'Yes, I am being paid for my services thank you, Rey.'

We spent the next five minutes discussing the medical side of my mother's condition and how she was being treated, when she was being seen by the doctor and so on. Once we had covered all of that, I felt much better that things were in hand. I could carry on with my work and know that things were in control. It was still a shock and one that seemed to have come out of nowhere. My mother had mostly been a beacon of light amongst people, even though she found it difficult. But she had never been a good enough mother to me. That I had known since I was young girl. And then after that, I had endured years with her blaming me. I wasn't sure if it was the drink that had done this to her, but it couldn't have helped, and for all her faults, for all that she had done and hadn't done for me, I still felt that she did not deserve this.

'So you will call again? And I can call you? To tell you how your mother is and if she becomes worse then maybe you can come to see her.'

I flinched at the prospect of flying back to France, to being near to where it all happened.

'Sure,' I said and we finished up the call with me promising to be back in touch in a few days. But already, the thought of seeing my mother at the lowest point she had ever been, was crazy. I still saw her as this glamorous party host in my mind, waltzing from room to room in her beautiful dinner dresses. Always a different one each time. Her wardrobes were packed solid with dresses of every shape and colour. I wondered if they were still there, or if my father would have disposed of them, the way he had disposed of everything of Franny's. The shock of that had nearly killed me. It was as though he had erased his daughter from his memory. Every picture, every item of clothing, every toy. All gone.

Disappeared in a second, just the way she had.

6

NOW

The alarm didn't wake me at 5 a.m. as I had set it to do because I was already awake. I looked around at the stark room I found myself in. I hadn't meant to stay so long. A late-night text session that ended with me leaving my flat at almost 11 p.m., taking an Uber five miles away to have an impromptu drink with a guy who had been pursuing me for months. I had been batting him away; the initial sexual attraction just wasn't there. The call from my mother, which ended with me speaking with Jolie after so many years as she delivered the staggering news, had sent my mind into a catastrophic cycle of self-punishment. How all this was somehow my fault – the way I had always been told – Franny's disappearance which had led to my mother living in a permanent state of stress, as though she were on a knife-edge, waiting and waiting and waiting. I had initially thought that her drinking would have been the catalyst to any poor health but then I realised it could have been nothing, or it could have been everything. I had gripped my phone as these self-sabotaging thoughts poisoned my mind and I found myself scrolling. I saw an image of the man appear in my Instagram feed, he looked different to how I remembered. More tanned, fitter. I went back to the texts we had exchanged a month or so ago, which I had allowed to fizzle out to nothing, and sought to re-light that flame he had started. He was online, and within minutes we were flirting outrageously, fantastical images rushing through my mind of the two of us together. He didn't need much convincing when I offered to 'pop in' for a nightcap, claiming I would be passing his house.

He took my mind away from things as I had hoped he would, but after he fell asleep and I lay there in the dark, listening to the unsettling sounds of a stranger as they slept, it all began to come back to me. And before long, the darkness was all consuming.

Eventually I must have fallen into some sort of fitful sleep, as the dreams were vivid, and I woke with a start as though I had been flipped over in my bed. I knew I had been dreaming of the water. I felt as though a weight was pressing hard on top of me and I tried to move my legs, but I couldn't feel anything. Perhaps this was fate, perhaps I had developed some sort of paralysis. If I could just reach my phone, I could call Sylvie and tell her the film was off. Then an image of the figure on the screen of my internet banking flashed before me, and those words printed about me in the report yesterday. As the night began to give way to day, I thought of my mother. The way she still treated me as though my life had not changed exponentially since I became Rey Levine the actor. She either refused to or didn't know how to make any reference to the work I did and the impact it had on my life and the lives of millions of others. To her, it always seemed as though nothing had changed. Perhaps this film might be the one to turn her head, for her to show some interest in me and my life. I longed for it yet disregarded it at the same time.

But for now, something more important was happening.

Today was the first day in a long time that I was going to swim.

Getting up in a stranger's house somehow felt easier than it might have done if I was trying to get up at my own flat.

I made it home in an Uber wearing the baseball cap I had stuffed into my bag the night before. The driver looked at me a few times in the rear mirror. My Uber account had been red hot this last year or so. They knew who I was, and most likely what I had been doing. But despite that I still tried to hide from what had been happening, and what I was fast becoming. And I was sure very soon become known for being.

The sun had started coming up already, so when I walked out of my flat an hour later, I wasn't expecting to see anyone. A man was crouched by a car just outside the flat. He was holding a huge camera.

Snap.

Instantly I thought about the Uber driver. The way he had seemed too preoccupied with me and I knew that he had informed the press that he had just driven me home. With the news story of Franny and our last holiday in Corsica fresh in the papers, I was obviously a hot topic and currently worth a few quid in column inches.

I put my head down and walked as fast as I could, but he was following me, that was for sure. For what reason? He had his damn shot. I headed up the street towards the market hoping I could lose him there but also to give myself some protection. I knew a few of the vendors there and they had pushed away a few paps for me in the past. No questions asked, and so as I edged my way into the market I began to feel the protection of just a few of them, an early morning delivery van and a few people opening their units.

By the time I arrived at the leisure centre I took one final glance behind me and saw that he had given up. I took a moment to breathe, I didn't want to arrive flustered or even appear so. But then suddenly he was there, snapping me in the doorway and instead of walking away – which I should have done – I pushed at the door. It was locked. I reached into my pocket and took out my phone. It was just before 6 a.m. They hadn't opened yet. I leant my head against the door, not wanting to turn around and face the fact that my life was about to be played out in front of the world.

Snap. Snap.

Damn it, I pushed my head away from the door and dropped it as low as I could, trying to make myself as small and as invisible as possible.

Snap.

The baseball cap was covering the top half of my face, but my taut and strained expression would be shown and that was what they would home in on. Not many readers would put this photo in perspective, at least not immediately. I would just be a miserable celebrity looking pale and pissed off.

I felt and looked like a cliché and the hat probably drew attention to myself even more. They didn't suit me. I don't know why I continued to opt for them. I supposed it was because I felt slightly more protected with one on. I wanted to turn and run back to my house, and I was just working out which way I would run, to confuse the photographer when the door began to open, and a tall dark-haired man stood there. He looked behind me at the photographer and grabbed my arm and yanked me inside the leisure centre. He locked the door behind me. I couldn't look at him and my head reached his chest. He was wearing a name badge: *Lloyd*.

'Are you okay?' he asked, bending down to see my face as I kept it down, not so much as in shame but out of habit.

Finally, I looked up.

Our eyes locked and I was momentarily stunned, transfixed by the darkness of his eyes.

'I'm used to it.'

I watched as he clocked who I was and his expression changed from concern to recognition. Here we go, I thought. One small act of kindness followed by a torrent of questions. He'll probably ask for a selfie. I wished that I had joined a private gym.

He had a northern, possibly Yorkshire twang to his voice. Despite my encounter, I felt soothed by his tone.

'Let's get you a cuppa.'

I glanced at him, waiting for him to move on, show me through the turnstile, wish me well with my swim. But he was still looking at me, waiting for a response and I realised he was serious. He was genuinely offering me a cup of tea at six in the morning.

'Our regulars don't get here until seven, so what will it be?' he asked again.

'Erm, coffee?' I said questioningly. He turned and went into an office behind the desk.

'Come through, tek a pew.' Then he turned and grinned at me. 'Hey, I'm a poet but I didn't know it.' He let out an infectious laugh and I felt my insides lift.

'It's only a naff machine mind, not espresso or owt.'

I followed him behind the counter and into a small office. The walls were painted a harsh green. The colour hurt my eyes.

'Sit down,' he said, 'you're allowed.' He tapped his badge, a hint of irony in his voice 'GM. I mek the rules.'

I smiled, though I felt more than a little awkward. I was barely awake. I had slept for approximately twenty minutes, and my mind was reeling with everything I hadn't managed to process yesterday. I probably still smelled of the man I had just been in bed with less than an hour ago. I had already decided as I lay there in the early morning light, that I would not be seeing him again. I had been hounded by a pap and now I was about to have tea with the general manager of my local leisure centre. All before 7 a.m.

I slipped into a chair as he was fiddling with an archaic-looking coffee machine.

'I'd say you need a coffee after that,' he called over his shoulder.

'Yeah, sorry about that.' I finally found my voice.

'Na, it's nothing. I've had to fight them off myself a few times, I've told them I'm not Zac Efron, but they won't have it.' He continued to fiddle with the machine until it omitted a squeal and then a whistle. Lloyd looked at me.

'That noise is good by the way. It means we're in business.'

He arranged two mugs under a spout and very slowly dark brown liquid trickled out and the air around us was filled with freshly brewed coffee.

Lloyd placed a filled mug down in front of me.

'Milk?'

I shook my head. He put his coffee on the table and took a seat in a decrepit upholstered chair.

'Me mate had a coffee shop few hundred yards down the way. It closed its doors for the final time last year and this was goin' begging. So I snapped it up. It's pretty grotesque, teks up half the room, like.'

He took a deep breath and looked at me. 'You okay now?'

'I am. I told you I'm...' I was going to say I was used to it again, but I didn't want to talk about myself as an actor. 'I only popped in for a swim.' I took a sip of my coffee. It tasted almost as good as it smelled.

Lloyd cocked his head back in surprise, his finger pointed downwards. 'What, here?'

'Yep.'

'Oh, crikey, sorry, I thought that pap had just corned you in the doorway and you were looking for somewhere to escape. Now I've got you in here drinking coffee.'

'No, no it's fine.' I cradled my mug. 'There's no rush. I'm not overly keen to get in there anyway.' I glanced out into the foyer.

'You'll have the place to yourself. Until at least seven. It's a good time to come.' He sipped his coffee. 'If you're looking for a bit of peace and quiet,' he added knowingly.

I nodded. 'Thanks. This was really good of you.'

'Don't go telling everyone, mind. They'll all want to get back here and sample my wares.'

I laughed, surprised by how he was making me feel. It wasn't just the coffee that was warming me up inside, Lloyd's kind words and demeanour were a welcome distraction from what I had already experienced so far this morning.

We looked at one another, I expected Lloyd to say something else, to make another quirky comment or joke, but he was silent, and then he looked away first.

'I should get on.' I stood up.

'Tek that with you if you like. Just don't tek it poolside, or you'll have me badge removed.'

'I won't.' I stood still holding my mug. 'And thanks. This was very kind of you.'

Lloyd walked me to the turnstile where I pressed my card to the infra-red spot next to it. I pushed myself against the bar, but nothing happened. I looked at the light which hadn't turned green. I let out a sigh.

'My card won't let me in,' I said.

Lloyd tutted and took my card and walked it over to the counter. He tapped away on the keyboard. 'Oh yes, it was Cheryl who set you up...' He continued to look at the screen, squinting and clicking. 'And for some reason she didn't...' He trailed off. He moved his mouse around, clicked a few more times then handed his card back to me. I realised maybe Cheryl had no clue who I was after all.

'That should be sorted now.' He walked back over and handed my card back to me. 'Miss Levine'.

I felt my body flush with heat. 'Thank you.' I pressed the card, this time easily making my way through, but with the tone of

Lloyd's voice ringing in my ear. I wondered, as I did with most people I met, how much he knew about me.

It could be apparent to anyone who had followed my work on screen that I hadn't been actively working and now here I was in a public leisure centre saving myself a few quid a month. I didn't feel like some other actors who just manage to pick up job after job, with no obvious breaks in-between. I remembered what Tammy had said yesterday – that I needed to own my past and not let anyone make me feel bad for what should just be part of who I am. But I knew that no matter what people knew about you, or in my case, pretended to know, that they would make their own assumptions, and spread them across the internet and social media.

I knew I didn't have long before people here would start talking, no matter how many goofy disguises I came up with. And that picture of me would be on the internet by lunchtime. Again, this time it would be accompanied by some more terrible words about my private life. My past. And so, I did what I always did and just kept moving forward.

Get in the water and start swimming, I told myself, but as I walked towards the changing room I couldn't resist one look behind me and when I did, Lloyd was still at the turnstile, looking right at me.

7

NOW

The changing rooms were empty, I stood next to the locker as the warmth of the moist air wrapped me in a blanket of empathy, encouraging me to stay where I was and not venture through the doors to the chill of the pool.

I pulled my towel around me for protection, unsure what or whom I would find beyond the changing rooms, and stepped through the door marked for the pool.

I let out a small sigh of relief that Lloyd was right and that I was the only nutter up and ready to swim at this time and took a few steps towards the shallow end. The water looked like a sheet of blue shimmery paper, so still, as the sun from a large glass window in front of me allowed a slice of light through from a panel along the top. The rest of the floor-to-ceiling windows were taken up with those classic public pool images. One of a male diver captured in mid-air just before he hit the water, one of a child under water, wearing goggles and grinning at the camera, their two top baby teeth missing. The final one and the one opposite me, and parallel to the lane I would be doing my lengths in should I ever summon the confidence, was a picture of a happy family. A mum, a dad and three children. All girls; one older and two younger. I stared hard and intently at the beautiful image, the visual reminder of a family of five. Three bonny daughters who could stop people in their tracks had been my life for sixteen years. I wondered who this family were, if they knew how many people stared at their faces each day. And if they ever considered the heart-stopping effect their perfect smiling faces could ever have on someone who would never pose with her two sisters ever again. Every fibre in my being was urging me to return to the changing room, get dressed and go home, where it was safe. I had overcome so much to get here already with the photographers and now this perfect family were staring at me, it felt as though they were mocking me. Laughing at me for daring to even think that I could do this. It was ironic really, to arrive here only to be greeted with some freakish mirror image of my own life several years ago. I was sure that if I scoured my mother's files I would find an image very similar to the one I was looking at now. My father was a stickler for capturing every family holiday, every Christmas, birthdays, even just a Saturday night in playing board games, he would set the camera up on a timer to capture us all. We would pull out our most inane grins for the occasion. It hurt my jaw thinking about it.

I looked around the still empty pool, aware of myself again and remembering why it was I was here and what I needed to do. There were two choices of steps. One was gradual, where I could easily walk forwards and the other was a silver ladder style which would see me climbing down backwards, unable to gauge what was beneath me. I knew which one I would be choosing and moved towards the first step. I had given myself an objective for today. Simply sit on the edge of the pool and dip my feet in. I didn't need to swim today, I just needed to get used to the idea of water again; it had been over a decade since I had even dipped a toe. Ridiculous now when I thought about it. I should have got straight back in the water again. At least I should have been put straight back in the water again by a parent. But one had been absent in mind, the other physically absent. No one wanted to think about the sixteen-year-old who was still there, when all everyone was thinking about was the six-year-old who wasn't. After Mum stayed in Corsica to wait – even then, as children, there was the general consensus between us that we didn't quite know what she was waiting for – Dad brought in a nanny to care for Scarlett and me. And that was the end of our experience with parental care. Of course, she was there more for Scarlett. I was off with my friends whenever possible, numbing the shock and trauma with whatever was given to me in liquid, pill or powder form, getting into relationships with lads who were way too old for me, until I got my place at the boarding school and enrolled in the theatre studies course I had been longing to do before Franny's disappearance, and that was my saviour. But I had never been able to return to water of any sort. Which had been awkward on a few girls' holidays away.

Now, the light reflected off the perfectly sleek water and it winked at me as if it were daring me to get in. I walked down one step. On the next step was an inch or so of water. I could do that, just let it graze my toes. I had bathed, I had showered, it was just like that. Just a big bath. And so I walked down the steps until my ankles were submerged. I knew it wasn't going to be getting into the water that would be difficult, but moving away from the edge to the middle, where there was little protection.

I reached the bottom step, the water now at my waist. This was progress, I began to feel a sense of relief and hoped that maybe this was going to be okay, that maybe things would get easier from here on in. I lifted one leg, then another as the realisation struck me: I was in water, I was floating. I felt my breath lodge in my throat, I could neither take in air nor expel it, it seemed. I was about to die and in a fucking council swimming pool. This couldn't happen to me. Not now. It was the flash of an image of a headline that drove me towards the edge of the pool, where I had been only moments ago. My arms flapped about as I grabbed and pulled myself to safety.

I leant against the edge of the pool, daring to rest my head back a little as I inhaled big lungfuls of air. When I brought my head back down again, I was looking at the perfect family of five all smiling at me, as they would have been looking directly at the camera when the photo was taken. I focused on each one in turn: mum's, dad's, the children's eyes all seemed to be right on me, this time, without mockery but enticing me into the water. I launched myself forward a little. This time I stayed afloat. I looked at the happy family in front of me and tried to plunge forward into any kind of stroke but my body was reluctant to play along so I dropped my legs and walked slowly forward, tentatively arriving closer to them. I was aware of my breath with every passing moment.

I looked at how happy the mum looked with her three beautiful girls. Images of my own mum alone in her flat wrestled with the perfection I was now seeing in front of me. She had never tried hard enough. An image of my mother walking past my room fell into my mind. It was late, I had been asleep, and then I wasn't. My eyes were wet with tears. I wanted to call out to her, and I was adamant even then, as the young child I knew I was, that we had locked eyes for a second, that she had seen I was awake yet she didn't come to me. Those memories stuck, made it hard to forget, to forgive her. She could be at her flat in Corsica now feeling confused and alone. When Jolie had told me about her condition, I now realised the emotion I had experienced wasn't the one you are supposed to feel when someone tells you that your mother has a degenerative disease. What I should have felt was total shock and horror, panic for what was to come. But in reality, what I actually felt was relief.

I stared at the family as I edged closer to them, wondered what this family in the image would be doing now, how old they were, what they did after this photo was taken.

Did they still speak to one another regularly? Were any of them missing, dead even? Did any of them live with debilitating conditions which prevented them doing something as simple as getting into a pool of water?

A loud splash reverberated around the room and the calm water I had been slowly wading through was now a ripple of waves. A little water went up my nose and I lifted my head further up and swivelled it to the right. There was a blur of a figure just under the water. As they came up for air a few seconds later I could see it was a male, in the fast lane, two across from me. He'd made it across the length of the pool and was ducking under the water to make a perfect forward roll so that he could continue back the other way. I had now reached the end of the pool and congratulated myself on completing one length. Even though I had kept my feet on the ground for most of it. As I held onto the side of the pool, I noticed a door on the other side that I had missed when I came in. Steam room. Maybe if I could manage a few more lengths, even just walking, then I would treat myself to a steam. But there was that urge again, that swimming alone wasn't going to stop this feeling that was burning inside me, the notion that there was something else, something bigger that I should be thinking about. Before the darkness engulfed me, I said quietly, 'It is enough.' I stayed close to the side still feeling protected by the swim hat and goggles. I now felt as though I were in a wave machine. The fast-swimming man was taking a rest at my end. He was heaving out a breath that was so loud it sounded forced and fake. I inwardly rolled my eyes. Jeez, what was this guy on. I was clearly the only person here, so was this performance just for me?

I began to make it to the other side of the pool, hearing the loud groans of the swimmer every time he stopped to catch his breath.

When I had completed my two walking lengths, I got out via the same steps I had entered and pulled my cap and goggles off. After I did, I spun around; the sensation that eyes were on me was like a spider crawling across my back. The man was leaning against the pool wall, but his head was turned towards me. Only the darkness of his goggles could be seen but it was clear to me he was looking straight at me. I looked down at my own swim hat and goggles in my hand and realised I was totally exposed. I moved swiftly to the steam room door, swung it open, and inhaled the eucalyptus smell. I took a few deep breaths as I tried to make myself comfortable on the hard wet bench. Eventually I scooted into the corner, enveloping myself in the gloom of the room and closed my eyes.

The creak of the door startled me, and I opened my eyes. Had I just dropped off for a moment? I could make out a figure in the doorway and then he closed the door and sat down. The steam had filled the room now and I was unable to make out if it was the same man from the pool or not.

Then he began to breathe, loudly. Occasionally emitting a small groan.

'It's so nice when they put the eucalyptus scent in. Council must have a few extra bob to throw about in this borough.'

I hadn't come here to talk to people or socialise in any way. I stood up, the squelchy sound of my swimsuit against marble tile making me cringe. I walked out of the steam room, grabbed my towel, and returned to the communal changing room. I decided a quick change was on the cards, the guy in the steam room could be right behind me. I walked down a long aisle, past cubicles and lockers. Only a faraway extractor noise could be heard and the wet slap of my feet on tiles.

I opened the locker with the wristband key, which I was glad to get off, it felt so awkward and bulky. Then I bent down to retrieve my clothes. I heard a slap of a foot on wet floor, and I looked to my left along the long corridor. There was no one there. I heard the far away sound of a shower starting up and I hurried into a nearby cubicle. I began dressing at speed. I only needed a few more sessions to get me confident enough to step into that sea in the Highlands and then I could be out of here.

I had just pulled up my jogging bottoms and was about to step into my sliders when a hand emerged under the bottom of my cubicle door, I gasped. The hand dropped a swim hat and a pair of goggles onto the space just by my feet. I heard footsteps walking away and then I let out the breath that had caught in my throat. It came out as a sort of cry as I scooped up the objects from the floor. I had left them in the steam room. The fast-swimming groaning man had picked them up. He knew I was the only other person here in the changing rooms. It was impertinent, what he had done, plain and simple. But he was long gone.

I emerged moments later, the door banged behind me and made me jump. As I made my way past reception, this time with just my sunglasses on, there was another young male staff member at the reception with Lloyd. The other chap looked at me in the way that people did when they knew who I was. I gave a half-smile, not wanting to encourage him but also not wanting to end up in some post on social media about what a miserable cow I was.

'See you again?' Lloyd called after me.

I turned briefly and gave a quick wave.

I felt as though I practically burst through the door and then I was outside, the sound of London coming to life as I headed straight towards Camden Market and immersed myself amongst the bustle of the early morning traders setting themselves up for the day. I walked past a crystal and ethical jewellery unit and looked across at the window display. How easy it would be to come here to work every day, to not have to be someone who people recognised, to not have to put on a hat and sunglasses, to not have to choose a public swimming pool because I had been out of work for so long and I was too proud, too stubborn to accept the money that came in the form of cheques from my father. No one sent cheques any more. But I had never given him my bank details, so it was his way of reaching me, financially. I would swap my life in a second sometimes, and instead of waking up each day wondering who I might be on screen and even off screen, I could just show up at the same place every day, to experience the ease of a simple transaction which would pay for the food in my fridge, the water in my pipes and the roof over my head.

But to live a life of such simplicity would be to accept me, to feel comfortable in every move I made and every inch I inhabited. That was never something I had ever experienced, even as a child. Especially as a child. But one is supposed to grow into one's self and feel more in touch with who they are. I had once been sure of a handful of things. One of those was swimming. It was something I needed in my life every day, the push and pull of the security it gave me, one minute feeling the meditative lull of the waves, which would calm me and coax me into their embrace, promising me they would protect me, only to change suddenly in the blink of an eye. I could be thrust under by a higher wave or caught in a rip tide. The sea was both a sanctuary and a place of peril. The sea was no longer a part of my life – in the same way I had chosen to block my father from my world, I had done the same with the sea. But now it was time for that to change. If I wanted my career back, if I wanted to know what self-respect felt like by exchanging countless hazy, drug-fuelled nights and early mornings for late nights reading and perfecting a script, I needed to face my fear. I had been waking up and each day choosing to be a multitude of people, faces, and characters so that I never once had to truly face who I was. But now it was time. It was time to find out who I really was. It was time to go back to the ocean.

8

NOW

I blinked at the screen a few times in case I was imagining it. Five simple words that seemed as though they might not be real.

Looking forward to meeting you.

From Dexter Rice to my Instagram inbox. It had been there for three days and I was mortified that I hadn't picked it up before now.

I called Tammy who answered after a few rings.

'I'm in make-up so can I put you on loudspeaker?' Tammy called to the room around her as much as to me.

'Absolutely not, this is top secret.' I hissed.

'Oh, okay, I'm listening.' Tammy's voice became suddenly smaller and directed at me only.

'Dexter Rice messaged me on Insta, and I only just saw it.'

'When did it come through.'

'Three days ago.'

'That's okay, you've been busy. Training!' She made it sound so glamorous. But one day in a cold and sweaty public pool trying to manage more than two lengths was far from glamorous and the furthest away from what I had envisioned my training regime to look like.

'What did he say?'

'"Looking forward to meeting you."'

'Kiss?'

'No.'

'Smiley emoji?'

'No.'

'Any emoji?'

'No.'

'That's fine. Reply now, it looks like you're super busy and important.'

'What do I say though?'

'Ask him when he's arriving in the Highlands. Drop him your number.'

'I can't.'

'Babe, Dexter Rice just slid into your DMs. Send him your number.'

'Fine.'

'Are you training today?' Tammy sounded distracted, her voice was far away, no longer just for me.

'I like the way you call it training.'

'Well it is. You're getting into shape for your best film yet.'

Preparing myself so I don't drown from fear, I thought so loudly I was scared I had actually said it.

'I'm swimming tonight. I figure late at night, less people to spot me.'

'Keep me posted on Rice-gate,' she sang before she hung up with a series of 'bye-bye-byes' that sounded out like a drum beat.

I laughed a little out loud at the way she had referred to Dexter sending me one message on Insta as 'Rice-gate'.

I fell into my sofa with a cup of instant coffee, because funds were seriously low now and the swim membership was an extravagance and I could now no longer justify heading down to my favourite coffee shop. But this was good for me. With my face in the news and the story emerging about Franny, I was glad to be keeping an even lower profile than usual. I opened Instagram back up and typed out a message, quickly because if I didn't think about it too much then that would be apparent at the other end when Dexter read it.

Can't wait to get cracking.

Then I added my number. And hit send.

Immediately a torrent of regret washed over me. I didn't even say 'call me' I just left my number and 'get cracking' could imply a host of things, none of which related to working together. I couldn't think about it any longer, what was done, was done. I opened my emails.

There was a new one from Sylvie.

Great news, you'll be in the Highlands in just over a week. Pack your bags! And check your bank account.

I felt a tremor through my body, a release of nerves. I was only one day in with my swimming and soon I would be heading to the Highlands. But this was good news on the financial front. I quickly checked my account and saw that there had been a transfer from Sylvie. Yes. I had been paid a portion of my acting fee. This was the start of it. I was officially back in business.

Tammy had organised a drinks thing in Soho as a *congratulations, you got a job and it's with Dexter Rice* kind of way, in a couple of days' time, which I felt was a little OTT but that was Tammy, and I would feel I was letting her down if I didn't attend. She liked to be a party planner; needless to say she wouldn't miss the opening of an envelope. But I felt better about going now, I could actually afford to pay my own way, and buy rounds of drinks for everyone else.

The healthy figure in my account that was now looking back at me made me want to dance around. I was suddenly looking forward to going out.

The leisure centre reception desk was empty when I arrived later that evening and so I was able to cruise through the turnstile without having to make eye contact or conversation. I had on my baseball cap, but I'd had to lose the glasses simply because the sun was beginning to set and I felt they attracted more attention.

The changing room was emptying out as I entered. A middle-aged woman, a more elderly man and a couple of teenagers, were all finishing up as I ducked into a cubicle. By the time I was packing my bag into the locker, the changing area was deserted. Which must have meant that the pool was too. I felt a small thrill that I was to be alone and as I made my way to the poolside, I saw the water was slowly returning to a mirror-like state.

This time the swim felt a little easier, the very moment I stepped into the water and the ripples distorted the perfect glass-like effect.

I was thrust back to the times I used to slip down to the beach alone whenever we stayed by the ocean. During our final stay in Corsica, I had relished the time there by myself right up until the time Franny vanished and my mother blamed me for her disappearance.

I looked across to the other side of the pool and greeted the picture of the perfect family. I thought that they might need a name. I called them the Smith family. It felt wholesome real, simple and approachable. This family looked as though nothing bad had ever happened to them, as if the parents loved the children unconditionally and the children soaked it up unconsciously, never aware that there was such a thing as types of love, or that it depended on the type of child you were at that particular time. This family looked solid as though nothing could ever break them apart.

I sought some comfort from the strength and bond that this family seemed to display.

The first length came easily; I focused all my attention on The Smiths.

Once upon a time – I heard the words in my head, the way I had heard them as a child. On the occasions I remember being read to, I remember feeling instantly soothed by those four words.

Before I knew it, I had begun imagining a life for this mother, father and three daughters.

There lived three beautiful daughters, all blonde, all fair-skinned and blue-eyed.

One length.

The youngest daughter was a firecracker. She was fearless, she was always ready to be what her elder sisters would or could not be. The middle girl was bookish, a people pleaser.

The eldest was liked by all. She was by far the most beautiful, but it was her sisters who turned all the heads due to their youth and vulnerability.

Their father worked hard and gave them everything they needed. Money, a home, fine clothes, and wonderful holidays. Their mother was adored by everyone she met, she was always so sociable and enjoyed parties most weekends. This was afforded by the father who worked all week long. He too enjoyed the parties which would sometimes go on all weekend long. The father liked to forget, and the parties were a way their parents came together, yet also separated themselves, as they retreated to their individual clans.

On Saturdays and Sundays, a nanny was employed, and the girls were whisked off to various activities and clubs. The weekdays were extra-curricular activities. Ballet, Girlguiding camps, ice skating, pony clubs and dressage. Every unit of every day outside of school was taken up with something, so that their little minds were always occupied, so they were never given an opportunity to think about anything else that might be happening. Of course, everyone knew this was purely to protect their tiny developing minds, which was what adults did.

And the children would never think to question that. They didn't question. Because that wasn't what children did.

* * *

Water in my mouth, it had gone down my throat. I was choking. I struggled to find the side of the pool and pulled myself against the wall, gasping for air. I felt so silly. I felt like a child who had just learned to swim.

I looked at the clock. I had been swimming for just under ten minutes. I had, for that time, been lost in the moment, thinking about the Smith family. I pulled myself out of the pool, and went into the steam room. I lay down, taking full advantage of the empty space, the excessive heat, and steam which had built up over the quiet period.

I made a promise to myself that I would swim more tomorrow and the next day. I had just one week to get myself to some sort of level where I could swim in open water. There would be a test shot needed of me in the water before I even had to properly swim for the real shots.

I lay on my back, my head tilted towards the door. The lights were low in the steam room, a pale blue framed the edge of the door, coming from the pool area. Even with my eyes semi-closed I sensed a sudden shift in light for a second. I opened my eyes. Had someone just walked past? Usually at this time of night I wouldn't have been surprised to see a member of staff walking through the pool area carrying out their daily duties and checks, even though this pool had no lifeguard at this time of night.

I also knew it was almost time for me to leave, and whichever staff member was on would not want me here for much longer and that notion that I was pushing precariously close to closing time was nudging me to get up, but I fought against it, putting myself in an uncomfortable limbo where I felt strangely safe and secure: that feeling I got when part of me wanted to leave, and the other part wished to stay. But the leaving part was more prevalent and urgent, yet I fought against it just for a little longer.

I lay there for a few more minutes and then felt the heat inch its way further inside me, and I knew it was time to leave.

The drop in temperature from the steam room made me shiver. I grabbed my towel from the hook on the way back to the changing area. It was all quiet in the cavernous rooms except for the background hum of the pool area. I scooped my bag from the locker and went into the closest changing room. The clunk of the door echoed around. I stood still, expected someone to come running to the noise that was so loud to the quiet background. I dressed quickly, suddenly aware of the time, and the club closing hour looming. Maybe I would speak with the reception team, let them know I'd be swimming at a late hour and then I wouldn't feel so uncomfortable. The sound of something like keys dropping on floor made me jump and I fell into the wall of the changing room.

'Someone in here?' came a man's voice. I pushed my wet towel and costume into my bag and unlocked the door. I popped my head into the walkway and there in the doorway to the change rooms was Lloyd.

'Oh, hey!' he said.

'Hi, I'm here. Just finishing up.' I suddenly felt vulnerable.

I knew I didn't look my full self, with wet hair stuck to my face and no make-up. But I was a character actor, I had appeared on screen in a myriad of guises, I was happier when I wasn't looking like an exact replica of one style of myself at all times.

'Don't worry, tek your time, I was just doing the rounds.'

I smiled and went to return to my cubicle to retrieve my bag. I noticed Lloyd didn't move, he looked lost in his own thoughts, and when I returned he was hovering by the door.

He gave me a half-smile.

''Night then.' I walked past him.

'Yeah, goodnight.'

I heard the jangling of keys and the sound of locker doors slamming closed, Lloyd going about his evening activities as I made my way to the door and out into reception.

I had just reached the front door when I heard a voice.

'Hey.'

I looked back and Lloyd was approaching me at speed.

'Are these yours?' He held out my keys.

'Oh my gosh, yes, they are. Thank you.'

I took them from him.

'You must have dropped them in the changing room.'

I didn't remember dropping them, I was sure I would have heard them. But I had been rushing and I was clearly nervous here. Maybe I might have time to change to a private pool for a few days, but even thinking it, I knew it was not really worth it.

'Well, thanks, Lloyd,' I added and he looked pleased at the sound of his name.

'You're welcome, Miss Levine,' he said and this time there was a definite lopsided grin. I felt a flutter in my stomach. Would it be so dumb, if I were to instigate a drink with this guy? Knowing that drink would quickly lead to much more. It wasn't unusual for me to squeeze in more than one date a week with different men. I was trying very hard to focus on my mission ahead, but there were still cracks where the bad thoughts crept in. I needed to quieten them with something else. With someone else.

'Are you okay, to get home?'

'I don't know, I might need a bodyguard?' I said hinting at what I knew he wanted to hear. I would be in the Highlands in less than a week, I could forget about this guy then. But just for tonight...

'Oh, well...' Lloyd looked around. 'I am just finishing up here, if you wait a minute, I could walk you home?'

'I'd like that,' I said with a tone that I knew suggested way more than what it needed to, and Lloyd heard it too. He looked as though he were struggling to breathe.

'Right, well, let me just...' He walked back to the office and began turning off screens, clicking off lights and grabbing a large set of keys.

We were out in the street within a few minutes, Lloyd locked the front door and pushed the heavy set of keys into a man bag which hung across his chest.

'Taking your work home?' I asked.

'Always,' he said. 'There is a lot more to being a GM than meets the eye.' That northern tone was fast becoming more enticing.

During the walk back to my flat my mind flipped between wanting to bring this total stranger into my domain and knowing that if I did, I could be stepping over an invisible boundary that I had set for myself. Never bring them back to your house. But the snob in me imagined Lloyd lived in a grotty bachelor pad. Not that I hadn't seen enough grotty bachelor pads, but these were grotty of a higher level, men who were high earners, in the industry, with enough disposable income, which was reflected in their life around them: left over pad thai, half-drunk orange juice carton from Waitrose in the fridge, some token Oliver Bonas pieces, a leather recliner on the right side of battered. These were levels I could cope with. I could have him out by dawn, explain I was on an early shoot. Keep the lights down low so not too much was revealed about me.

I opened the door to my flat. Lloyd wittered a commentary about the neighbourhood, the steps up to the garden and generally how much he liked it around here. I could have put it down to nerves, but he seemed pretty confident.

I put on the under lighting in the kitchen and pulled out a bottle of white wine from the fridge. I held it up to indicate if he wanted a glass and he nodded. I poured two and handed one to him. We sipped in silence.

'It's a lovely place ya got 'ere.' He nodded respectfully.

'Shall we?' I gestured to my massive corner sofa, at least if we did it there, he could leave immediately afterwards.

I lay on the sofa, leant back in Lloyd's arms. My top was off, my bra half hanging off. I pulled at a fleece blanket to cover our modesty and also, because it was late now, I was cold. Lloyd had been surprising. Not as forward as I would have thought, he held back, waited for me to lead. He was respectful. It was... nice. I was even thinking that I would like to see him again, that he was worth a second shot, he would probably loosen up more next time, when my phone let out an invasive ping. I leant down, felt Lloyd move behind me as I lifted up my trousers to discover my phone on the floor under them.

There was a message.

I think it's time we had a chat.

9

CORSICA, JUNE 2008

A golden light stretched across my bedroom, cascading from the wall to the floor, encouraging me to get up and embrace the warmth that was building outside. I was the early-riser of the family; I didn't like to sleep in too late here. I had always been up before anyone else. More so the last few years, I felt a need to be the one to make sure everything was as it should be. Even more so here in Corsica. Late nights would see the adults sleeping into late morning. My sisters were also at an age where they embraced lazy mornings, banking as many sleep units as possible, as if they were currency they might be able to exchange for school mornings.

I swept the sheets off me and stepped out of bed and headed straight for the window to get a glimpse of the sea. I spotted Jolie in the vegetable patch with a basket in hand picking produce for today's menu. The basket was already full of tomatoes of every colour and size, and cucumbers and lettuces. I raised my hand to greet her, but she didn't see me. She rested one hand on her hip, tilted her head to the sky and closed her eyes, absorbing the glorious first rays of the day.

But my first port of call was Franny's room. She was the

youngest and I knew Mum would not have checked on her before she went to bed last night. My heart began to race as I pushed open the door to her room. That ever lingering notion that something could have happened to her in the night. I catastrophised and had visualised some horrific scenarios from her accidently hanging herself on the blind cords, to sleepwalking and injuring herself. When I was around thirteen, I had developed a strong maternal instinct around Franny. As the door crept open, I could clearly see that Franny was sprawled across the bed, one pyjama leg over the sheets, the other under. Her long blonde hair tousled across the pillow. I could hear her breathing softly, even over the thumping of my own heart.

I found Jolie in the kitchen when I arrived downstairs.

'Ah, Rey. You are the first, as usual, come sit, I will make you special coffee and apple tart.'

It was a specialty of Jolie's, the apple tart. It had started as an accident, as all marvellous things do, when it had been made for the adults for dinner the night before once and they didn't finish it. Jolie had left it in the larder and we children had discovered it the next morning and devoured the entire thing. When she had found out what we did she wasn't mad, and we begged her for another one the next day. It had been a while since I had had a slice of Jolie's apple tart, and I had been craving it. I pulled out a stool and sat down, placing a novel I had brought with me to read on the kitchen counter. Jolie tilted her head sideways to glance at it.

'Is this a love story?' she asked as she poured boiling water from the Aga into a cafetiere of coffee. I looked at the front cover: *The Hunger Games*.

'Yeah, kind of.' I wasn't sure if I would even get around to reading it but carrying it around felt good, like a comfort blanket and like something someone my age should do on a villa holiday.

Jolie just laughed and sliced the tart, cutting an extra big slice for me and placing it in front of me alongside a steaming mug of black coffee. I had just started drinking coffee the last time we were here, and I had relished in the maturity of it next to my sisters, particularly Scarlett, who was practically spewing because they were too young to even get a sniff of the stuff.

I devoured the tart and cleared the plate away in the dishwasher, then took my coffee and book out to the pool.

I felt as though I were all alone in the villa, a few bird sounds, the whir of a lawn mower far off in the distance were all I could hear. I placed my book and coffee on a small table and lay down on the sun lounger. It was getting hot already. I knew when all my family finally rose they would be irritable from too much sleep and the midday heat. Except for Franny, she wouldn't be much behind me, and was never grumpy in the mornings. Or ever. I was looking forward to seeing Aunt Vanessa this morning. We didn't get time to catch up last night. The drinks flowed after that first one upon arrival and then before I knew it my sisters were ushered off to bed and my cousins disappeared to their room, leaving the adults to continue with their drinking. I would have been able to stay up as long as I wanted, my parents basically saw me as an adult now and had recently begun treating me like one, forgetting that I was still effectively a child and I still needed guidance and support. The desire to grow up and be free of them had quickly dispersed as I realised I was stuck in a weird sort of limbo where I was still reliant on them, craving their opinions and comfort only to realise that ship had sailed. As far as they were concerned, they had completed the task of raising one competent child, and what a good job they had done too. They didn't ever stop to consider that other figures in my life, like teachers, my friends' parents, and Aunty Vanessa and Uncle Rob, had played more significant roles than they ever had.

It was just after 9 a.m. and my skin was starting to prickle with heat as it had been so long since I had felt it. I loved sunbathing. I would often fall into a hazy half-sleep of psychedelic colours and sounds. When I finally woke, woozy but relaxed, I would be ravenous and so thirsty I would drink straight from the orange carton until it was empty. After the journey yesterday and the heat of the day already, I had some serious napping ahead of me.

I closed my eyes and remembered the apple tart I had just eaten. I licked my lips and tasted a sheen of sweat. I heard a shuffle of feet on the concrete next to me and I opened my eyes, thrusting my arm across my face to block out the sun. Wallace was standing in front of me. My heartbeat rose and then ebbed into a flutter as I edged my way into a sitting position and looked around to see if my aunt was with him.

'Morning, Rey.' Wallace loomed over me. I wanted to tell him to move, that he was blocking the sun. I wanted to tell him to get out of the villa, that he wasn't welcome here, that he needed to leave us all alone. I wanted to scream out to Aunt Vanessa that I wasn't sure she had made the right choice bringing a strange man into our world. I was on tenterhooks it seemed and I couldn't explain to anyone why, this man, Wallace, was not welcome around me or my sisters.

'Up early.' He didn't look at me as he spoke. He was staring past me to the pool. I hadn't really had a chance to look over him fully yesterday. All I knew was that before I left the sitting room, from the moment I set eyes on Wallace, I knew I had no intention of getting to know him. It seemed Wallace didn't have the same idea. I had seen him eyeing me after dinner and that was when I had made myself scarce, retreating to my room, to the quiet space Aunt Vanessa had thoughtfully placed me in. He had been waiting for his moment to get me alone, and now this was it. My thoughts shot back to Franny, to the sleeping angel I had just left. Aunt Vanessa's room was closer to Franny's room than my mother and father's. Thoughts of Wallace near my little sister brought a vile taste into my mouth that was a mix of stomach acid from the tart and stale black coffee. I could have leant over and retched if Wallace wasn't so close to me. He would be wanting to talk, say things like, 'I'm not here to replace your uncle' and, 'I love your aunt very much' but I wasn't going to listen to any of that. I didn't like Wallace, I had decided that the moment he appeared in that doorway yesterday and nothing was going to change that.

A short breeze swept gently across my stomach, reminding me I was still wearing a crop top and the shorts I had slept in. I pulled my legs into my chest.

Wallace took a step forward; I sucked in my breath as though he had stepped over an invisible boundary. He cleared his throat, and a sound came out, the beginning of a sentence. But he stopped and looked up towards the house.

'Darling, Rey. There you are!' Aunt Vanessa's usual greeting to me, that I was just where I was, as though it were a great surprise to her. *There you are*. I loved it, it made me feel so safe, so wanted. At the same time as Aunt Vanessa called to me, Wallace took a long step back and started to inspect the rose bush, which had just blossomed. Fat blood-red blooms stained across a background of green.

'Have you had breakfast, darling? Has Jolie looked after you?' Vanessa approached the sun lounger and leaned down and kissed my head. I closed my eyes, taking in the gentle touch of a female, the scent of her day perfume.

'I did. Apple tart.'

'Mmmm,' Vanessa said and moved across to Wallace. She slipped an arm around his waist, and he kissed her head.

'V, the roses look beautiful. We should ask Jolie to pick some for us.'

I felt my whole body go tense at his words. How dare he speak of Jolie as if she were some sort of slave. She was part of the family. Long before he arrived.

'I'll cut some,' I heard myself saying. I guess I didn't want Wallace to have any say in what Jolie should and shouldn't be doing and the thought of him slicing through the roses the way he had sliced his way between me and my aunt, made my skin prickle.

'Oh Rey, that would be lovely. I'll fetch my secateurs. Remember how I showed you?'

'I remember,' I said and glanced at Wallace. He was looking at me, a slight smile played across his lips, but then his eyes seemed to glaze over.

'I... erm, I need to...' He walked away. 'I'll look forward to seeing those roses, Rey.' His voice became smaller as he got further away.

Vanessa watched him and then turned to me. 'I'll fetch those secateurs, my love. And thank you again. That was such a sweet gesture.'

I sat and squirmed for what felt like an age until I realised Vanessa wasn't returning with the secateurs. I stood and went into the villa. I could hear the high, tinny sound of my sisters, playing against each other the way they did whenever there was an adult in the vicinity. It would be Jolie's attention they were both fighting for this morning as neither Mum nor Dad would be up.

I was therefore surprised to see Mum sitting at the kitchen island and Jolie spooning scrambled eggs from a pan into a bowl for her.

'Darling, good morning.' Mum stood up and made a show of cuddling and kissing me. I knew it was all for Jolie's sake because Vanessa was so generous with her affection and Mum would be suffering from a hangover and the instructions had always been never to come close or even touch her when she had a hangover.

I looked around for Aunt Vanessa once I was free from Mum's grip.

'Rey, would you like some more breakfast? Maybe some coffee?' Jolie asked.

'Oh, coffee is it, darling?' Mum hooted, trying out a joke which only fell on deaf ears. I narrowed my eyes at her, knowing she couldn't see me.

'Is it going to be a beach day today, Mum?' Scarlett whined. I felt my skin crawl, why was she whining? She didn't need to whine; she was almost a teenager. I caught a look on Jolie's face and for a moment we shared the awkwardness of my sister's tone.

I moved towards Franny, leaning over for a moment as she ate. Inhaling her sweet morning scent. I looked at her soft skin, her tiny, pursed lips, she was still just a baby.

'Leave your sister alone to eat.' Mum batted me away, her momentary show of affection quickly forgotten.

I looked at my mother, a hard stare formed on my face, and I had to physically wipe it away with two hands as one might rub tiredness from their eyes.

Mum didn't look at me, but I could sense an edge to her voice now. 'We need to see what everyone else wants to do. Maybe we could take a picnic. Do you have anything planned for lunch, Jolie?' Mum rushed her words out.

I thought of all the fresh salad Jolie had been plucking from the allotment earlier.

'Just whatever you want. I do picnic if you like. And a meal tonight when you return from beach.'

Jolie was always so accommodating, but I knew that was her job.

I looked at Mum, who was now focused on her breakfast, pretending that I wasn't still standing too close to my little sister. I bent down quickly and looked her in the eyes. They were sparkly and inviting, like two little paddling pools I could step into. My mum shifted in her chair and emitted a small sigh. Franny looked at me and grinned a goofy smile. It pleased me and I ruffled her hair and edged away as my mother had insisted.

* * *

My cousins surfaced just before midday. Dad was in the drawing room looking through the English papers that had arrived from the local town that morning. He was a day behind, but he didn't mind when he wasn't at work.

I went over to my father knowing that there was always a moment when we were on holiday that he would finally acknowledge me. Because he always had done. The holiday was his time with his family. Holidays were when families became close, weren't they? I had just approached the desk and Dad's head had lifted, and our eyes met, he looked as though he were going to give me one of his special smiles, the ones he always used to give me and so I took a step closer. This seemed to unsettle him, he looked flustered and ruffled his paper, moving it closer to his face and losing eye contact. I knew I had stepped over some sort of invisible line, but I felt I wanted to keep pushing it. I was discovering more and more about myself each day and my desire to push boundaries, to become someone else other than who I was and I knew my father didn't like it, but it gave me some kind of thrill. I didn't want to be just Rey any more. I needed to be more than her.

Cormac, my eldest cousin, appeared in the doorway behind me.

'We're going to play cricket, on the front lawn.' He looked from Dad to me. It had been a while since either of us had played and I knew that part of Cormac was asking my dad as well as me.

'That sounds jolly good fun, Rey, you go and kick those boys' butts for me.' There was a command to his voice that I thought perhaps only I detected. And with Cormac here as an audience, I decided to push it further.

'You're not coming?' I asked, trying to persuade him with the backward way I had asked.

'I have a couple of phone calls to make actually.' Dad shook his newspaper.

'Ah, that's a shame.' I looked at Cormac looking at me; his awkward gangly manner becoming more so with this interaction between his uncle and cousin.

'You'd be good at cricket, Dad, come and give us a game.' I felt a smile edge across my lips. My father didn't shift, he remained silent as though ignoring me would make me disappear. I didn't want to leave the room, for this already felt like a game and he had won because the silence buzzed in my ears until I marched from the room and ran, tears that burned in my nostrils were long gone by the time we reached the lawn.

The cricket was set up and Faren was already there looking bored. When he saw me approaching at speed, he looked lively and began to swing the bat around.

'We'll need Scarlett, to make an even team,' Faren said.

I looked around. Scarlett was sitting on a low branch of a nearby tree, her legs swinging to and fro.

'Where's Franny?' I asked.

'I'll play,' came a voice and I looked right to see Wallace making his way over to us. Franny in tow. I lowered my head like a wild cat about to pounce at the sight of my younger sister with this stranger. Franny was holding Wallace's hand and I felt my gut tighten. *Let go of her!* my body screamed but I couldn't make the words come into my mouth. This wasn't supposed be how this holiday panned out. It was supposed to be just us with Aunt Vanessa, and I was the one looking out for Franny, not this weird man with his massive hand on my sister's tiny hand.

'I love cricket, perfect time to play too before it gets too hot.' I couldn't help but feel he was talking only to me when he said the last part about the heat, as his eyes darted to me and back again to the boys. Franny released herself and ran to a spot on the lawn, suddenly entranced by an insect or something.

Faren looked excited that a male was going to be playing. I glanced at Cormac; his brow furrowed. Did he not want Wallace around either? Maybe I wasn't alone in my concerns.

The boys played with fierce enthusiasm, as though the temperature wasn't about to tip thirty degrees already. Wallace appeared to be trying too hard, although I barely knew the man – it could have just been his default personality. I wanted it to be. Because I sure as hell didn't want to suddenly discover something likeable about him. I ran as little as possible, opting only to bat. There was a level of sibling closeness between my cousins and I, but I did not feel comfortable running in skimpy clothes around this strange man. So I was content when the game was forced to an end when Vanessa appeared at the door with a large wicker basket giving us all a ten-minute heads-up for the beach.

I showered and changed into a blue sundress, threw some essentials into a straw bag and left my room. Because I was situated at the very end of the corridor on the second floor, I had to walk past all of the children's rooms before I reached the landing, where it led off to my aunt's bedroom. I had one foot on the stairs when I heard my aunt Vanessa's raised voice.

'You will never be like him,' she said and I shot a glance into the room. Wallace appeared in the doorway, I saw a glimpse of my aunt sitting on the bed behind him.

I opened my mouth, to ask my aunt if she was okay, but Wallace looked firmly at me. A glare that suggested I should leave and not ask any questions.

I knew Vanessa would not want me lingering and asking after her, so I bowed my head and hurried on, my sandals slapping against the tiles as I hurried away.

* * *

Everyone was slowly piling into two cars in the driveway; floaties, bags with towels spilling out of them and crates of drinks were all stacked around the vehicles. Scarlett was in the car, half slumped over a seat, half on the floor. Dad was hollering at her to get up and move and Mum was trying to look as though she were moving things whilst Jolie did all the heavy lifting and Dad stood between the two cars looking at his mobile phone, lifting it occasionally trying to get reception.

'This looks like fun.' Wallace's voice behind me made me jump. 'Do you think we should help or just let them fathom it out between them?' There was a hint of laughter in his voice and if it had been anyone else speaking to me I would have laughed and engaged them in the conversation, I relished any moment to mock my family, and this would have been the perfect moment. My aunt had loved my uncle Rob with every fibre of her being and now here was Wallace trying so hard to fill that big, beautiful space and he was failing. And I was glad. I was so very glad.

10

NOW

There was a line of shots in front of me, and Tammy stood to my right. On my left were two other girls, Mabel and Acacia. They were more Tammy's friends, two make-up artists from shoots she had done. But they were good girls, and I always enjoyed their company. Acacia in particular. She was a six-foot British Nigerian with high braided hair and perfectly sculpted smooth biceps. She had a laugh that attracted a thousand looks and a stare that would deter a thousand men. Or anyone who crossed that invisible line between girlfriends on a night out and any outsider, be they man or woman.

Even though I was a known face, there were famous faces to be spotted everywhere, but there were also the spotters of the faces, the ones who came out just to see who they could sidle up next to and get a selfie with. Acacia seemed relaxed and present, but I could also see the way she would look out of the corner of her eye when she felt someone new approaching.

'Now are you sure you're going to be okay?'

I screwed my face up at Tammy.

'Because of what today is? I want to celebrate, I asked you and you said yes. Don't say I forced you, I just want you to be okay?'

'I'm fine. I need this. Today more than ever.'

'Okay.' Tammy accepted my response. 'Then this is for you.' Tammy began handing out the shots, placing one in front of me. We had commandeered a round table with high stools close enough to the bar that we could shout our orders over if we wanted to.

'To you and your new job, for being so brilliant and patient and never giving up and for getting in Dexter Rice's pants in the next few weeks,' Tammy squealed.

'And now the whole of this bar knows,' I sighed.

'They'll know soon enough, listen, get drinking.' Tammy shoved my shot closer.

Then she counted down and we all drank at once. Mabel winced loudly. I wiped my mouth and felt the burning of the alcohol as it ran down my throat. But it felt good to be out, good to release my inhibitions, good to know I had money coming in again, good to know I had a job and good to be around my girls. I had ignored the message on my phone for now I knew what it was about and I wasn't ready to think about that yet. This was all because of the article in the paper. I would of course deal with it in due course. Just not now, not tonight. I needed to let loose and just feel like myself again. I had put a few posts out on social media and a few stories on Instagram, trying to be the self-promoter I knew I should be when it came to being an actor. I had posted an image of me from a while ago and as I scrolled through the hundreds of likes, I spotted a heart like from Lloyd.

I was feeling a little bit pleased with myself for managing to get into the pool, twice already. I wasn't sure if any of the experience was made a little easier with Lloyd, but his presence certainly had piqued my interest and I thought about how I should maybe message him, perhaps suggest we pick up where we left off.

'This is for you.' Tammy was handing out another shot.

'Where did these come from?' The hit of the alcohol was in my head, as though I had just inhaled poppers, my body felt light and fuzzy.

I felt my phone vibrate in my pocket. I was reluctant to look at it. Maybe I should just switch it off. I opened my bag and took a look, not wanting to take it out, not wanting to commit to it fully. There it was again. The same message. Repeated. This was the third message with the same wording.

We need to talk.

A pink-coloured liquid was placed in front of me this time. I laughed at the absurdity of it, and as I did my head moved to my right, and I caught a glimpse of a woman staring at me just a few feet away, standing among the crowd. She looked in her late twenties, early thirties with scruffy, longish dark blonde hair, which made her look as though she could be a surfer or a snowboarder. She had that nomad look about her, as though she could work away all winter, and pop back to London in the summer to inhale up some of her roots because she never truly forgot where she came from. I knew a few like this, who spent months of the year away, but something about the capital always brought them back – as though they had been sent a homing signal.

There was a look in this woman's eyes that was intense. People stared all the time, but in an inquisitive way, or a friendly way as though they wanted to make contact but were too scared. And I felt a flutter in my heart, I needed to take a deep breath and then I looked back at the table in front of me where Tammy was preparing us to down the pink liquid. When I looked back the woman was still staring. In that same intense way, as though she were trying to communicate with just her eyes. Someone bumped into her on the way to the bar and her body just took the impact, she barely moved, her focus remained on me. I felt her stare on me like a hand pressing on my head, then down to my neck and on my throat. I felt the urge to run outside for fresh air. Tammy was pressing the shot into my hand, and I brought my attention back to my group of friends.

'Three, two, one!' everyone chorused except for me.

Shots were approaching lips. I brought mine tentatively to my mouth but chanced another look to my right to see if the woman was still there. I didn't see her and the spot where she had been was already tightly packed again with other bodies and I wasn't sure if I had imagined it, her expression and intensity. If it was the alcohol, the heat of the bar on a summer's evening in Soho, or if she had indeed been there at all.

A cigarette break was called. I was no longer a smoker, I would only have one or two with a drink on a night out. We went out in pairs whilst the other pair held the table. I was with Mabel who was petite and already quite unsteady on her feet, so I took her arm as we made it outside the bar. She expertly lit two cigarettes and handed one to me, then she leaned against the wall, one foot propped up against the brickwork and inhaled.

'I can't believe actual Dexter Rice! I asked Tams to repeat it when she told me like, I thought I needed my ears syringing. That dude is smokin' hot, and he is on fire. I also think there is a lot to learn from someone like him, he seems like he would teach you things, you know what I mean.'

'Well, I could teach him a few things too,' I said and whilst I didn't mean it in a double-entendre kind of way, Mabel was whooping with laughter. I was sick of people raving about how lucky *I* was to be working alongside Dexter Rice when maybe it was *he* who was lucky to have landed a job with me.

I wasn't really listening to Mabel, she was always on her own agenda – which I liked about her – but there was something about the way that woman had been looking at me inside the bar that had unsettled me, and Mabel's words were bouncing right off me. They were like a hard rattle in the background and part of me wanted to shout out 'stop' to her, but I withheld myself. I just needed a few long drinks to calm myself down, those shots had got me all riled up. People were people, they were always going to stare, there was nothing I could do to stop them. I smoked furiously on the cigarette not really needing it or wanting it. It was part of the ritual when we went out, to buy a couple of packets of fags and smoke whilst we drank. I enjoyed it when I did it, but I wouldn't ever become a real smoker. But tonight I wasn't enjoying it at all. I would be cursing myself in the morning for taking even one cigarette. I always wanted so badly to be healthier than I always was.

Mabel's voice had now morphed into a background soundtrack to my thoughts and the vibration of my phone in my shoulder bag dragged me away from the moment altogether. I was sure it would be another message with the same words. But it wasn't. This time, when I opened my messages and I saw the name of my sister there, all the background seemed to fade to nothing.

Scarlett's name appearing on my phone always brought the same dread that it did since she was thirteen years old. A year after Franny's disappearance, she was given her first mobile phone. She would text me all the time, then as she grew older it became less until finally, she only ever texted me four times a year. Once on my birthday, once at Christmas, once on Franny's birthday and once on this day every year. The anniversary of Franny's disappearance. I hadn't forgotten. It had been etched in my brain. The nineteenth of June 2008. But once Tammy had announced that this evening was about a celebration I thought that for once I could forget about the negative association because it was all I wanted to do. I didn't want my life to be ruled by my past any more. Especially with the rate the press was hounding me. But I knew it was not possible to live as though nothing that had happened in my life could not get to me any more. I had just wanted this one day of the year to not be about her. I thought about Franny daily, sometimes several times a day.

Fifteen years today. Always in our hearts, never forgotten. One day we will be reunited. I know that day will come.

All the shots felt as though they were back in my throat and thought I was about to puke. Scarlett always wrote these messages as though she were writing to someone else who had not suffered the grief as she had. They always reminded me of something that I would see on a tombstone. I didn't understand her reasons for communicating with me this way. I saw her intermittently after I moved out, but it had been almost seven years since I had seen her properly and had a conversation with her. Our mother was still in Corsica, our father in the family home alone and Scarlett lived in Bristol, I believed, the last time I had heard; we were no tight-knit family. We certainly never were before, but people would have believed what they wanted to see, three beautiful girls, an immaculately presented mother and a father who earned enough to provide for everyone.

But what was weird about this particular message from Scarlett this year, on this day, was that it sounded as though she were making reference to Franny being alive. Scarlett had once believed when she was younger that Franny was out there somewhere; like some weird sibling thing, she referred to be being able to feel her presence. Scarlett had developed sleep problems the day Franny disappeared. Sleepwalking, paralysis, insomnia. We put all of her ravings down to the sleep diagnosis. But why now, why would she imply that Franny was alive, reunited one day? I didn't know how my sister was health-wise. Our interactions had just slowed right down. We never really had much of a bond when she was little. I looked out for her, and I tried again when she was older but she didn't accept my interactions as an elder sister looking out for her younger sibling. Scarlett had definitely been the one who had missed out the most on the unconditional love, because I had not been able to give it to her at such a young age. When I was old enough to realise the power I had as an elder, it had all gone on Franny. I cared for them. Despite my skewed perception of love. But I felt what I believed was love, for my aunt Vanessa, my uncle Rob and the love I felt for Franny. She was so young, so innocent.

I had so many intentions of being there for her, for always making sure she was safe. But I screwed up.

And in the end, I couldn't protect her either.

11

NOW

I don't remember exactly how the night ended but I knew there was a lot more drinking involved than I had ever intended. I woke at 10.45 a.m., parched as anything and with a massive cloud of anxiety hanging right over me. I knew it would be a late evening swim as that date to go to the Highlands was fast approaching and if I didn't swim, I would be landed with this fuzzy unnecessary feeling all day and into the next.

Scarlett's words were of course dangling at the forefront of my mind, making me feel that there was some sort of shift happening, some unexplainable event that was long overdue. Like a bad remake of a familiar movie.

For now, I would need to get up and face the day in some way.

My phone rang out too loud and trill. It probably wasn't any louder than it usually was, but my eardrums were incredibly sensitive. There had been a club last night, I was sure of it.

Sylvie's name was on my phone, and I picked up, unable to disguise the craggy tiredness in my voice.

'Rey, you sound like shit, sorry to dump this on you this early but the papers are back at it in full force.'

'What now?' I croaked.

'It's your sister. She's done an interview.'

I sat bolt upright.

'She's bloody what?'

'I know right?' Sylvie totally got that I was practically estranged from all of my family.

'It's all about you and Franny. And that day, in Corsica, when Franny went missing.'

I felt sick rise in my throat. How could she do this? But then I didn't know Scarlett any more; the person I knew had been a doe-eyed rabbit, always looking as though she had been caught in the headlights.

'There is a whole story about the summer your little sister went missing.' She took another deep breath. Mine was shallow and low. I felt as though I couldn't quite get enough oxygen. 'She is saying that she doesn't believe that Franny just disappeared, she believes there was more to it. She wants everyone to know that she is still alive.'

I let out a sound so alien I barely recognised it had come from me. But it made perfect sense that Scarlett would have done this feature, then sent me that text.

'I think you should read it. Then we'll talk.'

We were both silent for a few seconds.

'I'm sorry, love, I really am.'

That bitch. That absolute bitch.

'Expanse, have you, I mean are they—' I could barely finish the sentence.

'I've been on to them already and I have a conference call booked around midday. I think they will be fine with this, I just need to ask, there was nothing sinister or illegal that happened, that maybe I need to know about? It's just newspapers stirring stuff up isn't it?'

As my mind was half in the present, half back in that kitchen the night Franny disappeared, I felt my stomach drop. What the hell had Scarlett seen, what the hell had she told the press?

'It's just newspaper stuff, Sylvie. I'm due on set in a few days,' I said, panic rising in my throat.

'I know, I know, even if it's not blown over by then, I don't think you'll have too much to worry about.'

'But I'll be hounded? I just wanted to disappear into the Highlands, not worry about stuff. You know?'

'I know, and like I said, I think this will be fine, it will blow over. They found out you're in a film, they've only got this to create headlines. That's all it is. But don't worry you'll be protected.'

'It's my fucking life is what it is!' I felt the weight of my body on the bed, and the terror began to run through me, the anxiety that was only slightly there before had now spiked and was whirring into a hurricane within me. Christ, I couldn't breathe. I flung back the covers and ran to the window and flung it open. This was bad news for everyone. But mostly for me. I couldn't believe it. I could just about handle that little feature and dig in the paper the other day, but this was going to be epic in comparison. It could take a long time to go away. It might not ever go away. Fifteen years of this had just been another one of those stories, of a missing girl on holiday. Now it was focused on us as a family, and me as Rey Levine the actor. The problem was not with the timing of this, and yes of course I didn't want the filming to be jeopardised by fuckwit journalists scraping around for any bit of evidence. But what evidence might be found as a result?

'Are you okay?' Sylvie was using her calming voice.

'I'm fine,' I lied, sucking in great lungfuls of air through the open window – the heat of the morning was not helping. I felt as though I couldn't breathe still.

'Okay let me do this call and I will get straight back to you. Then we'll make you a plan, okay. Nothing bad is going to happen. This film is still going to go ahead, okay? And like I said, you will have protection.'

I felt the emphasis of her words. She was right. The film would go ahead. But it was everything else that Sylvie couldn't control that I was trying to deal with in my head.

'So I'll buzz you after lunch. Have a shower, eat some food. Drink some water!' she added with greater emphasis, and I knew she was referring to the hangover from hell which was palpable down the line now.

'I will.'

We hung up and I stayed by the window for a few minutes, trying to bring my breathing back to normal. Trying not to fall apart. Trying to remember what I had told myself all those years ago. It was a sad and sorry mess, but Franny was in a better place now. And most importantly, no one could or would ever find out.

I pulled up the article on my phone and speed read it to the end. It was hard to read about the last summer we were all together as a family, and it was strange hearing it from Scarlett's perspective because I had only ever had it on a loop in my head from what I remember. Once I had got over the shock of my then twelve-year-old sister remembering an inordinate amount of information from the night our sister disappeared, I got to the bit that could potentially make my life even harder than it was already. Scarlett talked candidly about waking up in the middle of the night and hearing Franny being taken.

I had fallen asleep in the playroom, a little space downstairs in the villa that my aunt had made into a sort of play/craft room. I was a restless child and didn't ever want to be sitting about. I had woken in the night and went to get a drink and maybe scour the place for some left-over food. I knew I shouldn't have been up at that time of night. I heard a noise come from the hallway and I peered around the kitchen door. The lights were off so I couldn't really see anything, but what I heard were a lot of hushed voices, mainly an adult voice telling someone to be quiet. And then I heard my little sister's voice. She was asking for my elder sister. She was asking for Rey.

I threw my phone down. The bitch, she was lying. She was lying. I had barely heard a word from Scarlett in years and now this. Why now? Because she had seen that my career was on its way back up, and she wished to sabotage that. Or was this punishment for what I didn't do for her when we were younger. Was this because I took Franny under my wing, something I tried too late at and failed at with Scarlett. It wasn't my fault.

'It wasn't my fault!' I shouted so loudly that Freckles jumped off the bed with a startled meow.

But I knew that the events of that night came down to the one simple act I had chosen to do.

Franny disappearing was my fault. Only one other person knew the details and he had been trying to get in contact with me.

After a minute or two of sobs that echoed around the room so loudly I was sure someone would come knocking, I picked my phone up again and looked at the message from yesterday. There had been no more after that third one. But I knew what I had to do. I hit dial. The phone only rang for two rings as though he had been sitting there waiting for me to call.

'Hello,' he said without question. His voice was deeper now than it had ever been, and it bore a stronger Irish tilt.

'Cormac,' I said.

12

NOW

It had been a long time since I had spoken with my cousin. Not as long as the rest of my family. I supposed I could blame it on the dry spell of work and falling into a pattern of destructive behaviour, which thankfully even I could recognise for what it was, that had caused me to forget about Cormac for a while. To forget about my responsibility to him and to us and to that night in Corsica.

The accent he had tried to acquire to fit in with all the lads at his new school in Ireland was now prominent and real. He had moved there just after his father had died. It was a new start for Aunt Vanessa and her boys. A way to forget what had happened. But then she met Wallace, and everything changed for the worse. I felt a shivery sensation when I heard his voice because despite the accent he had developed I could still hear the old Cormac beneath it. I both longed to hear that voice and loathed to.

'Are you well?' he asked. He even arranged his words in that wonderful way the Irish did with that lilt that only slightly went up at the end.

'I'm good.' It was the default response, even when I was doing so well. But how could I tell Cormac anything else, he knew every inch of my psyche. He knew my darkest secret. It was a surface question. How was life treating me right now? I'd had a dry spell, but I was back in business. I was a well-paid, well-known actor. I could not complain.

'How's Vanessa?' I said. It pained me to speak the name of someone who was so unreachable, that just uttering the syllables of her name was torture.

'She's well.'

Ghosting my aunt after Franny's disappearance was not something that I had intended to do. But her relationship with Wallace had complicated everything. And now we were perfect strangers. Except for Cormac.

'How long has it been, since we last spoke?' I asked, daring myself to hear the answer.

'Nearly a year, Rey.' Cormac spoke in monotone. He was disappointed that we had not kept to our promise.

'How? How has it been nearly a year?' I asked but I knew how easily twelve months could slip by when you were falling out of bars, into strangers' beds.

'Because it has.' Cormac sounded a little short. 'Look, I'm glad you're well, I'll skip the small talk just 'cos, well, you know what's going on.'

I thought about the newspaper article. I never read anything about me. But maybe this was different, maybe I had needed to read it.

'It's Scarlett. She's being a little so-and-so as usual. She must be skint. Daddy's funds dried up maybe.' I hated how spiteful I sounded. I knew I hadn't tried hard enough to be there for Scarlett, but in the end, it had been futile. I couldn't be what either of them needed.

'Or maybe she just loves being the centre of attention, you

remember how she was when we were kids, she used to pretend that she was fainting or something.'

Cormac made a sound down the phone as though he might have been agreeing but I wasn't sure. This didn't sound like the usual Cormac. But it had been a year, as he told me, even though I couldn't quite believe it.

'Scarlett said things. In the article.'

'I know!' I felt my heart begin to quicken. 'I read it. But listen, Cormac, there is nothing to worry about. It was a long time ago'.

'She's said that she believes Franny is still alive.'

I pushed out a long breath.

'She's said that all along, Cormac, this isn't news to us. She sent me a cryptic message yesterday on the anniversary. She said, what was it now...' I tried to recall the message.

'It doesn't matter what she said to you, Rey. You and I promised we would stay close, stay in touch. I've been trying to get through to you for months. I gave up, but I couldn't let this feature bypass us. We need to do what we promised one another. We need to stick together. If the police come knocking—'

'Police! Why would the police come knocking?'

'Because, Rey, the article, Scarlett says she remembers something vital. Things went on that night that we... by some... miracle, we have been able to keep to ourselves. So maybe she is right. Maybe she does know more than she ever let on, more than she let on in that article even. Maybe she knows what we did?'

13

NOW

I felt as if the ground were sucking me in, a tiny inch at a time. I could feel the movement, but it was slow and torturous. There were many things that I thought about on a regular occasion, like remembering to feed my cat, and buy him food, remembering to eat and to call my friends instead of just texting. And then there was that day. That was the day I thought about the most more than any other thing I did or experienced.

I ended the call with my cousin prematurely because of the overwhelming sense of panic and the notion that I might throw up. Cormac was understanding and I promised to call him back once I was feeling better.

'And don't be leaving it another year now,' he added before we ended the call and I found it hard to believe that he could make any sort of quip under the circumstances.

I went to the kitchen and made myself a strong cup of sweet tea and then I sat down at my dining table and found the same story but by a different news source.

Star of *Cry Baby*'s Rey Levine's, secret missing sister.

Fifteen years after she went missing, Frances Levine's sister Scarlett believes she is still alive.

Franny, as she is known to her family, went missing on a family holiday to Corsica in 2008. Rey Levine, is the eldest sister of both Scarlett and the missing sister, Franny.

Scarlett was often tasked with keeping an eye out for her younger sibling whilst holidaying at their family villa. Owned by Levine's aunt and late uncle, the nine-bedroom mansion was considered a safe area and the children were often given the freedom to roam the grounds and local beaches. The idyllic setting was a backdrop to the worst nightmare that any parent could go through. Franny disappeared on the night her sister Rey was at a beach party. The well-known star had left the villa that fateful evening to go to the beach with her cousin and had been in the water having a swim when her sister was discovered missing from the villa. A search by French police that lasted over two days was unsuccessful. Franny has never been found.

To this day their mother, Felicity Levine, remains in Corsica, believing that one day her youngest daughter will be found.

Scarlett Levine, now twenty-seven, said she too believed that Franny was still alive and recalls the night she saw her sister Franny for the final time. Recently, she has been experiencing flashbacks to that day and now remembers hearing her sister late at night in the hallway being led away by an adult and calling after her sister. She hopes to be able to have the case reopened and help the French police with their investigations.

Rey Levine is about to begin filming with heart-throb and all-round good guy, Dexter Rice in the Highlands for a new project which is set to be released in 2025.

I let out a loud sigh. I was thankful that Sylvie had batted off journos, but they had managed to squeeze in that ridiculous photo of me outside the leisure centre which was irrelevant and plastered it everywhere making it look as though I were guilty just by the expression of fear across my face. It was 6 a.m., I had just stepped out of a stranger's bed and was trying to get into my local swimming pool. And what was all this nonsense about flashbacks? Scarlett had not once mentioned anything about flashbacks to me or anyone as far as I was aware. I know we hadn't exactly been close for much of our childhood or when we became adults, but something as important as remembering new details should have meant she came to me first. But what if the sleep problems she'd developed had prevented her from remembering. And now it was all coming back to her. The way I was feeling gripped by terror ever since I knew I had to step into the sea for my job.

I was fuming. And so I picked up the phone and dialled my sister's number. Unsurprisingly she did not pick up. She had seen my name and had been too terrified to answer the call, undoubtedly. I returned to thoughts of why Scarlett would make such a claim at this juncture. And after I had exhausted all my anger, all I was left with was that suffocating layer of guilt and sadness. The same way I ended up feeling every time I spoke with my mother. The everlasting cycle. When would it end? With me? If I didn't have any children, then I had broken the curse.

By eight thirty that evening I had started to feel as though I could crawl into a ball and fall asleep again. I had pretty much snoozed all day but knew if I didn't take myself off to the pool then I would be failing myself. I needed to swim, I needed to be good enough for myself and for the film in a few days.

I walked the half a mile to the leisure centre, getting in there just before nine. I needed to attempt a good half-hour swim, really properly swim this time, not just walk. Not only for my mental health, but to strengthen my muscles. This job was going to wreak havoc with my physical health if I didn't stop drinking, and start feeling a little healthier. At this rate, I wouldn't survive ten seconds in the North Sea.

I looked down at my phone briefly on the walk, seeing all the messages from friends, all telling me they were thinking of me and that if I needed anything, I was to call.

No messages from my mother. But I thought about her in that little flat and the iPad she kept charged, ready to be connected to any piece of news anywhere around the world at any time. I could not bear it. I couldn't bear to be here walking along a street unable to do anything whilst they spouted things about me, which I had no control over.

When I arrived at the leisure centre, I was relieved if not slightly embarrassed to see Lloyd was working. Another employee was next to him at the counter when I arrived.

'Good evening,' Lloyd said, his face a broad smile, but his eyes were telling me something else. He had read the news story. He knew that I was the woman who was once a girl on holiday with her family when one of her sisters went missing. And we had seen each other naked. This was beyond awkward.

'Evening,' I said. I hung my head not wanting to engage with Lloyd. Any spark that had been there, I was certain would now be extinguished by my sister's story. Because people always believed the family members, didn't they. Especially an innocent sister who had only been twelve at the time. Lloyd probably thought I was a mess, and what must he have thought about me and my family. What sort of people went on holiday and let their youngest daughter disappear?

I went to go through the turnstile. I heard the sound of muffled voices.

'Well you could have clocked off four hours ago, mate,' came the mocking sound of one of the male staff.

'Do some work or I'll have you for insubordination,' Lloyd

retorted and he sounded cross. I looked around and the other guy was walking away, and Lloyd was standing there. Smiling at me. I smiled back.

In the changing rooms, there were two older women dripping wet at their lockers, too engrossed in their conversation to care about the cold. I nipped into a changing room near to them, taking comfort from their conversation, as they talked of their grandchildren and their plans for the weekend.

By the time I came out they were each in a cubicle and the changing area was once again quiet and deserted. I felt a sense of safety that Lloyd was nearby and maybe perhaps even watching on some CCTV. I felt a flash of shame that I would be swimming so badly and wished that I could swim the way the fast man had been the other day. I was like a tortoise in comparison.

I showered by the poolside and pushed my way into the water. A short man exited the pool as I went to take my first length and then it was just me. I looked around and spotted the camera. I almost lifted my hand and waved, certain that Lloyd would be watching me.

I walked through the water until I was no longer able to touch the bottom then I lifted my legs. Images of Scarlett were in my mind, I felt the fury still as strong as it was, surge through me and before I knew what was happening, I was swimming across the pool. Don't think about it, don't think about it, I promised myself as I slowly made it towards the other side of the pool. The Smith family were beaming back at me, their story begging to be told. Okay, I said to myself. Whatever passes the time. Anything to distract me from what was really happening, and the anger I felt at Scarlett.

The Smith family were a beautiful family, I think I mentioned this already. The daughters were often likened to fairy dolls with their blue eyes and blonde hair. Yet the mother and father did not see themselves quite as lucky as others, for it was a son that they wished for.

The mother and father met at a charity dinner. The mother was escorted that evening by a friend of the family that everyone was hoping she would marry. He was very keen on the mother, but the father was also there that evening. And he was wearing his favourite tie. Later he would refer to it as his lucky tie because he had been so blessed to have met the woman he would marry.

They hit it off at the bar, the mother worrying her hands at her neck and her necklace until the father told her to stop. Which she did at once.

'Because your neck is so beautiful, I want to see it.'

Two days later the father sent a car for the mother who was waiting at her front door, waved off anxiously by her parents. She stayed with the father for three days and three nights and on the third night when he asked her to marry him, she agreed. The ceremony was three months later. It was lavish and showed everyone exactly what the father was made of and showed the mother, of course, what was to come.

On the first evening in their house together as a married couple, which had already been the father's house, the father turned to the mother and said, 'Now that we are married, I should tell you, I do not cook and never intend to.'

The mother didn't look too fazed by this. 'Well, I do not cook either.'

The first day of their married life, after a ten-day honeymoon in the Maldives, the mother presented the father with a toasted cheese sandwich. Which the father ate silently. The next day the mother presented the same meal and the next day. On the fourth day a lady arrived at the house upon the father's request. She was there to take care of the house and cook meals. The mother never had to lift a finger ever again.

To some, this would sound idyllic, never needing to work, or do any tasks around the house, but too much time on your hands can present a whole host of other problems, much worse than never being able to cook anything more than a toasted cheese sandwich.

And so, with the marriage bit completed, and not needing to do anything to tend to her own house, the mother took well to hosting. She became the best host of dinner parties and soirees in the borough of London and people came just to taste the exquisite food – prepared by a Michelin-star chef, and the tastiest cocktails around – shaken by a professional mixologist. But it was all in the planning and timing and pairing the right guests with one another. That was a skill the mother was proud to say she could do. No one left the Smith house hungry, sober, or unsocialised.

I suddenly came to and looked at the time. It was nine forty-five. I had been swimming for almost half an hour, and I hadn't known it. Wow. I felt I should congratulate myself somehow. I could go and sit in the steam room if I wished. I had earned it, but it was almost ten and the centre would be closing soon. I didn't want to hold the staff up. Particularly, Lloyd. He was... nice, but leisure centres weren't my usual place for picking up men. I had reached the point that I knew there was a problem because I had to be drunk. However, I thought about the other night with Lloyd and how I had been very sober.

I shivered as I made my way to my locker. I bent down to retrieve my items when suddenly all the lights went out and I was plunged into darkness. I fell forward into the locker, hitting my leg on the door, and I cried out in pain. I was practically blind. I let out a wail, I could feel the panic rising in my chest, taking over. I couldn't think straight. I searched for a speck of light, pulled my towel around me and slowly and carefully followed the fire door sign. I yanked at the door, which opened onto the reception.

'Hello?' I called. My voice was shaky, but I was suddenly so thankful to see the light. 'Hello!' I shouted louder. I pulled my towel tighter and went to the reception desk. 'Hello!' I screamed this time. I could see through into a back office and beyond that, another door which opened, and Lloyd walked causally through. When he saw me standing there in just a towel, he looked shocked.

'Oh, are you okay?'

'No. I am not. All the lights have gone out in the changing room and I can't see anything.'

'Hold on, let me, erm...' Lloyd looked at me in just my towel and costume for a second too long. Then he opened a drawer and pulled out a torch. He scooted round to the front of the desk, looked me up and down again, then pulled an apologetic expression, and hurried in front of me. I kept close behind him, following the torch light. We located my locker, and I retrieved my items.

'I'm so sorry, I don't know... I'll check this out in a minute and see why this has happened.'

I stood redundant, not knowing what to do.

'Do you want me to, erm, hold the torch whilst you—'

'No!' I snatched the torch from his hand. 'I'll take this.'

Lloyd reached into his pocket and turned his phone light on.

'Okay, well, I'll be at reception.' He pointed the light to my leg. 'You might need me to see to that'.

I looked down at my leg, there was long trail of blood running down it from a gash just below my knee.

'Oh!' I dabbed at with my towel, but the blood still dripped.

Lloyd looked at me with concern etched across his face and left the changing room.

I put the torch on the bench in the cubicle and dried myself as quickly as possible. I pulled my clothes on, leaving my jogger above my knee as the blood was still fresh.

I held the torch in front of me as I made my way to the door. A clanging of metal made me spin around and shine the torch down the walkway. There was another locker door wide open down the end of the walkway. I stood for a moment, holding the torch and waited. I would not have been surprised if someone else was there;

I had that sudden feeling that I hadn't been alone in there in the dark. The door opened and I spun around.

'You all done, or were you going for a hair-dry as well?' Lloyd said po-faced and I spat out a laugh. A rush of guilt came over me after our very intimate contact.

I followed him through to the office and took a seat on the same chair I had taken last time to drink my coffee.

'I'm sorry I was rude before.' I was thinking of the changing rooms where I had just shouted at him.

'Don't be. It's a pretty big gash. I can get you an email address if you would like to contact someone to put in a complaint.'

I looked at the now dry cut and the thick plaster Lloyd was putting on it. The tips of his finger grazed my skin so softly I opened my mouth just to breathe in.

'I've been through worse,' I said and he stayed where he was on his knees, his finger still on my leg and looked up at me. He sucked in a breath as though he were going to say something. We both looked at one another for a few seconds. Lloyd realised his position and quickly got off his knees. I was worried he was going to start talking to me about the story in the papers, but he didn't and I was grateful for his silence on the matter. There was, after all, a very good chance that he had read the full story. The full story that the papers had presented to the world.

'Sooo, are you getting on okay here? Is there anything I can assist you with? Obviously more plasters are always at your disposal.' He laughed in that infectious way, a little to himself and I liked it. I liked him.

'I think I'm doing okay. I'll only be here a few more days and then I go to the Highlands.'

'Wow, the Highlands. That's a way.'

He leant against the desk; his legs crossed at the ankles his arms crossed across his chest. His head tilted to one side. He had really good skin, I thought.

'Yeah, not sure how I manged to sign myself up for that. But actually, my membership? I won't need it any more at the end of the week.'

'Okay,' he said, a hint of sadness betraying his voice. He cleared his throat. 'It's a touch of a button. Consider it done.'

'No hidden charges?' I asked.

'No hidden charges.'

'Thank you.'

'You're welcome. I can assure you nothing like that will happen again. For some reason, the lights had been put on a timer and the timer had been changed. They usually go off at ten thirty. Gives everyone a chance to get out. If they aren't, it's a not very subtle way to get them out. Like I said, please feel free to put in a complaint.'

'Thank you. Obviously, I won't.' I wasn't thinking about taking out a formal complaint, I was being plagued by the sensation I had felt when I was in the changing rooms. That there had been someone in there with me at the end. I had played a character in a thriller in one of the last pieces of work I did before things started to fall apart. I knew all the classic signs of not feeling as though you were alone in a room. My skin had prickled, and not just from the temperature and my damp skin, it went deeper than that. I'd had an unexplainable feeling of a presence, an energy that was close to me. Lloyd telling me that the lights shouldn't have been off, made me instantly think that it wasn't a weird fluke. I also knew that there was a chance that it was nonsense and these things happened. I was overtired and stressed about so much. My mind could have been playing tricks on me.

'Come home with me?' I asked Lloyd, words I had never had to utter before, it was always being offered to me, men were always so upfront. Lloyd nodded, shut down the office and we walked out of the door.

As Lloyd was locking up, my mind raced back to the changing rooms, and the person I was sure was in there with me. But how could they have been, Lloyd and I were the last ones out.

I was so sure about it, because it wasn't the first time this had happened to me or that I had experienced it first-hand. The times it had happened in the past had been so significant, that I could put dates and locations on them. I was adept at knowing when someone was in the room with me when they had not even breathed a word. I thought back to the holiday in Corsica, and how I had that feeling, that fear had almost suffocated me at times and when I thought about that fear, the face I saw belonged to Wallace.

14

CORSICA, JUNE 2008

'Do tell us all about how you two met?' Mum was pouring wine into a plastic wine cup. Dad was lying down on a sun lounger, his eyes shut, a sun hat pulled down over his forehead. The beach we had chosen today was busier than my father would have liked it to be, I could tell from way he couldn't seem to lie still, and the tone of his voice had become hard and brittle. There were a group of French guys playing volleyball a little closer than I guessed my father would have liked. There was a small beach bar a few hundred yards away, and I could hear the solid thump of dance music.

'She told us last night, Flic,' Dad said drolly. 'My God, were you that drunk?' he murmured, as though he thought no one was listening. But I was always listening. He turned to me and winked. I felt something rush through me like a shock of electricity, that one moment between us that no one else saw. It was ours. He had ignored me so intently in the study the other day that I was shocked he had wanted to even acknowledge me now. But I knew my time was up with my father, I was no longer the favourite and hadn't been for a long time. And in a way, I knew it was all my own doing. My mother had chosen to ignore the awkward tense conversations between my father and I which, had begun when I started to grow up, as soon it was clear that I was no longer a little girl who just did what she was told. My father didn't like it, but he had accepted it. But after that, we were left with nothing. He didn't even try to scour amongst the scraps of my younger self to find long lost anecdotes to share with me, to use the memories to bind us together. It was just then, and now.

'May I tell it this time?' Wallace sat forward on the picnic blanket where he had been spreading soft cheese onto a crusty baguette.

'Oh, please do, I love a love story. I do, don't I, Digby?' Mum called over to my father. He grunted and turned his head away, not needing or maybe not wanting to hear what was about to be said. But I felt a jolt of sadness that he wasn't going to share in his annoyance with me, that there would not be another moment like that. It was probably some sort of fluke, he was on holiday and he had forgotten himself.

'I am a teacher, theatre studies at Cormac's school,' Wallace began. My ears pricked up. This was totally new information. I did not know that. Or rather, I had not expected that. I had presumed that Wallace and Aunt Vanessa met online, or at a golf club on one of her country retreats with her friends.

Wallace looked at Vanessa who was sitting in a deck chair, a smile so broad across her face I wondered if it would break her in two.

'And, well, Vanessa came to watch the play we had put on.'

'*Les Mis*,' Vanessa added with the softest tone and glimmering eyes.

'Ambitious,' I heard myself say before I could stop the words coming out.

Wallace laughed wholeheartedly. 'Yes, Rey, it was ambitious. It was a rather condensed version of it, shall we say. But it worked.'

I looked away, unable to believe I had just instigated that interaction.

'Neither of the boys were in the play, but Vanessa brought Faren along because they had offered to serve the refreshments during the interval.'

'I was doing my best, but hospitality is not my forte.' Vanessa had pulled her feet up onto the chair and was hugging her knees.

'Oh, Vanessa, you're a wonderful host!' Mum chimed.

'The best customer service in Ireland.' Wallace gazed at Vanessa, and I was moments from standing up and walking away.

'I was running out of wine and I had more in my car.' Vanessa picked her way back in.

'Hey, I'm telling it!' Wallace said in a mock whiny voice.

Vanessa laughed, put her hands up and I found my mind wandering back to the moment between them in their bedroom and wondering what Wallace had said or done to annoy her and to make my aunt compare him to my late uncle.

'I was in the car park, getting in a sneaky cigarette because well, directing a play of sixteen and seventeen-year-olds is stressful. I was just putting my cigarette out when I heard a yelp.'

'Damsel in distress!' Vanessa quipped.

Wallace let her interjection slide this time. 'I ran in the direction of the cry and discovered Vanessa, half hanging out of her boot and balancing a busted-open box of wine on her knee. I grabbed the wine, obviously and helped her carry it back in. There was an instant attraction, we hung out after the show.'

'I gave him my full critique,' Vanessa piped up again.

'She did,' Wallace laughed. 'And we've been inseparable ever since.'

It seemed I was the only one who heard the slight clearing of a throat and when I turned, I realised it had come from Cormac. Our eyes met for a second, and in that moment, I tried to convey

a question. What is it? But he looked away, back down at his
phone.

'Oh, Vanessa that is a lovely meet cute.' Mum hugged her knees
and looked longingly towards the horizon.

'Meet cute?' Dad spat. 'Have you been on the sherry, Flic?'

'Oh, Digby,' Mum's voice wavered; she was beginning to feel the
force of his irritation. 'Have you never seen *The Holiday*?'

Dad didn't reply.

'Well, this was some meet cute,' Wallace said in an American
accent, nailing the line from the scene.

Vanessa and Mum erupted into laughter, there were plenty of
'Oh Wallace's' chucked around and when I couldn't take it a second
longer I stood up, brushed the sand from the backs of my legs,
picked up my sandals and headed towards the bar.

As I walked away I felt the presence of someone behind me.

'Rey.'

I turned and saw Scarlett. 'You okay?' I asked. We walked
together until we reached the bar. It was unusual for Scarlett to
seek me out.

'Wallace...' she said.

I furrowed my brow.

'Is he like Uncle Rob?'

I laughed. 'Hardly. No one is like Uncle Rob.'

'Oh,' she said, sounding more upset.

'But I'm here. You have me,' I said hearing how pathetic it
sounded.

'What can you do, Rey? You're just a child.'

She looked back towards where our family was gathered.

I shook my head. 'I'm nearly seventeen, Scarlett. I'm nearly an
adult.'

I didn't know what else I could say to her. There were so many
unspoken words that could have passed between us as sisters, but I

thought she was too young, and I that much older than her. I felt my role lay as the protector of Franny, because she was so young and innocent. Scarlett was at that age where she was never sure if she needed guidance or mentoring. I should have known that she was more vulnerable than she made out. But at sixteen I didn't know enough about life. And I was selfish. So incredibly selfish.

'I'm going to the bar, Scarlett.' I felt a rush of adrenaline reach my throat as I walked away from my sister.

'Yes, please,' the barman asked me in French. I turned and looked at him. He was handsome and young, and I thought I looked old enough now. Even though I was welcome to drink wine with Mum and Aunt Vanessa, I fancied ordering a beer at the bar alone. I didn't really have high hopes that the barman would serve me but he was looking at me in that way that men had started to look at me. I used my best accent, the one I had promised Aunt Vanessa that I had been practising, along with my perfected French and the barman gave me a swift look up and down – the all-in-one black swimsuit with the dramatic plunge at the chest had worked some extra magic – and a beer appeared in front of me.

I turned back around, half expecting to see Scarlett still standing there waiting to continue our conversation. But she was gone. Part of me was relieved, but another part supressed emotions. Feelings that lived deep within me were trying to force their way out. I shoved them back down where I could only feel them like a low vibration.

I sat down on a stool and looked out to sea.

'Can you get me one of those?' Cormac's voice from behind me. I spun around.

'You're older than me,' I said turning back to my beer.

Cormac sat down next to me, sighed and tilted his head to one side, then gestured to his attire. It was obvious out of the two of us who was more likely to be served right now.

'Fine,' I sighed and returned to the bar. The barman gave me an inquisitive look but served me another beer. I carried it over to Cormac and placed it in front of him.

'I thought I was about to spew so I had to get away.' I took a long gulp of my own beer. 'How many times have you heard that story? Their *love* story?'

Cormac looked agitated.

'Too many times, I'm guessing.'

'Yep.' He began to peel the label off his beer.

'Look, you might not want to talk about this, and now I've heard their meet cute, I just think, well, do you think it's a little too soon? It's not that... it's not my place to say, I know. He was your dad, but he was also my uncle, and we were close, and I don't know, I guess I feel a little let down. That she's moved on.'

'Welcome to the club.' Cormac shifted in his seat and pulled his features in a strained expression as he looked out towards the sea.

'And, I don't want to be annoying or anything, but he seems, a bit, like, I don't know, maybe it's because he's not Uncle Rob, but I... I don't want to like him.'

Conrad sucked in a deep breath then took a swig of beer.

'Should I not like him?' I added.

'I can't speak for you, Rey.' Cormac looked at me. 'We just have to get on with it. I'm not thrilled.'

But I wanted Cormac to speak for me. I wanted him to tell me it was okay, that yes Uncle Rob was gone, but this man Wallace was here now and everything was going to be just as it was.

I paused and thought about when I had walked past Aunt Vanessa's door. Did Cormac know that they fought about my uncle? Or perhaps it was just a one-off. Or maybe the beginning of the end, I secretly hoped.

I cast my mind back to when Uncle Rob was here and how close he and Cormac had been. I had never once heard them argue.

Perhaps they did away from us, the cousins, and my parents, but life with Uncle Rob had always been good. Safe.

I looked fondly at Cormac and saw he had nearly finished his beer.

'Shall we have another one?' I asked, already knowing the answer.

'Yeah. Let's get wasted,' he said and gave me a wicked smile.

Cormac ran into the sea first and I followed. Pulling off my shorts just before we reached the shoreline and dropping them on the wet sand before splashing my way clumsily into the sea behind him. Cormac did a pristine dive despite the five beers he and I had just finished. He surfaced and then went for another dive. He made it look so simple. The water was so cool and turquoise blue, I could see the sand beneath my feet. I was never a particularly good swimmer, but the way my cousin dived and resurfaced made me want to give it a go, plus I was buzzy from all the beer and quite frankly, I felt invincible.

I must not have noticed how choppy it had become because from where we had been sitting gazing out to sea it looked like a glass mirror I could have walked across.

I threw myself under the water in what I hoped from the outside would look like a clear and perfect dive, but immediately something felt wrong. I had opened my eyes and they stung like mad which caused me to become disoriented. I tried to surface only to get knocked back and when I tried again, I was unsure which way was up. I felt like I was locked in a game of push and pull with a wave for an eternity, eventually raising my head enough to gasp in some air. That was when I felt an arm around my ribs.

Later Cormac told me I had not seen the big wave and had dived right into it, surfacing as it was breaking.

We walked out of the water together, Cormac with his arm still around my waist. I scanned the beach for where everyone was; I could just see them, Mum and Vanessa were packing everything away, my sisters were jumping from sand dunes behind. I wasn't sure if my father had witnessed anything because he was just turning away when I looked at him. And then there was Wallace. Wallace was standing, his back to everyone, looking straight at Cormac and me, a look of frustration etched across his face.

As we reached him, Cormac let me go and walked over to his towel to dry off.

'Drinking and swimming is a pretty dangerous combination,' Wallace said quietly to me as I began to walk past him to the charade of packing that was happening behind him. I imagined he would have separate words with Cormac later. But for now, I felt exposed, completely ashamed of my performance. But no matter how I was feeling, I didn't want to accept any of those words from Wallace. He hadn't earned the right to speak to me that way and he certainly did not get to try and piss all over my fun with my cousin.

The words were out of my mouth like venom from a snake. 'You're not my dad, you're not even my uncle so why don't you butt out.'

Wallace didn't flinch at my words or retaliate. In fact I was certain his expression moulded from frustrated to a look of pure sorrow. And that was even worse. I had no intention of ever trying to impress Wallace or win his affection, but to see that look form on his face was worse than anything.

I barely touched a thing at dinner. Jolie came and brushed a hand across my forehead at one point, checking for a temperature the way she did when I was much younger. If she had opened her arms, I would have climbed into them, exactly as I had done five or six years ago. Such was the dichotomy of being a teenager, needing the space and freedom to grow, yet always wanting to return to someone who was older and wiser for comfort and security. I found my way to bed before anyone, including my sisters. I fell into a fitful sleep, waves climbed over me as I gasped for air. And beyond the waves, I could see my sister, Franny. I was trying to reach her, but she was too far away and each time I thought I could make it over a wave, it overtook me until eventually, I could no longer see her. I had lost her.

I woke up sweating and crying, trying to find a way out of bed sheets that had wrapped themselves around me. I squinted at the moon pouring its light into my room and stepped out of bed. I stood next to the shelf and looked at the dolls lined up, pristine and perfect.

I heard a noise from along the corridor and I knew it was Franny. I stepped out of my door without hesitation as I was closer to her room than my parents' room.

I stopped dead in the hallway as I saw by the half-light, a tall male figure. He was outside Franny's room.

Wallace.

I walked right up to him, not caring about the hour or the lack of light around me.

'What are you doing?' I hissed.

'Franny – I was checking on her. No one else got up. Your mum is comatose.' He looked at me. 'I presumed you would be too after the amount you drank at the beach today.' Wallace gave me a hard stare. Accompanied by the strength of his tone, I knew this was not the sort of conversation to be had outside my little sister's room at 2 a.m.

I turned to go back to my room, but I went slowly to make sure Wallace returned to his room. When he had reached his door, I heard the sound of my father's voice, then the two of them talking and then each man closed their respective doors. And suddenly and without warning I was overwhelmed by a sense of security, that there was a real man and a proper parent looking out for my sister tonight.

The next morning, I woke with a fierce determination. As though a veil had been lifted and I could see clearly. I would return to the sea. This time sober. I was not to be defeated. I was not going to let a silly thing like yesterday scare me from going near the water again. Just the thought of this made me see how I was protected here. Uncle Rob may not be around any more, but everything was going to be okay. And so, because I had fallen asleep so early, I rose at dawn, took a bike from the shed and cycled the distance down to the beach alone.

15

NOW

I would be in the Highlands the day after tomorrow. Sylvie had called back the very same day and reassured me things were going ahead as planned. Assuring me again of my protection. The damn news feature was not going to mar my job. Scarlett had still not returned my call and I had pent-up frustration I needed to expel in one line with her. *What were you thinking?*

My accommodation was booked and there was even a thumbs-up emoji response back from Dexter Rice, which eased my embarrassment and made me feel hopeful for our meet.

I decided I would get a swim in today, and as I thought of heading to the pool, images of Lloyd and I flashed through my mind; I felt a weakening in my gut, followed by a fluttering. I laughed out loud at myself.

'Oh, no you don't,' I told myself. Lloyd was a GM in a leisure centre, I was a worldwide famous actor. This was not *Notting Hill*. There was undeniably a connection with Lloyd and I felt that he was keeping an eye out for me. But I knew I would be in the Highlands soon, surrounded by hundreds of cast and crew. There was no need to try and pursue anything or make things complicated. It had been fun.

Because of the hype around this story, I chose to stay indoors in the day, taking myself up to my oasis for sun and relaxation. I had a gruelling filming schedule ahead of me and I needed to feel okay. I had, by some fluke, managed to read most of the script and had familiarised myself with some of the lines I would need to know between myself and Dexter. But fortunately, it was mostly sea shots and very little dialogue required for the time I was needed in the Highlands.

Tammy, also by sheer fluke, was working in London, and so between shoot times she delivered me food and drinks. That way I was able to avoid the photographers. Or so I thought. When I arrived at the pool that evening, there were two men waiting outside.

They started taking photos straight away.

'Bit late for you tonight, Rey, you kept us waiting, all right,' one said, as he dared to get close to me.

'Any news on your sisters?' the other said and I was about to turn and throw a punch when Lloyd was at the door and was pulling me inside.

'Get in,' he said firmly and I felt a flutter of excitement at the tone in his voice. He pushed me inside and then closed the door, staying outside to say something to the photographers. I watched them walk away. Lloyd came back in.

'Wow, you must have a real way with them. They don't listen to me.'

'That's because you're the bait.' He moved closer to me and a breath caught in my throat. 'Are you okay?' he asked in a deep and sincere voice and I thought how strange this was, that the manager of a leisure centre could make me feel as though I were being protected by Jason Bourne.

'I am now,' I said and I took a step closer to him.

'Where do you want these, boss?' one of Lloyd's minions came out from the office carrying a pile of flyers.

'Just... just anywhere for now,' Lloyd called over his shoulder and the minion went away.

'I should...' I pointed towards the pool.

'You should.' He nodded.

'Pool's empty,' he called after me, motioning to the screen in the office. I hadn't noticed it before. But of course, I knew that it was there and that there was a possibility he had been observing me. I thought back to yesterday and the light flickering off, the presence of someone in a dark room with me, not making themselves wholly known to me.

'Great. I'd better crack on.'

'See you in a bit.'

* * *

I admired the mirror effect of the water, my favourite part about being here. I looked at my goggles and swimming cap in my hand and tossed them to the ground. I didn't need them today. It was just me. And Lloyd. I went to the shower and took my time under the water, raising my hands and running them through my hair as though I were in some hair advert in a tropical location. I looked up to where the camera was on the corner wall and held my gaze there, wondering if he was there, if he was looking. Watching.

I hated disturbing the beautifully still water, but I was feeling more confident. I looked at the Smith family and heard their story calling me once more.

Once the mother had perfected her skills as a party planner and hostess, she wasn't sure what else she was supposed to do with her time. There had been little talk of children, they did not plan them and no one had given her any advice about taking the pill or putting in a coil. So when she became pregnant it was as big a shock to her as anyone else. The mother was now a mother for sure, in the physical sense, but she did not feel that way in her mind. She herself was an only child, her own father had been absent for much of her childhood, immersing himself in his career, only re-emerging as a ghost of a figure in her life when she was much older. The mother had played with dolls a lot to occupy herself when she was young. She was sure she would know how to be a loving parent because although her own mother was present, her mind was often elsewhere and never with her. When the mother was growing up, she had seen how it was done in movies and adverts. She dressed her dolls up in the most beautiful clothes. She knew her child would be the best-dressed child around.

The daughter was born. She had bright blue eyes and a flash of blonde hair. The mother was tired and was never sure if she was doing anything right because the daughter cried all the time. And when she wasn't crying, she was fussing and being sick and did not ever seem to respond well to being held. The daughter spent a lot of time with the housekeeper until the housekeeper complained that she was not a nanny and left.

The house fell into disarray. The father worked more than ever, always staying late at work. Whenever the mother called him on the office phone, his receptionist answered, even when it was ten o'clock at night. Sometimes, she was sure she heard giggling just before she put the phone down, but she was so very tired. Eventually, new help arrived, and the mother was able to relax and sleep. But the new help didn't stay for long and soon the cycle began again: the sleepless nights, the terrible mess in the house. The father wanted to entertain again, he said it had been too long. The mother was a mess. She felt sad all the time. So she went to the doctor and the doctor told her she could take some tablets if she wanted to. Sometimes she didn't even feel as if she was in the room, as if she was real. But she felt that being this was better. She could tolerate the little things, *like the endless nappy changes and the late-night phone calls to the father's office that ended with a curt goodbye from the receptionist. She could tolerate the crying, so much so that sometimes she could go for hours listening to it and not even really hear it in the end.*

When a few years had passed, the father asked the mother for a son. She thought it queer, as though he was asking her for a loaf of brown bread and not white, and she could simply pop to the shops and fulfil his request.

And when the next daughter, was born, the father was simply unable to disguise his disgust. He left the mother to her own devices most days and even began to take long weekends away, only spending any time with his wife and daughters on long family holidays where he got to show off the two blue-eyed girls he had helped to create.

Such a lucky man...

Such beautiful girls...

The comments that people made about the daughters were like someone was talking to him about someone else's children. For the father did not feel lucky.

One day, many years later, a third girl, was born, and the mother looked into the eyes of her husband, silently pleading with him to love her and their daughters. Something seemed to change in the father that year his third daughter was born, for finally, he began to see what everyone else could see. He saw for the first time that what he had were three very beautiful daughters. And they belonged to him.

It was almost ten when I had completed over fifteen lengths. I had beaten my personal best and I was feeling okay. I dressed and made my way out to reception just as Lloyd was getting ready to leave.

I took in a deep breath and smiled. 'You just closing up?'

'Yes.'

'Did—' I went to speak and Lloyd cut me off.

'Look. I want to ask you out, for a drink or something. But I'm not going to, and it's not because I don't want to – I'm not asking you out, because I do want to. Does that make sense?'

I nodded. 'Perfect sense.'

It didn't. But I got it. I was too much for him. He didn't want to get involved with someone like me, someone who came from a family as messed up as mine.

'We could just skip the drink part,' I said as confidently as though I had just delivered a line in a film, surprising even myself that I hadn't had to be fuelled with alcohol to say it.

I wasn't proud of what I did, with men, the way I could just give myself to them. Until now, I supposed, the way Lloyd was looking at me, I couldn't decipher it, I couldn't work it out. It felt too much, I was overwhelmed by his intensity. I only knew how to love intensely for one night. But I felt as though it was all I had. It was my default. Yet I'd had two nights with Lloyd. This could be the third.

Lloyd put his hand to his head. 'Woah. Okay. I... this is going to sound so daft, but I'll have to decline. It's not that I don't want to, I—'

I took a step backwards. There was a flicker of something in his eyes, like desperation, not for me per se, but for what could have been. For what he maybe wanted to say but was choosing not to. And I was a colossal mess when it came to men. It's okay, I thought. He's just another man.

'Thanks for everything.' I instantly regretted the words which sounded so final and over the top.

'I'm sorry. And you're welcome. Take it easy now.'

We both stood for another beat, each of us not daring to speak.

'I'll be seeing you.' I turned and walked out of the door.

Once I was outside a rush of fresh evening air hit me and I gasped an inhale. And as if the sudden shock of oxygen had given me clarity, it came to me. I felt a pang in my chest and in my gut. My breath became laboured, part of me was walking back into the centre, the other half was already walking down the street. I blew out my breaths as though I were blowing out a candle as I walked, trying to join the two parts of me together. Lloyd was nice, and there were plenty of nice men about. Weren't there? What was this feeling and what did it mean. I didn't know how to deal with this emotion. I had felt so comfortable with Lloyd, he was funny, being with him felt good, he made me feel safe even. I had enjoyed this level of flirtation and what felt like a genuine connection. My God, the list could go on. I had played a myriad of characters my entire life it seemed, even off screen. Get a grip, Rey, what was it? What was this over whelming pain searing through my chest? I stopped, bent down and pushed my hand against my thighs as though I had just run 5k without stopping. I stood up and it was as though I saw it, clearly. When I was with Lloyd, for the first time in my life, I felt authentic. I felt as though I was being the person I was supposed to be. I felt like me.

16

NOW

When I landed in Inverness there was a woman standing in the arrivals with a card with my name on it. She looked hard but sincere.

I approached the woman who was wearing a black bomber jacket with blue jeans and Doc Marten boots.

'Rey Levine?' she said to me and I nodded.

'Em,' she said and for a second I was waiting for her to finish her sentence. Then I realised Em was her name. She had that chiselled model look about her and I felt as though I already knew her in some way.

'Oh, Em. Nice to meet you. I wasn't expecting you.'

'Protection, ma'am. For the sake of the film and your own personal safety.'

This was my protection? Wow. The film company had gone all out for me. I felt relief flood through me. I looked at her: muddy blonde hair tied back in a tight ponytail, not a free strand in sight, her flawless skin... she couldn't have been much older than me, but she was tall and sturdy. Athletic. My eyes fell to the small logo on her jacket. A blue and red criss-cross pattern.

'I believe we may have a lift.' I began to look round, and as I did, I saw a woman racing towards us.

'Sorry, sorry, the parking is weird here.' She laughed and looked at Em and then me. 'It's no Heathrow is it?'

I raised my eyebrows in sort of agreement. I didn't want to upset anyone in hearing distance.

'I'm Layla.' Layla moved everything she was holding into one hand to shake hands with us both.

'Hi,' she said to Em.

Em nodded and looked at me.

'Security,' I said.

'Oh, right. Yes. Okay.' Layla was carrying a phone and had another one around her neck on a shoe string. She opened the phone in her hand and began scanning through. She looked back up at both of us; she seemed flustered she was late. She was young, too. Younger than me it seemed.

'I'm new. This is my first week.' Her face flushed and she grinned.

I dared a glance at Em, her face softened only slightly and I felt that we were both thinking the same thing. Would we even see the accommodation today?

'Right!' Layla clapped her hands. 'Let's get you to the Glenside.' She threw her hand over her mouth. 'Oops. I didn't mean to say that out loud.' She flushed again and looked around to see if anyone had heard her. 'Let's just get to the car,' she whispered as the phone in her hand began to ring.

Inverness airport was small but once we stepped outside, I took a moment to take in the vastness around me – the mountains in the distance and the huge blue sky dotted with little clouds.

'Lovely, isn't it?' Layla said to me, her phone to her ear, half listening to a conversation she had apparently just been conferenced into.

'It's beautiful.' I looked off in the distance, at the mountains I had seen out of the window just before we'd landed.

Layla led us to a black Mercedes and took a seat in the middle section. Em ushered me into the back and once I was in a warm and comfortable car, I watched the landscape change dramatically until mountains were practically hugging us either side. I was tired; I knew I should make conversation with Em or at least Layla, but I found myself nodding off. Layla spent a lot of time on her phone, checking in with us occasionally. About an hour and a half later, the car stopped. We had driven down a remote driveway and reached a clearing. A huge house looked down at me. I had seen plenty of big houses in my time, I had acted within their walls, but something about this house felt different. It seemed as though it was looking at me, the way the two larger windows on either side of pillars appeared like eyes, as though it was human and had been expecting us. I wanted to laugh, to say my observations out loud but they felt childish. And Em was so serious, she didn't seem like the sort of woman I could have a laugh with.

Besides, I realised I was super tuned into my senses, my personal alarm. Or at least I was trying to. It had to be the upset with the feature. I was feeling vulnerable. And suddenly I looked at Em for some reassurance. Her face revealed nothing and instead she stoically went about getting me out of the car with my baggage. Layla, finally ended her call, and sighed.

'Well, here we are.' She was still holding on tightly to both her phones as the driver opened the door on her side.

'You'll be pleased to know there's a pool in the house, so you can get some extra training in.' Layla smiled at me as we stood and took in the house for all its splendour. But I still saw those eyes staring down at me.

'A pool,' I said. The Smith family popped into my mind; they were the ones I had spent so much time with in Camden, swimming with every day. They were the ones who had got me through the last week. Although I wouldn't have their physical image to look at when I was swimming, their story had begun to embed itself in my mind and I found I was looking forward to being reunited with them, albeit it in a different location.

'It's an Edwardian manor, built in 1912, so not a ghostly house or anything like that.'

'Why would you say that?' I looked up at the house. 'I mean, about the ghosts.' I looked at Layla who was looking at me blankly. 'I mean, soon as you mention a ghost, well, you've mentioned a ghost.' I laughed and looked at Em for some encouragement. She looked back tight-lipped.

'I said there are none,' Layla said, looking back at her phone where she had been for the last few hours since she met us at the airport.

'But how do you know?' I said raising my eyebrows, half jesting. I had stayed in so many different locations for my work, a lot of them were much older than this place. And I would always tune into the house to see if I could sense anything. I rarely did.

She shook her head and sniffed out a laugh. 'Come on. Let's get you settled.'

We walked up the steps into an ornate hallway, with a huge fireplace and two statue heads on pillars on either side. On the walls hung pictures of long forgotten people who now only existed in portrait form. The wallpaper was a dark shade of green with undulating patterns that made my head spin.

'Well, it's certainly got character,' I said, wondering what I would find in my bedroom. I thought of all the ancient houses I had visited as part of the National Trust and imagined a bed that breathed out dust when it was sat upon.

'There is a housekeeper and a chef,' Layla continued. 'Nothing new there. You'll be picked up at 5 a.m. tomorrow.'

I winced.

'Sorry, they want to get a couple of early shots near the water.'

I shuddered at the thought. Would I be expected to go into the water tomorrow, I wondered. Or would they give me a bit of break on my first day. I had been swimming for only a week, and to suddenly make the transition from pool to sea was something I knew I needed to do at some point, but I had been trying to pretend it wasn't really going to happen.

'Will I be in it?' I asked casually.

'What?' Layla frowned.

'The water, am I going in it tomorrow?'

'Oh, I don't know'. Layla looked flustered again and began swiping frantically at her phone.

'Don't worry. Forget I asked.' I looked at Em who was standing just behind me. 'I presume we have a room for security.'

'I'll just go and find out.' Layla hurried away leaving me standing with Em. I turned to her.

'So is this the sort of job you do a lot? Work with actors and what not?'

'Usually. I've done some royalty and I do high net-worth individuals in Saudi Arabia.'

I nodded. 'Nice. Keeps you busy then.'

'Sure does.' Em held her hands in front of her in a clasp.

'So it's Em as in Emily? Emilia? Or is it M as in the letter M. Like in James Bond.' I scoffed a little. It was the first time I'd ever had my own security and I wasn't sure how to treat this situation.

'It's Emma. But Em is easy. One syllable. Easy to say.'

'Or holler, I presume, if I'm being swept up in a sea of paps.'

Em nodded. 'It's not unusual. When they get hold of a story, they don't want to let it go. Your story interests people, because it involves a missing little girl.'

My heart clamped when Em said the words 'little' and 'girl'. My sister Franny who had been trapped in time would forever be a little girl. Whenever people spoke of her, I always thought of my last moments with her. It was a terrible pain that I would never be rid of, playing the same movie scene on repeat had become the bane of my life.

'And you think they might come here?'

'I think they will find a way to find you if they really want to.'

I let out a breath as a way to fill the void between us.

I heard the clip-clop of Layla's boots coming back down the hall. 'There's a room along the corridor from yours for... Em, was it?'

Em nodded.

I looked at both women. I was eager to get away from them. I wanted to get a swim in before dinner and then have an early night.

'There are a few of the crew here, plus Rose, Andy and Mia.' Layla reeled off the names of some of the supporting cast. 'And Rice,' she said and then paused before she glanced at me.

'Dexter is here?' I asked, quite surprised. I didn't think he would want to bunk up here, I presumed he would have somewhere solitary. But then, it's not as if you can just book into a Travelodge in the outback of the Highlands.

Layla looked at her phone. 'Yes, he should be arriving in the next few hours. He's driven from the Lake District. Family place there.'

I nodded, grateful for a little heads up and insight into his life, although I felt a little apprehensive about meeting Dexter. He was so hot right now, his face was everywhere: magazines, billboards and all over the socials. You couldn't get away from him. It occurred to me that Em was more valued than I had initially thought. If Dexter's fans tried to find him here, then I wanted to feel safe.

'And you?' I asked.

'I'm in the lodge. Over the back. It's hidden.'

I looked behind me and the driver had brought in my bags.

'Thank you,' I said.

'Right, I'll see you at dinner.' Layla began walking, one hand dragging her case, the other pressing her phone to her ear 'Your room is the second floor, third on left! Em's is final room at the end next to you,' she called as she walked away.

I took a deep breath and glanced around. The driver was loitering in the doorway, he half looked at me and then turned and walked back to the car. It was just me and Em in the stark hallway.

'I'm going to have a look around,' Em said and left me with my case where it was.

I also wanted to have a scout about, but I waited a moment until Em had set off so we wouldn't be together, still feeling a little unsure of how I needed to be around her.

I looked around the bottom floor. There was a huge dining room, already laid for dinner. I stepped out quickly, feeling as though I shouldn't have been in there. There were several lounging rooms scattered around what appeared to be a large study or conference area with a huge desk. As I walked towards the stairs I could hear the clattering of plates from behind a door and figured that was the kitchen. I walked on and followed my nose until a long corridor opened up into a sunroom with a swimming pool behind the glass. It looked very inviting, clean, and fresh and I was surprised that I felt eager to get in, to be close to the Smith family again. Even though their images were back in the Camden pool, I wondered if their voices may have followed me here. Besides, I wanted to be the best I could be for the shoot, whenever that moment arrived that I would need to step into the sea. I didn't want there to be anything to come between me and my work. The fact I had been able to stay out of the water for my job until now was nothing short of a miracle.

I went back to the hallway and found my case was gone. I took the stairs two at a time. After a minute I had to stop and catch my breath. The staircase was long and as much as I had been swimming recently, I was not fit by any means. I found my room and walked in. There was my case in the middle of the room and there was Em standing by the window looking out. She turned when she heard me walk in.

'Hi,' I said and looked about the room. I wondered if Em had brought up my case. 'Everything look okay?'

Em didn't answer. Instead, she turned from the window, spent another minute looking through the wardrobe, under the bed and along the skirting boards, where she ran her finger and occasionally stopped to press it hard against the wood.

She got up and walked to the door.

'Do you think we might be bugged?' I asked knowing it wouldn't surprise me if we were.

Em took a final glance over her shoulder. 'Everything is okay,' she said. 'I'll be next door. I'll see you at dinner.'

I closed the door.

My room had a king-size bed, a heavy-looking duvet, even though it was summer – I was in the Highlands now and I had already sensed the change in temperature from what had been the stifling streets of Camden. I went to the window and looked out over a vast immaculate lawn, eager to see what Em had been looking at before me. Beyond the lawn was a less tended to wild area, which fell away and eventually became a wood which looked dense and eerily inviting.

I went to my suitcase and began to pull items from it and as I was here for over a week, I knew I was going to make myself at home a little. I had packed a hot water bottle, not knowing how cold the nights might get here, even in June, and as I went to place it on an ancient chest of drawers, which looked as old as the house itself, I stopped, as I felt drawn to the window again. This time I didn't see an empty lawn, but a man, with a dark beard standing in the middle staring right up at my window. I inhaled quickly and shot backwards, tripping over my suitcase and banging my head on the bed.

'Augh.' I let out a loud groan.

The door to my room flew open and there was Em standing in the doorway. She took two long strides and she was next to me, hauling me up from the floor.

'I fell over my suitcase,' I said feeling foolish, but I was keen to see who had been on the lawn just then. Em stood back and once I had I righted myself I went back to the window. When I peered out of the window from a distance, the lawn was once again empty. The words in the newspaper article were racing through my mind and I thought of how many people would have read it. Maybe it was Em's presence that was making me paranoid. Social media was already awash with images of Dexter and me. The location had been named as the Highlands, but who knew if anyone had leaked where we were. There were hundreds of people involved in making this movie. I had once thought Scotland was gargantuan, yet just driving here to this remote location, I felt we had pretty much driven in a straight line and so I was beginning to realise that maybe we weren't so remote, that maybe it wasn't going to be so difficult for people to find us. But what was bothering me was why Scarlett had decided to talk so openly about what had happened. Why now?

I wanted so much to just concentrate on being here in Scotland and focusing on my job, but people were probably out there making all sorts of assumptions about Corsica, Franny and why she never returned from our last holiday. Including Lloyd. I had seen it;

I had felt it. I could replay the night over and over, yet it never changed what happened.

The words that my mother called out to me when she discovered me at the beach.

It's all your fault.

And the secret Cormac and I clung so tightly to together.

17

NOW

I put one toe in the pool and took a deep breath. The water was beautifully warm and inviting. No public pool facilities here. It felt like an indulgence I was ready to accept. I had swum several lengths back in Camden, and although it was a different pool, a different location, I was sure I could do this. The Smith family had kept me distracted with their stories, I was sure if I tried to summon them, they would be here for me now.

I was ready to lower myself in when my phone rang. Anticipating a call from Sylvie checking in on me, I felt a wave of calmness wash over me. I was protected out here – not just by those that were here but by my team back home.

I looked at who was calling. This time it wouldn't just be for a chat and catch up and to air her stresses at me.

I allowed myself to reach my guilt default setting as I answered the call.

'Hi, Mum.'

There were no words, just tears. I listened to her cry for a few seconds. I thought about what I always did, my life so far removed from the life I'd had as a child. I was about to shoot a film with one of the most well-known actors right now and it should have been the first thing we discussed. Like mother and daughter. But she wouldn't mention anything. She would skirt around it, even when I made reference to elements of my life which incorporated my work. It had always been the way since I landed my first role. She had brushed over it as though I had told her I had taken a job as a filing assistant. All it did was bring back memories of the way she could manage to pretend things weren't happening when we were young. Instead, she found her answer in the bottom of a margarita glass.

I thought about the mother I knew when I was a child. I'd stopped knowing her when I was almost seventeen – when I left Corsica, and she didn't. I thought how angry that had made me at the time, how desperately I wanted her to come back to England and be with us. To be with me. I had needed her but she had chosen one child over two. And not just one child, but one missing child. But even then, I knew it was more than just about Franny going missing. It was my mother's way of escaping. She had always wanted out. I knew that she had tried to be a mother, a wife, but it never came naturally to her.

Franny disappearing was her get-out clause in a way. Finally, she was free of the shackles of domesticity. She didn't need to pretend any more. Before Franny went, when it was it still the five of us, I had heard her cry many times behind the door of her bedroom, always when my father was away, her never thinking or perhaps believing that we might be able to hear her. But I would often just stand outside the door, listening to her sobbing for what felt like a long time. I had wondered so much then, why she cried behind closed doors. I never went to her or tried to comfort her, because whenever *I* had cried behind closed doors, she had never once come to me. I was glad she was still in Corsica, so she didn't need to pretend at playing mummy dear and I didn't need to think I needed her still. In a way, I had never really felt as though I had a mother. She was always a presence, a figure of certain importance in my life, but never someone I would want to go to for comfort, certainly not when I crept out of my childhood years and began to make my way into becoming an adult.

Yet somehow, always in the back of my mind, there was that longing, that tugging back to the past where I lay in my bed, waiting for her to come to me, to hold me, to stroke my hair like I had seen other mums do with their children. It still stayed with me, no matter how much I tried to dismiss it, to tell myself, I'm an adult now, I didn't need her. That wanting, or maybe it was needing. I was never sure. I just knew it wouldn't leave. And when the day came when my mother was ready to depart this world, I knew that was what I would grieve, the love that never was.

Finally, my mother's sobbing subsided.

'I take it you've seen the papers.'

'Seen them, Rey? I'm living the papers. My life is the goddamn papers.' My mother's voice was high and strained. She was breathing loudly down the phone. Fuelled by her anger and frustration. Not just from her missing daughter, but from the missing parts of herself, the parts she gave unwillingly to the family she could never really look after.

'They are here every day. I opened the door one day and there they were. They haven't left me alone since. I kept thinking they would go, but they just stay here, or they go and come back. What was Scarlett thinking? Do you know? Do you two know something? They keep knocking and asking for my side of the story, "What happened to your daughter all those years ago?" they ask. "Why have you never come home, do you think she is alive?" All these questions? I presume they are asking you questions, too? Following you around?' Mum asked, slowing her speech. 'Because you must know more than me. If Scarlett claims she is alive... then. Oh, I just don't know any more. I'm completely dizzy with it all.'

'I've managed to bat most of them off,' I said but I began to piece together an image of a face. It had been the night Tammy had organised drinks for me in Soho. There had been a woman in the bar, it had been the way she had stared at me that had bothered me. It was a look that had gone on for too long, as though she knew me and not just from my face on their TV screens. But I imagined that my mother was getting absolutely battered by photographers and journalists, maybe more so than me. But was I supposed to feel sorry for her? Was I supposed to empathise with her? I couldn't summon the feelings. There was the permanent blockage of anger and resentment that prevented me from accessing the feelings which were normal between a mother and daughter.

'Well lucky for you. I can't afford that privilege. I suppose you can pay for your protection.'

I snorted at this comment.

'What do you mean?' I asked.

'Don't you get haughty at me, young lady.' My mother's tone had turned bitter, and I recognised the change as something that was going to turn ugly. My mother had changed. It was the illness taking over.

'I don't have a security guard, Mother,' I said, omitting 'Mum' because she was making me angry and I wanted to separate her from me as much as possible. And it was true, I didn't have a security guard. One had been hired for me by the production company. I didn't raise the issue of the lack of funds she had referred to. She was doing okay, I knew that my father would still be settling up with her each month. There were only two daughters to tend to and we were both adults now. I knew that Mum wouldn't ever need to worry about money again, even though they no longer spoke. My suggestion to my mother on our last phone call that she should live with my father was taken badly by her. But they were as bad as one another; they deserved to be living together. Without us. What neither me nor my mother ever discussed was that after she stayed behind in Corsica, I went to boarding school and studied acting and dance. I never returned home after that. I hadn't seen or spoken to my father in over ten years. But from the cheques he tried to send to me, and the comfortable life my mother led, we were both going to be okay financially. Except I had ripped every cheque up and thrown it in the bin. We were the absolute epitome of a broken family. A production company would have been overjoyed to get their hands on a script about my real life. And not just the bits they got to read about in the papers.

Eventually the conversation petered out. My mother was tired, she was on edge and no doubt would be looking for something to medicate those feelings with as soon as we ended the call, if she hadn't begun already. How odd it was that here I was in a beautiful old house, in a lovely part of the UK and I couldn't even bring myself to mention anything about it to her. It was as though my life as an actor was a myth to my mother; everything I had done seemed to have just passed her by. She did not want to acknowledge it at all. But despite her inability to parent me, to protect me, all I felt was a raging desire to succeed. I had done it all alone, without her unconditional love and support. As hard as getting into the water had been, as difficult as I knew sea swimming again would be, I knew I would do it, because succeeding and pushing past what my body didn't want me to do was weaved into the very fabric of my being.

However, the entire relationship with my mother on her side was based on her need to expel any lurking demons that she had within her, towards me. Whether she was looking to me to fix things, I don't know. There was one tiny scrap of glue that still bound us together and that was the memory of Franny and the memory of that day.

18

CORSICA, JUNE 2008

Empty beaches always gave me equal amounts of joy and shivery fears. It felt similar to when I was watching the film, *The Shining* – I desperately wanted to be immersed in that world, but something terrifying was about to happen. It was a sort of agoraphobia, coupled with claustrophobia, looking around, not a person in sight just the sound of gulls, the rush of the waves, yet I knew it was a place of safety. It could bring me equal levels of calm. It was almost unbelievable to me how this beauty continued to exist when there was no one to witness it. Like would a tree make a cracking noise when it fell if no one was there to hear the sound?

I sat on the sand for a few minutes and watched the sun continue to rise.

I stripped to my bikini and ran to the water's edge. I was in before I had time to think about it. I was swimming and diving beneath the waves and it was joyous and exhilarating and all the fear and that anxiety that I woke with most mornings had evaporated and it was just me and the elements. And this was where I was happy, feeling the fear and embracing it all.

I dried myself off knowing I had absolutely done the right thing.

As I walked away, I looked at the waves roaring and crashing. I felt their force and I still felt what they could do to me.

* * *

When I returned to the villa, Jolie was in the kitchen, preparing breakfast.

'Oh my, you're here already?' She looked momentarily panicked, as she put on the coffee and began to scour about for some food.

'Don't, I'm fine. I'll eat later. It's still early.'

I headed back to my room, which was on the other side of the stairs to where the adults slept. As I approached the top of the stairs I heard whispered voices, it was just after seven which was early for anyone to be up during the holiday, and all the adults had stayed up far too late again judging by the mess I had clocked as I passed the drawing room.

I hovered near the top of the stairs for a moment, singling out voices until I knew that it was Vanessa and Wallace I could hear and that this was their room closest to the stairs. I paused and tried to tune in; I could decipher sobbing and a soothing voice. After a few seconds, it was apparent that the sobbing was Wallace and after another beat, soothing words of Aunt Vanessa. Wallace began talking a few muffled incoherent words. Suddenly the door flew open and Aunt Vanessa was in the doorway, her face a muddle of emotions. Shocked and surprised to see me stalled on the stairs, but also embarrassed and frustrated even. As she wrangled with a suitably benign expression for her favourite niece, I began heading up the stairs.

'Are you okay?' she eventually asked softly.

'Yes, good, I just got up, had a swim that was all,' I whispered back as the hour was still early for most.

'Oh lovely, good for you.' Aunt Vanessa's usual jovial tone was back. 'I'll see you at breakfast, shall I?'

'Yes.' I turned before I headed down the corridor to my bedroom. I heard the door close to Aunt Vanessa's room and the sound of her pattering downstairs. In my room I took a shower in the en suite – one of the other perks of being so far away from everyone else – and lounged on my bed, snoozing until my stomach began to tell me it was time to eat.

Downstairs there was a low hum of chatter, and as I walked through to the kitchen I was already anticipating who would be there. My sisters Franny and Scarlett were sitting at the kitchen counter and Jolie was already hard at work tending to their needs. I noticed a jug of freshly squeezed orange juice so I took it and began to fill my sister's glasses as Jolie wrestled with croissants scalding from the oven. She gave me a look of thanks and so with juice and food in front of them my sisters were quiet.

'Franny, are you okay?' I asked quietly. 'What happened last night? You were crying in your sleep? Do you remember?'

'Somebody woke me up,' she said in a small voice. I didn't need to ask any more questions. An image of Wallace outside her room flashed in my mind. My stomach was twisting and turning, the smells of the breakfast were sending waves of nausea down to my gut.

'What are we doing today?' Scarlett asked through a mouthful of croissants. She must always know the agenda and was never satisfied with doing nothing. Jolie had turned one of the downstairs rooms into a games and crafting room just for Scarlett when she became beside herself with boredom and we could no longer abide her whinging.

'I want to go to that water park,' Scarlett said.

'It's too far,' Franny said, repeating the words she'd heard our mother say yesterday. Scarlett looked at me, and we shared a knowing look because Scarlett was now old enough to understand how to read the subtext. Mum's excuse was formed when Dad refused to drive. Something they didn't think we had heard. The park was forty kilometres away. Mum passed her test but wouldn't drive abroad. Jolie was too busy. If I were old enough, I would have driven them myself.

'We could go the lake, take the paddle boards.' I suggested, diverting from the water park. The lake was not really a lake, more like a bay with a short, old wooden pier and a rustic, grey sandy beach where the ocean threw up slimy seaweed and pale driftwood that looked like old animal bones. Three years ago, when we were last here, we found a half-dead seagull and tried to nurse it back to life. We wrapped it in a towel, but it died. We buried it and built a gravestone out of shingle and thick oval pebbles. A part of me wanted to see if it was still there. A reminder that we had tried to do a good deed, that we had tried to save something.

'Yes!' both my sisters yelped in unison.

'Eat some fruit, girls.' Jolie put a platter of fat red grapes and galia melon chunks on the counter and I dived towards the glistening treasure.

'We can take a picnic, you could take your drawing pad, do some sketches of the dunes, Franny?' I suggested and she nodded enthusiastically. Sometimes slipping into the role of mother felt so natural and easy, and when I did it, it made me feel good, like I should do it more, and I knew I could. But often, I rejected it, even though I knew my sisters craved that constant chivvying, those few words from an elder that made them feel as though they mattered. Because I still, even after all these years, expected my mother to step up to her post, to assert her role of primary caregiver and to show us the matriarchy of the family started and ended with her, the point at the tip of the triangle.

The air shifted as I felt another presence in the room. When I turned my head, Wallace was leaning against the doorframe, his eyes flitting between me, Scarlett and then Franny.

'This looks cosy,' he said and whilst the sentiment was there, his expression was blank, his eyes lifeless. The man who had been excited to meet his girlfriend's family was another person, not this hollow version I was seeing this morning. Not the man I had encountered in the corridor between all our bedrooms last night.

'Good morning, Wallace.' Jolie was wiping down the counter as though she were a server in a cafe, ready to greet her next customer.

Wallace moved slowly towards the counter. When he reached me, I saw his face was blotched and red, he didn't look as though he had slept at all and I had an urge to prod him with my finger to see if he might break.

I thought about him outside Franny's room last night and the way I had shouted at him. Was this my doing? He was a man of substantial stature and the way he had been so animated at the beach the day before was such a stark contrast to the shrivelled man I saw before me. My own father had a small range of emotional settings. I had never seen him cry, or even seen his eyes well up at events that my mother would openly weep at. To even think my dad could or would ever cry was so far removed from my understanding of my real life that to see this man, standing in front of me looking hollow and weak, was an alien experience. I found I was studying him hard, pondering over the look of him, so raw and exposed, his emotions were so on show and there for all to see. There were no barriers, he was not attempting to hide how he felt. I had never witnessed such a display before, I had only ever heard the sobs of my mother from behind closed doors. And I knew this was what was bothering me about seeing Wallace today. I knew it shouldn't, I knew I should not be feeling this way, yet looking at him all weak and pathetic this morning, was not only shocking but was, in fact, disgusting me.

I felt the last drop of energy slip out of me after I hung up from the call from my mother. She was ill and I had noticed the changes happening slowly but I had chosen to ignore them. We were essentially estranged. I hadn't travelled back to Corsica to visit her. I was never the one who called her, she only called me and I only thought of her in the past tense, not as someone who was in my life now. If it hadn't been that I was ready to swim, I wasn't sure I would have done. But I closed my eyes and calmed my thoughts, then cleared my head of the words that buzzed around in my mind always after we spoke.

I looked at the new surroundings, the luxury of the ceramic tiles, and the clear water that I imagined had barely been swum in. I slipped in and began my strokes. Like a muscle memory, the image of the Smith family in the leisure centre came to me, as did their story. I let my mind fill up with their world, allowing me to escape from the challenge I was embarking on.

The father went to work. The mother stayed at home. That was how it was. The mother did not complain, for she knew what she had signed herself up for when she married the father. He was a popular man, *always in demand with work and socially. The mother found it a bitter pill to swallow at times; the perfect family scenario she had imagined before they were wed was a dream that had just evaporated, something she was never going to be able to touch.*

There were times when the father was away for long periods of time and the daughters were hard work. They demanded all of her time. But the mother found that giving part of herself to her daughters was very difficult. She found love and affection were tricky to manoeuvre and the woman she had envisioned herself to be was a mere shadow. Sometimes she would watch a film and see how the mother interacted with her children and she would try and emulate that behaviour. But it felt strained, and she was never able to keep it up for long enough. Her mind was often a muddle. She thought of the father and what he was doing when he wasn't with them. But after a while, she resigned herself to her situation.

Her mind would wander to other things, to other places and she was rarely in the same place in her mind as her children, and when the father did return home, he would appear vexed at her vacant expression. But what was a woman to do with herself if she had no job and a nanny and a housekeeper to take care of her children and her home?

The husband liked to keep a well-stocked bar because when he was back at home for the weekend, he liked to entertain. This was where the mother came into herself once more. This was where she came alive. The father was pleased when the soirees were revived. He loved to be seen, and the mother felt seen. By the guests and by her husband. The husband would praise her ability to organise such an event, loudly and proudly in front of the guests.

Even though the mother knew that actually, she had not been the one to organise much except who was sitting next to whom and how to decorate the table. She took hours over this part of the event. It was, after all, her soul purpose, except for being there, next to the father.

She knew the children would often get up and sit on the stairs and listen and watch. The father knew this too and now he had come to terms with his role, he would often head to the stairs, take whichever child was there by the hand and lead them back to their beds where he would stay with them for a while, not caring that he had guests downstairs that he had neglected in favour of his daughter. When he returned to the dinner table, he would make his apologies, tell his fellow diners that he had been doing his father duties, and the entire table would praise him loudly, so joyously and so triumphantly, the mother felt she were in some kind of theatre and the audience were applauding a show.

The mother tried to bring herself into the joyous rapture, to feel some of its embrace for she could see just how it lifted the father. His time with one of his daughters followed by the congratulation, he was a different man. She would say he was even glowing.

It was hard for the mother to witness that change in her husband and to see how he had bonded so easily with their children, albeit in fits and spurts, but the ease at which he went to them only highlighted how little the mother had been able to replicate such unconditional love. She felt a heavy burden begin to weigh upon her, much more than the feeling she had experienced when each of her three daughters was born. This was a harder, denser, all-encompassing feeling, and for all her lack of mothering knowledge, she knew she needed to dispose of this feeling at once. And so, she looked around her, at the abundance of alcohol and she took her wine glass to her lips and she drank. And she drank. And she drank.

Footsteps slapping against the floor stopped me swimming and I stood up in the pool. I went to swim to the side of the pool, to grapple for a towel, for my phone but I couldn't move. It was the man I had seen on the lawn earlier. I went to speak, to holler for Em, but my mouth was dry from the chlorine water, only a small, hoarse sound escaped my lips. I looked towards my towel, then the door, calculating his proximity to me and how quickly I could get there.

'Hey.' His voice was soft. I had half expected a gruff tone to match the look of him with his scraggly beard and crumpled clothes. It wouldn't have been hard for him to have bypassed security or somehow find his way in through the woods. I looked around for a camera and then opened my mouth to scream.

'Howdy.' He lifted his hand in a wave this time and as I reached the end of the pool, I quickly lifted my goggles and rubbed at my face with a towel, so I was able to see a little clearer. I stayed where I was in the middle of the pool, Somehow I felt, that I had the upper hand as no matter which side of the pool he stood, I would always be the same distance away from him.

He approached the pool side and was looking out at me. I could see then that there was something familiar about this man.

'Dexter Rice. It's Rey, isn't it?' His voice echoed around the room.

The fear evaporated and was replaced with a rush of embarrassment.

'Dexter.' I half swam, half walked to the edge of the pool and hauled myself out in a most ungainly way. He reached down to help me and then changed his mind, and there was a moment where neither of us knew what we were doing with our hands, as Dexter remembered I was partially dressed. He moved his hand to his head and ran it through his hair which was long to his ears. The beard, which was what had thrown me before, was unkempt and wild. But it looked good, now I knew he wasn't a mad psycho come to accost me.

Once I was out of the pool, Dexter handed me my towel and I wrapped it thoroughly around myself. I knew I would soon be playing out scenes with him where he would see more of me beyond a swimming costume but I thought we should get this meeting out of the way first before we started stripping off.

Dexter held his hand out and I took it, and he gave it the smallest of shakes.

'The beard,' I said touching my own chin.

Dexter's hand went automatically to the mass of hair on his

face. 'Ah, yes, I am pretty impressed with what I have achieved here. Months of this in the middle of summer anywhere else would have been hell, but I reckon I can handle it up here, with these temperatures.'

'God, yeah, it's a bit cooler that's for sure.'

'Talking of which, you must be chilly now. I heard a rumour they were serving tea and crumpets in the parlour, I mean, it doesn't get any more *Downton Abbey*, if you fancy it?' Dexter sounded so incredibly English I almost laughed.

'Okay, I'll see you in a bit.'

I edged my way awkwardly around him and he took a hurried step back to let me pass.

* * *

I found the parlour through following my nose to the scent of freshly brewed coffee and toasted crumpets. As I entered, I found Em sitting on a table in the corner. She looked up at me and nodded. I gave a swift nod back but not before Dexter, who was already seated at a table with some of the crew, had spotted our slight interaction.

'I took the liberty of ordering us a little jam,' Dexter said, moving to sit opposite me. I liked hearing a richness to his voice that I didn't hear so very often these days, living in Camden and not having had a job for some time. I had become used to my own little circle of friends and hearing the way we spoke. I had almost forgotten that there were people out there who spoke and acted like this. The way my parents had and the way I had. It seemed we had both come from a privileged background and I couldn't help wondering what Dexter was really thinking of me, and the feature, the stories that continued to suggest I should have been looking out for my younger sister.

There were smiles and hellos from the others as I sat next to Dexter.

'Is she here for you?' Dexter said without even looking at Em, but I knew he was referring to her.

I cleared my throat. 'Yes, I believe she is,' I said with a hint of laughter in my voice.

'Why is that funny?'

'I've never had security before. I guess you might have seen all the papers? Well it was deemed necessary that I should feel a bit more protected out here.'

'Well, I'm sure she'll do a damn fine job. Better than the two turnips I passed at the front gate. Not as fit as your lady.'

I looked at Dexter.

'I don't mean it like that!' He looked boyish, and it was endearing. 'I just meant that these chaps I saw like their beer. Not like your girl here.'

'I don't know. I've barely spoken to her.'

'What? Why?' Dexter held a pot of tea and a pot of coffee up. I pointed to the coffee, and he poured some into my cup.

'I don't know what to say to her? I'm still coming to terms with her even being here. I feel silly if I'm entirely honest. But I was told by my agent I would be protected, so here she is.'

'You've been practising your swimming, I see.' He poured tea into his own cup and I was suddenly conscious of how very British we were being, the tea, the crumpets, the light chat.

'I have.' I nodded and poured my milk, offering some to Dexter but he shook his head.

'I must get in there tomorrow, I'm a bit stiff myself. I used to sea swim in Norfolk; that's where my family home is and we also have a place in the Lake District. I just love it further up this way, don't you? There is no one to bother you.'

'I agree. I haven't spent any time this far north before. I spent my summers in France as a child...' I hadn't realised what I was saying, the words spilled out of me and I felt cold and exposed, as though he might probe me with questions about Franny.

Dexter cleared his throat and lifted his cup.

'I had heard there had been some story that the papers got their hands on. I'm very sorry about that. It shouldn't be the way. Your past is your past. You're here to do a job and a bloody brilliant one at that, so I hear!' Dexter very craftily acknowledged the elephant in the room and then turned it on its head, so it was a celebration of my life, my craft. I couldn't help but smile; it was sweet and clever, and I was warming to him so much.

'And you're ahead of me in the training department, so that's amazing.'

'Hold on, you said you were a sea swimmer?' I said, stopping my cup halfway to my mouth.

'That I did, but once you're out of the water it can take a long time to get yourself back to fitness level again, and it's been a while for me. I injured my leg, my mother was unwell...' Dexter waved his hand. 'A whole host of reasons that really should not have stopped me swimming, but they did.'

I nodded, feeling an affiliation with Dexter. My reasons were more severe than his but still, there had been something that had taken me away from the water in the first place and I was only just getting back to it now.

'Well, I can't say I've been much of a water babe myself these last few years, but it takes a good job to come along and give you a kick up the arse.' I hope I sounded sincere with my excuses.

'And a great co-star', Dexter said so quietly and almost mumbled it into his teacup.

I thought it was funny and he was clearly being cute, but then Dexter's face changed, he wasn't looking coy and cute, he was looking stressed and alarmed, and for a microsecond, I thought it was my own social skills that had offended him, but when I saw he was looking past me and towards the glass doors, behind which opened up onto the garden, I spun around. There was a man at the doors, holding a long lens camera, and he didn't look like one of our crew. He was aiming the camera at me, and Dexter and I just knew he had got his shot the moment I had turned. I could see the headline already.

'Fucking paps.' I slammed down my cup and stood up and immediately faced away from him, I wasn't about to give him his second money shot. Two out of breath security guards arrived just as Em grabbed the man, put him in a head lock and threw his camera to the ground.

'Holy shit,' Dexter said before I turned and ran out of the room and he followed suit. We both ran, headed for the corridor and up the stairs to what appeared to be a billiards room. We closed the door behind us. We were out of breath, but I began to laugh.

'I can't believe they found us.' I gasped.

'Did you see the size of the security guards? They were hardly going to be able to stop him. He was a whippet; he would have got passed those two no probs. But your girl got him, good for her. Didn't miss that for a second. By Jove, I'm unfit,' Dexter said, leaning over and panting.

'I know. It doesn't give me much reassurance.' I looked about the room. It was cold and I was missing my hot drink.

Dexter changed his demeanour and went into full thespian mode. 'But, my dear, that is why I am here, to protect you from thy scoundrels.'

Dexter seemed to have a way of making me feel very present, and even though I knew there were photographers still trying to pursue the Franny story, and that it was now obvious that people knew where we were, I allowed myself this time to just feel this moment with him. Because I liked it. And I liked him.

'Me and your security guard anyway. Shall we go back?' Dexter asked. 'Or we could play a game? Are you any good at snooker?'

I looked at the colossal table in front of us. 'I mean, it is rather big. I'm more of a pool girl.'

'Oh, come on.' Dexter fetched the cues and chalk and handed one to me. 'Couple of games before dinner.'

* * *

The distraction was exactly what I needed and after Dexter beat me, twice, I was pretty tired and ready for a lie-down.

He walked me back to my room. 'There you are, madam,' he said and he did a little bow. I was thankful that Dexter was so far showing himself to be a fun and agreeable man to be around. I was sure we would be fine together. Em appeared around the corner.

'Not leaving you for a second is she?' Dexter said quietly to me. 'Hello.' He turned and smiled at Em. 'Right, I'll see you at dinner then?' He said it as a question and I saw a slight twinkle in his eye. The warnings I'd heard from Tammy and the girls came reverberating back to me. I had batted away the absurdity and now here I was at the receiving end of his charms. I knew it was exactly the sort of thing that would destroy a working relationship, but as I looked around the stark hallway, and an image of swimming in the North Sea began to torment me, the prospect of finding comfort in the arms of a man like Dexter was one I was becoming more inclined to welcome.

* * *

I opened my eyes.

Bang, bang, bang.

I sat up and took in my surroundings. I was in the Highlands; I was on location. I had fallen asleep, and someone was at the door. I looked at my phone. It was just after 7 p.m. I was still clothed, thankfully, so I went to the door and tentatively opened it.

Standing there was Dexter.

'Evening.'

'Ah, it is,' I said, embarrassed by my bed-head and having fallen asleep.

'This looks like it was left for you.' Dexter produced a small envelope and held it out to me.

'What's this?' I asked, my voice thick with sleep.

Dexter smiled and raised his eyebrows. 'I wish I could see through paper, but alas it is not one of my talents. And I have many.'

I took the envelope from him, slightly perturbed by his wittering as I was neither properly awake nor entirely invested in the banter he was offering. He stayed where he was and I wondered if he was waiting for me to open the thing in front of him.

'Right then,' he said after a few more uncomfortable beats. 'I'll see you in the dining room.'

'Great, see you in a bit.' I tried a wide grin, but it didn't quite reach where it needed to. My heart was pounding, because I knew that a letter with my name on it seemed an entirely odd thing to have been found outside my door.

Dexter waited another second, eyeing me carefully before he turned and walked away. I closed the door and ripped at the envelope. Inside was a small piece of paper, a small logo on the top, some sort of hotel and spa and then in the middle, in scrawled handwriting:

Watch your back.

20

NOW

I arrived in the dining room wearing a smock-style dress and a smile. Em was just behind me. I had wanted to ask why she hadn't seen the person who had left the envelope, why it had been delivered without going through her first. I knew there were no cameras in the house, except perhaps at the front of the driveway with the useless security. I didn't want Dexter to think anything was wrong either. So I tucked away the concern and hoped that the night could lead to something more than a few laughs. A bigger distraction that I was craving and needing. My face was all over the newspapers, my past had been dredged up. He was being more than gracious. I obviously didn't want to discuss what was in the letter, but I was conscious that he might ask. Only because of the interest around me and the fact this was supposed to be a hidden location. No one was supposed to know exactly where we were. My gut churned like a washing machine on a high spin. Em took herself to the small bar to sit on a high stool looking out at the dining room which made me feel like a complete idiot that needed babysitting. I took a seat opposite Dexter.

'Menu looks... interesting.' Dexter perused the A5 sheet with an amused expression. I could smell something meaty and spicy; my mouth began to salivate but not out of hunger. I swallowed hard, and took a long drink of the water already poured on the table.

Without lifting his eyes from the menu, Dexter asked, 'Everything okay?' I looked to my left, a group had just arrived in the dining room, I didn't recognise them. Then I saw Layla at the back with some of the crew from teatime. She clocked me and waved. The crew were already looking over at us, making observations at our intimate dining arrangement. But I was thankful Dexter had chosen a small table for us. I was tired and not up for much socialising. They all seemed thrilled to be working with us but keen to get a look in and clearly ecstatic to see both Dexter and I together. I looked around for alcohol but couldn't see any.

'Don't worry, I've a bottle of vodka in my suite.' He looked up at me. 'For later.'

The grinding in my gut halted for a moment and I felt a stirring. Was it that simple? There was not to be any effort involved. Dexter was going to invite me back to his room tonight and we would be at it. We'd become an item, and the newspapers would love it, then we'd deny it but they'd capture us kissing outside a Starbucks in LA clutching gigantic Frappuccinos.

But tonight... I thought for a second. I didn't need to think beyond tonight. I could escape dark thoughts and feel something else. I could be taken away from all the newspaper features, photos and threats and melt into the arms of a rising star. Thoughts of the sea were whirring through my mind and as always, beneath that, that feeling. Like an impending sense of doom. Worse than stepping into icy northern waters, worse than facing my fear of the sea, having never swum since the night Franny was taken. This was something else, it had been coming for me in Camden, and it had followed me here.

I took a long sip of water desperately hoping that wine was on the way.

'You have a suite?' I asked casually.

Dexter nodded smugly. 'I do. There's only one in the entire house and they gave it to me. What can I say.'

'Fine. I'm not bothered,' I said, wanting it to sound playful, but it came out slightly aggressive. I looked down at my menu. I felt Dexter's foot reach my leg and he gave it a playful nudge.

'Oww!'

He looked perplexed then laughed.

'I bruise easily,' I said.

'Don't we all, darling.' He brushed his hair back theatrically. I smiled. Suddenly a lady with a greying bob was by my side. She was wearing a black apron stretched tightly across her chest and stomach; this must be the caterers.

'Good evening, Miss Levine, Mr Rice.' She spoke softly in a Scottish accent. Her face was flushed and there was a smell emitting from her, the same meaty, spicy smell I recalled from earlier.

'Can I offer you some wine?'

'I would love some wine. Do you have red?'

'Indeed we do.' Her flushed face seemed to redden further.

'Then I will take a bottle.' I looked at Dexter.

'Two glasses,' he added. Then he looked up at his server, suddenly remembering his manners. 'Please.'

'No problem. I'll be right back.'

'Any of this take your fancy?' Dexter was looking back down at his menu again. 'Haggis bonbons. Whatever they are. Neeps and tatties, venison, they've gone all out on the Scottish front tonight.'

'I think it's because we're in Scotland,' I added. 'I don't think they're pretending to be Scottish just for us.'

Dexter's face changed to one of mock horror. 'All right, smarty pants! Are you very au fait with the Scottish pallet?'

'No, I am not. I'm not hungry either.'

'Well you can't go glugging that entire bottle of wine without something inside you.' Then he raised an eyebrow in a seductive way.

'Bread. I'll eat bread.' I took a roll from the basket between us and slathered it with butter. Another eyebrow raise from Dexter. He was doing well to distract me but every now and again little spikes of terror would attack my gut and I would be reminded that I wasn't allowed to relax. I didn't even care about the letter. It was probably one of the security, or that journalist that got in. Let them carry on with their nonsense. It wasn't the first time I had received a message like that, either cyber or in person. Mostly these days though it was cyber, as that was the easiest way to get to me. I didn't think I was in danger here. I was surrounded by enough people and Dexter seemed to be pretty savvy. Besides, the signals he was giving me meant it was unlikely I would be on my own tonight, and maybe if I told him what was in the letter, perhaps he would insist that I stay in his suite.

Our server arrived back with our bottle of wine and took Dexter's order. He ordered the same for me and gave me a knowing, almost fatherly look when I tried to protest.

'You have to eat something for Christ's sake, you have a job to do tomorrow,' Dexter scolded.

'Better not make it a late night then. We're up at the crack of dawn.'

'Don't I know it. Hope you've brought your lard.'

I frowned. 'What?'

'The stuff you rub all over you to stop the cold getting to your skin.'

'I believe it's goose fat, but I think that's a myth.'

'Wow, you know your stuff. Have you been doing much other

prep for the role other than breaststroke and slathering your body in goose fat?'

I looked at Dexter and laughed. He was cute, he definitely had something going for him. I was happy to make all the small talk, just for the next hour, until the wine had done its thing. I watched Dexter pour for us.

'How old are you?' I asked after a long drink of wine.

'I'm surprised you've not googled me.'

'Far too busy for that.' I slung back another gulp. Dexter eyed me carefully but, I noted, with intent and interest.

'I'm twenty-seven.'

'A baby then,' I said before I knew it.

'And you're thirty... one? Hardly much older is it?'

I shrugged. I felt much older. I felt old. The last decade or so of my life had been enough for two, maybe three lifetimes.

'Almost thirty-two,' I added, thinking about my birthday next month.

Food arrived in front of me, and I picked at little bits, finishing the bottle of wine with ease and ordering another.

Dexter said nothing, he watched me drink but didn't have nearly as much as I did.

I ordered a brandy after the wine was finished and I knocked it back, feeling my whole body go tingly. I leant forward across the table.

'Shall we?' I said and then stood up. I wobbled and nearly lost my balance. I saw Layla and some of the crew watching. Em was on her feet and by my side.

'I'm fine.' I put my hand out towards her. 'You can go, you're dismissed, whatever it is I'm supposed to say to you.'

Dexter looked awkwardly at Em. 'It's fine. I'll see her back to her room.'

I began walking towards the stairs.

Dexter was right behind me and I began the ascent.

'God, I needed that drink,' I said as we reached the top of the landing. I looked left and right. 'Where is this ridiculous suite then?'

Dexter had hold of my arm and was guiding me along the corridor. It took me a moment to realise that we had stopped outside my room.

'Goodnight, Rey, see you in the morning. Early doors. Set your alarm.' And he walked away, leaving me standing there feeling as though all the life had been sucked from me. Suddenly all the other feelings I had been hiding behind as I had been anticipating my seduction of Dexter Rice came flooding back. And a dark cloak wrapped itself around me, I felt myself sinking into it, unable to escape the weight. There was no space for regret or mortification because Dexter had turned me down. Very soon I would be in the sea and whatever invisible force was trying to get to me was coming. I needed to accept my fate. There was no escaping it.

21

NOW

I was on a shuttle bus with several crew at ten minutes past five in the morning taking me to the location we were shooting from today. A beautiful idyllic beach that was more like a loch, I had been told. But my mind could not compute with those words. It was true that I was in a remote and wonderful part of the world, my job took me to some amazing places, I was lucky. I should feel lucky. I should feel happiness. But all I could feel was this relentless panic and worry that it wasn't just the sea I should fear, but something far more threatening.

My throat felt as though it had a golf ball in it since I woke at 3 a.m. I hadn't been back to sleep since and this, I knew already, was going to be a hard gig. I tried to think about the sessions at the pool in Camden and how I had managed to even make it into the water after so long. I tried to think about how well I had done and how far I had already come by just getting into the water. I thought about those journeys to the leisure centre, and then I could see Lloyd in my mind's eye. His words had tormented me at the time, yet I had managed to forget about them. But really, they made little sense. How could someone act as though they fancied me and then refuse me? That had never happened before. I felt as though I had become trapped in a rapid downward spiral since then. Although Sylvie offering me the job had been the catalyst.

But then Lloyd rejecting me, and now Dexter. This was becoming a habit. I felt silly the way I had been dropped off outside my room last night.

Was this all because of the stories, was it maybe because people thought I came from a dysfunctional family and that because little girls did not go missing every day, that there must be something seriously wrong with how I was raised, which meant that there must be something very wrong with me? I was now repelling men and I wanted it to stop.

The shuttle bus jolted as it headed downwards towards the beach, and I felt my gut tighten. The strain sent a wave of nausea through my body ending in my throat where the golf ball was still lodged. At the motion of the bus I must have made a sound of some sort.

'You okay, Rey?' came from Layla. A concerning question laced with a hint of malice I suspected from her non-concerned tone and the way she had been observing Dexter and I last night. Perhaps also from the story she had read about me.

I couldn't think about this, not at this time of the morning when I could feel the swell of nausea making its way through my body, threatening me with a full body convulsion followed by expulsion of last night's red wine, bread and haggis bonbons. Just saying the name of them in my head was enough to make my mouth fill with saliva. Realising I hadn't brought any water with me, I looked behind me.

'Is there a bottle of water anywhere?'

Immediately one was passed down to me by one of the crew and I sipped at it tentatively, not wanting to overdose and upset my stomach further.

Dexter was curled up in the corner of his seat, his baseball cap and sunglasses on. Probably getting a nice relaxing forty winks before we arrived on set. Not thinking about the end to last night's dinner or feeling any level of shame, the way I was. The finger of mortification had been nudging me since I opened my eyes this morning and I would physically shudder each time I recollected our dinner, the amount I had drunk and what my intentions were towards my co-actor once I had consumed enough alcohol.

'You okay?' came Dexter's voice and I physically recoiled at his tone.

'Yep,' I called back at him. I managed to turn my head just enough to notice he hadn't lifted his head, or taken his baseball cap off, or removed his glasses. Was he psychic?

The shuttle bus rumbled down a small track and just when it began to slow I thought I was going to be sick.

The doors opened letting in some much-needed air and I inhaled big breaths.

I spotted the catering station and made for it.

The aroma of the coffee was the antidote I needed.

'Never regret. If it's good, it's wonderful; if it's bad, it's experience.'

I turned and saw Dexter edging his way towards me.

'It's not wonderful and I've experienced enough hangovers, so are there any other options?'

'Coffee is always the answer?'

'I'll take that and the coffee.' I looked at the woman who was waiting to serve me. She looked familiar. We often see the same catering crew on different sets. I smiled at her, always wanting to remain professional and amiable, even though my brain felt as though it were trying to break free from my skull.

'Do you want one?' I asked Dexter.

'I'm going for the full Scottish. Fancy watching me whilst I eat it?' Then he laughed demonically, and I felt a slither of a smile try to edge its way across my lips, his laugh was penetrating.

'I'll sit with you,' I said taking a coffee from the woman and noting how she looked intently at me for a second. Then I observed with horror as haggis, black pudding, eggs and tattie scones were piled into a cardboard takeaway box and handed to Dexter with a huge smile. She suddenly seemed like a different person and I realised it was because she had not smiled for me. I understood that Dexter was probably the bigger superstar here, that he was the one people were here to see in action. The catering team were here to do a job, but to get to hang out with up-coming actors like Dexter was one of the perks of the job and me, the actor who hadn't been seen on screens for years, well I was probably of interest to them, but that was all.

There was a large, tented area with seating and I sat down next to Dexter, moving my head to the side to stop the waft of breakfast hitting my nostrils.

'How are you feeling this morning?' Dexter asked and I felt my breath catch in my throat.

'I have felt better.' That was all I wanted to say about that, but Dexter seemed intent on pursuing it.

'Do you drink a lot?'

I laughed 'No more than most.'

'But the papers and their stories, it must drive you to distraction. It's not fair on you is it? Dragging up the past like this?'

It was the first time Dexter had made any reference to my past being splattered across every paper. I wondered if I should tell him what the letter said. I wondered if I should be more concerned than I actually was. Dexter seemed as if he wanted to talk – he was opening up the conversation to talk about me and what was going on in my life. For someone so young I thought this fairly admirable. He could have continued to pretend it wasn't happening, when we both knew it *was* happening, and that would have made for an awkward relationship. No more awkward than if I had managed to get into Dexter's suite last night, though.

'Are you here to give me advice? The sun hasn't even properly risen yet, I've barely had a sip of coffee.'

'There's no right time to have a conversation is there. I just thought you might like to talk. But also just know we all go through it; you think it's not happening to me?'

'I don't know, Dexter; they all seem to like you here. That caterer couldn't have smiled any more if she tried. I didn't get quite the same reception.'

'She probably fancied me,' he said nonchalantly and began spooning haggis into his mouth. I had to look away again.

'We're in this together, Rey, and we're going to be stuck up here in the Highlands together so we might as well try and trust one another. I can tell you don't trust me.' He didn't look at me when he spoke, just pushed food into his mouth.

'What? Said who? Why would you say that?' I was dumb-founded.

'Because you think that I was the author of that letter you received yesterday.'

It had occurred to me on several occasions during dinner last night that Dexter was some sort of prankster, a young kid, fresh out of an all-boys school and straight into RADA, who felt we needed to adopt schoolboy tricks as part of the bonding process, to separate the wheat from the chaff.

'How did you know it was a threatening letter?'

'I didn't. You just told me.'

I went to speak and closed my mouth again. I wasn't sure what was going on here. One minute he was inviting me to his suite, the next I was being dropped outside my room. Now he's playing games with me about the note.

'I didn't say that I thought you sent it,' I finally responded. It didn't make sense that Dexter would do such a thing. He had no reason to have any gripes with me.

'I didn't say you did. I said you're thinking it.'

I shook my head, swallowed hastily and looked away. 'Too early for being cryptic. Besides, it doesn't matter okay, I have a lot going on right now, some you are aware of and others, not so, but I just want to concentrate on getting this right. I'm not worried about silly notes.'

Dexter scraped up the last bits of his breakfast which he had practically inhaled since we had been sat here.

'Sure, I get it. Me too.' He put his spork into the cardboard container and sealed it and then wiped his mouth with a paper napkin. 'You could just tell your Em. Is it Em as in Emily or M as in James Bond?' he asked.

'Emma,' I said.

'Right'. He nodded.

'Morning, guys,' a friendly voice came from behind me and I turned to see a young woman in dungarees and a red fluffy jumper underneath beaming at us.

'Did you want to see where we'll be shooting from today? I'll take you down to the water?'

I felt a storm brewing in the pit of my stomach and my knees felt weak. I gulped down another sip of my coffee. There was nothing I wanted to do less.

'Sure,' I said and jumped to my feet.

* * *

The walk down to the water was practically treacherous. It was rocky and steep and I had to go very carefully to keep my footing on the makeshift steps.

'Is this factored in for insurance?' I called back behind me, where dungaree girl was laughing hysterically and for a weird moment I felt as though I were in some sort of surreal dream. It had been so long since I had been out of my comfort zone, this was playing hard with my senses. Everything about it; the early rise, the drop of the cliff, the feel of the mountains all around me as I began to experience their presence... It hadn't necessarily occurred to me yesterday, but today they felt ever closer, ever nearer to my soul, as though they too were leaning over me and judging me for what I had done. I looked around at the dark weather approaching from the distance and my heart raced fast in my chest. It was coming for me, I suddenly thought, and had to stop myself from panicking with three long deep breaths.

'You okay?' she called. 'Nearly there.'

I had my phone tucked into a zipped-up pocket in my jacket. When I felt it vibrate, I stopped walking and pulled it out, stared at the message from my cousin.

You ghosted me.

I hadn't called him back after I said I would. I quickly texted him.

I arrived in the Highlands last night. Been a bit distracted.

I hit send.

I'm glad you're distracted. Because I'm not. I'm thinking about this all the time. What we did. What happened to Franny.

I looked down at the steep drop below me. My heart began to thud. I pulled my phone closer to my chest, in case someone might have seen the words even though there was no one around. I wanted to call him immediately, tell him he couldn't just send me messages like that, that anyone might be able to see.

I felt the lump in my throat become larger and swallowing felt weird. Cormac was never like this. He was usually placid, had never spoken this way before.

Why are you being this way? Don't you think I know this; don't you think I think about it every single day? She was my sister. I wanted to protect her.

I bashed out the words quickly as I saw the dungaree girl had reached the descent and was looking back up at me.

His response came back faster this time.

Well, you didn't protect her. Now people are talking about this.

We rarely spoke of Franny, but she was the connection that had kept us together all these years, the contact we'd had.

Not as two cousins but as two accomplices.

I glanced again at the last text that had just come through from Cormac.

They will find out what we did.

22

CORSICA, JUNE 2008

I had been both fascinated and distracted by Wallace's behaviour for most of the day. He had been among us, but he hadn't. Vanessa had hovered around him, making him camomile tea and presenting him with a plate of fruit and nuts accompanied by hushed words like *brain food* and *these will help.* I found myself looking away whenever Vanessa said anything to Wallace. I felt as though bugs were crawling under my skin and I wanted to scratch them out. The sight and sound of his sudden and very obvious frail movements, hunched shoulders and lack of spark in his eyes was not something I could bare to witness. It was not something I was used to seeing in any man. Not in my uncle and not in my own father. Men weren't supposed to look this way. Or if they did, should they be letting children see them this way?

But the food was left untouched, and the tea barely drank. Wallace moved from place to place around the villa, pulling a cardigan around him despite the constricting heat. Whether purposely or not, his presence had shrunk, he was no longer the force that had greeted me on the first day. I found that my behaviour unconsciously mirrored Wallace's and I took to retreating around the villa, not bothering the adults. Slinking into corners with iced drinks and a hand fan. My sisters and cousins did the same. Dad was absent for most of the day, utilising Vanessa's study for his own needs. Mum made her opinion about this vocal on more than one occasion through the day, then eventually, around 4 p.m., as the heat finally began to subside by a few degrees, she was distracted by Aunt Vanessa with a large glass of white wine and a few reassuring words. I began to wonder who was looking after Aunt Vanessa, the one person who needed to be looked after based on what she had been through – losing Uncle Rob only a few years back and this being her first visit to their family holiday home since. I began to see us and Wallace as nothing more than a burden that she did not need.

I found Franny in a corner of patio, shaded by trees and trellising. She had a stone and was scratching it onto the concrete. I heard my mother's voice in my head, as she would have asked Franny to stop immediately, as it would ruin the aesthetics of the villa. And in that moment, even without my mother present, and her voice a mere echo of past experiences, I thought how much it mattered to her how things looked from the outside. She never wanted anyone to see what was behind the perfectly positioned veil. I often thought about what people would think. That veil was within my reach. I could whip it away at any moment and scream to anyone who would listen, *Come and see, come and look. This is who we are.* And I could see their faces, the look of horror, disgust and eventually pity on their faces.

'What are you drawing there?' I asked, but already I could see it was two figures she had scratched out with the edge of the stone. She didn't reply, but carried on focusing on her work. As the two figures developed, I could see that one was much taller and clearly a man. The other was small with long hair sticking out. Was this Franny?

Their hands were stuck together, and I thought about Wallace at the cricket game, with his hand clamped firmly over Franny's. I put my hand on Franny's head. Stroked it for a moment.

'Shall we go and get something to drink, little one?'

She put her stone down, turned and looked and me with her bright blue eyes.

'Yes,' she said. I took her hand, knowing this was right, that she was safe here. But it was still my responsibility to keep looking out for her.

The day passed too slowly because no one could decide what they wanted to do so we all ended up sitting around, becoming irritable with the heat and each other's company. My sisters eventually retired to Aunt Vanessa's 'pop-up' craft area and emerged hours later with brightly coloured bracelets made from plastic lettered beads, each spelling our names. Even Wallace was presented with one from a slightly coyer Franny, who despite her usual fearless tendencies, had sensed the changes in Wallace. Scarlett handed mine to me. 'Rey' spelled out with blue beads on one side and white on the other.

'It's beautiful,' I said and for a moment she looked proud. I looked at the green and white beads on her own wrist, spelling out the name 'Scarlett'.

Only my mother seemed not to adapt her behaviour to suit the darker mood of the villa that day, still engaging Wallace in conversation as though he hadn't just shrunk down inside himself. Even his lacklustre approach to the day and stilted responses did not deter her. But even then the notion of mental health was an alien concept to me. It was only several years later when I edged into adulthood that I would come to understand that for my entire childhood I had in fact been submerged in a world of mental health disorders of varying degrees and severities. Although I didn't have a name for everything I witnessed and experienced growing up, I always felt that whatever was underlying with both of my parents was a part of us; I could never escape it. It was who we were. I knew that Aunt Vanessa would be sad because her husband had died, but I didn't understand to what extent, and what repercussions would follow. I didn't understand that my cousins, who had lost their father at such a pivotal moment in their development, would be so affected, and how that would change their behaviour and how they saw the world. And I certainly had no name to give to the condition that this new man, a replacement for my uncle, was suffering from. Nor did I know the repercussions of that, and how it would affect my family. But I was to understand very soon.

23

NOW

I stood at the little bay and watched the water lapping just up to my feet. I thought about the games we played when we were younger, running towards the waves and then turning and running back so they wouldn't catch us. We'd play it for hours and we'd naturally grow tired and so, soon enough, they did catch us. Because you could never outdo nature. It was a force that could not be reckoned with. And it was always there, just like these mountains, watching us. Sometimes the sea protected me, sometimes, it was my own enemy. But no matter how many times the ocean chucked me under or caught me out, or worse, enticed me towards it, taking my concentration away from something so precious that I ended up losing it, I always returned. The last fifteen years, I had not stepped amongst any waves, Mediterranean or English Channel, and soon I would be venturing into the North Sea, one of the cruellest and harshest seas I had known yet, and I wasn't sure if I was ready.

'Pretty damn cold even in the summer,' dungaree girl said.

'It's pretty though,' I said. 'We could be in the Mediterranean here couldn't we?'

'Oh, you really aren't from these parts are you.' She chuckled loudly. She was a bit of a breath of fresh air this morning and the antidote I needed to my hangover.

'Used to the hotter parts of the world I suppose,' and I heard the way her voice trailed off on the last word. Of course she knew too about the feature, she would have read it like everyone else. She would know that I had holidayed in France as a child with my family. I was a little rich girl, the one who had made her sister disappear.

I looked at her as though to give her that sign that she could carry on, she was okay to mention things that people thought were bad for me or might make me uncomfortable. I wasn't going to melt like the wicked witch in *The Wizard of Oz*, but she was already looking away across the water, straining to see something that probably wasn't there.

'Might I catch a glimpse of the Loch Ness Monster?' I said to change the mood.

She looked back round at me as though nothing awkward had passed between us a moment before.

'It's said that only very special people are blessed with a sighting of the rarest creature on the planet. You might!' She smiled.

I knew then that I wouldn't. I wasn't special. I certainly wasn't deserving of catching a glimpse of one of the world's greatest mythical creatures.

We both looked out at the vast water that was hugged by a mountain on either side. We could be in New Zealand.

'Is the water very cold?'

'It's not warm,' she chuckled again, 'but then I swim in it all year round.'

I felt a surge of envy. I was once so obsessed with the sea. How could I have let it all stop? I should have stepped back into the water long ago. But I had allowed it all to consume me.

But even if I had, would I have been able to have stopped this extra force that was building up around me, playing with my mind?

I had been thinking about the Smith family, the three beautiful girls and the mother and father and I was anxious to get back into the pool at the house, so that I could return to their story. Because it brought me great comfort, and that was something I craved right now. I had never felt so exposed and so out of my depth in so many ways.

But I couldn't just quit. I wondered how much longer I could keep pretending, keeping up the façade.

I wondered how much longer I had until I was discovered for exactly what I was.

24

NOW

The relief when I was told that I wouldn't be entering the water today was enough to lift my spirits that I could just focus on what the rest of the day would bring, including nursing the mother of all hangovers. It had been a stupid mistake to drink so much last night and Dexter had done the right thing by ditching me.

Dungaree girl had introduced herself as Brie. 'They like to break you in slowly,' she said after she revealed that the swimming wouldn't happen today and I breathed out so loud she had chuckled.

I texted Cormac during a break and he called me straight away.

'We need to come up with a plan.'

'What plan?' I hissed into the phone on the other side of the trailer where I hoped I was far enough away so that no one could hear me.

'What we're going to say about that night?'

'We were kids, Cormac. No one is going to say anything to us or start digging up anything.'

'But what about Scarlett, she says she remembers something.'

My heart galloped at the mention of my sister's name in context with that evening and I was suddenly there again, reliving the last few hours before Franny's disappearance.

'We do nothing, Cormac. Nothing. We wait for it all to blow over, and it will because it's all because of me making this film. They have somehow picked up on this story from so long ago and decided this is how they are going to punish me. And so we just ride it out.'

My gut churned from lack of food, too much alcohol and now the reminder that yes, I was responsible for what happened. I was selfish, I wanted to get out of the villa, to go to a party and be with young French men and dance and drink and smoke weed and forget about my life. I put my own needs first.

It was all your fault.

'Let's just leave it at that, yeah? I will keep in touch and I will make sure I tell you if I hear anything. And vice versa, okay?' I felt this was a good way to end the conversation so that Cormac went away feeling as though he had an objective.

Dexter found me at the back of the trailer. I was about to call my mum. After Jolie had told me she was now her carer, I felt I had more than an obligation to check in on her, to make sure she was doing okay. She had sounded okay on every occasion I had spoken to her, she was fine in the sense that she was still the mum to me that I always knew but looking back, her effervescent personality that she revealed on social occasions had left and her bad moods had increased. Now I know that this is synonymous with dementia, I just hadn't recognised it or put the two together before. Funny, how I was way more astute as a child and able to pinpoint things like her alcoholism and bulimia, even before my limited vocabulary had names for them.

'They just want us to shoot one more scene, down by the sea.

You up for it?' Dexter appeared round the trailer and I was instantly suspicious that he may have heard my conversation with Cormac. But as he was an astounding actor it would have been impossible for me to tell.

* * *

'So, if you could just hold her face with your left hand and then speak the line,' came the sound of the director's voice.

'Ooo, our first smushy scene. Don't go too weak at the knees, Levine,' Dexter whispered and I felt a smile lift at the edge of my lips. Last night had essentially felt like a rejection from Dexter, but maybe tonight might be different. I needed it to be different. I couldn't just go to bed alone with my own demons.

'And action!' came the call from the director and Dexter's hand was on my cheek.

'You've been through so much, you and I, we're much the same. You just have to let me show you.'

Dexter delivered the line impeccably and with a class A Scottish accent.

'Cut!' came the call again and Dexter stepped back, was himself again.

'So up for some more haggis bonbons tonight?' he said with a wicked grin.

'How else will we pass the time up here?' I said.

'Great. It's a date.'

* * *

When I got back to the trailer I pulled out my phone knowing that now would be a good time to call my mother, or maybe I'd get through to Jolie, but either way, I was feeling slightly less hungover and there was some promise of a half-decent evening with Dexter tonight.

There were three missed calls on my phone from Tammy.

'Shit,' I muttered. What had happened? Tammy had the key to my place and was popping in to feed Freckle and let him out a little on the terrace. I hit call back and she answered straight away.

'Rey!' She sounded breathless and urgent.

'What!' I said.

'Some fucker's broken into your flat.'

'What!!!' I screamed and I felt my legs weaken. My flat. My life that I had built up, my personal space. What? Why?

I rubbed my hand across my face, no doubt ruining the lovely work of the make-up artist.

'I'm calling in the cleaners and then the organisers. This is on me, babes. I feel like this is my fault.'

'Why?' I didn't know why Tammy was blaming herself.

'Because you left me in charge.'

'Yes, but you locked up properly?'

'Yes, yes, this is a break-in, they took the door apart.'

'Fuck.'

'You didn't have an alarm?'

'No. I don't.'

'But you have the doorbell video thingy?'

'Yes, I have that!' Just the thought of looking at my flat on the camera made me feel eerie. I didn't want to know.

'Well it happened anytime between five o'clock last night and just now when I got here, if you want to ask your neighbours. Police aren't going to do bugger all obviously. But they asked if they could see the doorbell footage.'

'Thank you for bringing in the cleaners and the organisers.'

'Obvs. I feel like a total failure. Thank God Freckles is okay.'

'Can you give him extra cuddles?'

'I'll be with him until the place is back to normal.'

'Thank you.'

'You're welcome. Now go snog the face off Rice.'

I ended the call, but was not ready to look on my phone to see who had been lurking around the place. I was too terrified, the doorbell footage gave me the creeps at the best of times, let alone when I was potentially about to see who had just broken into my house.

It would have to wait until I was in my room back at the house later.

* * *

I took a long shower in my en suite and then called my mother.

We discussed the feature again for a while until finally she said, 'I suppose Jolie has told you then?'

'About the diagnosis. Yes.'

'I'm too young, Rey.'

'I know,' I said, trying to think ahead about what else I could say to her. 'There are drugs. They are finding ways to combat the symptoms all the time.'

Silence.

'It's all because of you,' Mum finally said after an awkward pause between us.

'Who?' I asked, but I wondered if she were referring to Franny. The last fifteen years had been about waiting for her. Had the waiting been what had harmed her, what had brought the dementia on early?

'I did everything but it wasn't enough.'

'Mum,' I said sternly.

'It was all because of you! I wish you had never been born!' Mum screamed and then a loud smash as she must have dropped the phone on the floor.

'Mum... Mum.' But she had gone. This was exactly the sort of thing I would expect my mother to say to me, without the dementia.

I waited another minute and then I hung up. Jolie had texted me her number so I dialled it next. She picked up straight away.

'Hello, Rey, I am with your mother.'

'Oh, thank you, Jolie.'

'I arrived here just when you called.'

'Okay. Is she okay? Did she fall?'

'No, she only dropped the phone. So she is fine. I will make her a coffee and we will sit for a while.'

'Okay, that's great. Thank you, Jolie.'

I felt a swell in my throat as I thought about Jolie and the night Franny went missing from the villa. She had been distraught. She had not been able to console herself, and had needed medical intervention in the end.

'Jolie, I want to ask you, I have wanted to ask you for so long, how you are?' I said meekly.

'I should same the same for you, Rey. I know they blame you. But you must understand this was not your fault. You were just a girl, Rey.'

I felt my breath catch in my throat and dared not breathe in case I cried. Of course she would say that. She didn't know anything.

'But you, Jolie. Are you okay? Were you okay after?'

'Yes, I did okay. I had a baby myself, with a man here and we are married. We moved away to the other side of the island. But we just returned this year. I did okay. I think about Franny all the time, and of course I blame myself, it was a terrible thing for all of us, for you and your family to go through. For your poor mother.'

'But you have had a good life, yes?'

There was a pause.

'Yes, I had a good life, Rey. I feel guilt to say this to you. But I did.'

'Please don't feel guilt, Jolie. You were so good to us for so many years. We loved you so much. I'm sorry it ended the way it did and that we never got to keep in touch.'

'I am sorry too. But I am here now, and I will stay in touch with you. And I am here now for your mother.'

It was a weight off my shoulders. I needed someone to be there for my mother, and I knew it could never be me.

'Thank you, Jolie. I'll be in touch.'

'Okay. Bye now.'

A loud rap at my door and I opened it still with my phone in my hand and my body wrapped in my towel, to find Dexter there.

'Now are we going to dinner early – because I am famished and also, I think I'll be asleep by nine.' He eyed me from head to toe, a small smirk on his face.

'Okay, I'll meet you there. Half an hour.'

'Don't be long and no falling asleep again.' He looked down the hallway. 'By the way, Em is on the prowl.'

'Right.' I looked down the hallway and saw Em walking up and down, but she was on her phone and she looked stressed. She clocked me and stopped walking and then hung up her call. She gave me the solitary nod again and disappeared around the corner.

I closed the door and took a seat at the window. I opened the doorbell app and found the footage from last night. I held my breath as I watched from round about the time when Tammy said I had been broken into. I was almost falling asleep when I saw something, a figure appear in the corner of the screen, then they became fully visible. They turned to face the camera and looked at it long and hard, for a full five or six seconds. I kept playing it back staring at the face over and over, their features becoming more engrained in my brain, sparking the synapse and triggering a memory. A memory of a face, in a club not so long ago. After a few minutes of staring it was clear to me that the face I was looking at was the same face of the woman who had been staring at me in the bar in Soho.

This wasn't just some random break-in, this had been planned.

25

CORSICA, JUNE 2008

The next week was the hottest on record that year, according to Wallace. He had come out of his dark mood, which had been unsettling to say the least, but his presence which had been stifling was now replaced by a heat that no one could seem to cope with. Least alone the adults, who were hungover and tired from drinking and partying.

My father was finally out of Vanessa's study and seated at the table, still with a paper in hand but he was amongst us ready to see out the rest of the holiday with his family. Mum seemed to be ecstatic about this, flitting around him like a little wasp, bringing him toast, topping up his coffee – even when Jolie tried to do it, Mum took the pot from her, puffing her chest out with pride at being the one to serve her husband his breakfast. She was rarely able to do this at home; Dad was up before us all and came home when we were all in bed, sometimes never coming home at all.

Jolie came down with sheets and whispered to me, 'Scarlett wet the bed last night.'

But Mum was returning the pot to the coffee station and heard.

'Wet the bed? She's nearly a teenager. She's never wet the bed at home?' Mum rattled on, eventually retreating back to my father's side. I glanced over at him and he seemed to me as though he were trying very hard not to look up. He didn't look as immersed in the paper as he had been.

When Wallace and Vanessa arrived for breakfast my father tried to make excuses to leave the room, mumbling something about needing to check the car before Wallace drove us down to the lake. But Mum made him sit down, because we hadn't all been in the same room together for breakfast yet.

Wallace seemed back to his old self, although a little wary of the level of noise in the kitchen coming from my sisters.

'I've nudged the boys, told them we're leaving in half an hour,' Vanessa said to my mum.

'Typical boys,' Mum said flippantly, and I wasn't sure even she knew what she was referring to as typical for a boy, when she and all of her daughters were all partial to a long lie-in from time to time.

Scarlett seemed particularly annoyed by life this morning, taunting Franny, making silly comments and not saying please or thank you to Jolie.

'Someone's tired this morning.' Mum made the comment without even looking at Scarlett. 'I think an early night is in order, don't you think, Digby?' She looked to our father.

'Noooo!' Scarlett began and then my dad simply stood up and said, 'Early night, Scarlett.'

She suddenly bowed her head so she was looking at her knees and my mum looked as though she had been awarded an accolade because she had received backing from her husband, and to anyone who had witnessed it, they were a team.

Dad left the room, probably happy with the distraction that allowed him to slip out.

'So, off to the lake again today?' Vanessa said, pulling enthusiasm for all of us.

'Yes, they can't wait – can you, girls?' Scarlett was silent, still staring hard into her lap. 'Shall we go and pick some clothes out for you, Scarlett?' I said.

'No,' she barked and jumped down from the stool and went upstairs.

'Sometimes, I despair with that girl. Middle child syndrome is it? You are the middle child aren't you, Vanessa?' Mum asked as she took a seat and sipped her coffee.

Vanessa looked momentarily flustered, and I wasn't even sure she would answer.

'Yes, Digby is the eldest and...' She paused, put her knuckle to her mouth as though swallowing something invisible. 'Lottie is the youngest.'

'Ahh, and how is she these days?' Mum said with such joviality in her voice, I saw my aunt frown.

'She's still in Sage Forest, Flic,' Vanessa said flatly. I saw Wallace reach down and take her hand. I looked at my mother's nonchalant expression even when she was being given the news that her youngest sister-in-law was still in a psychiatric unit.

'Ooh, yes that's right. Poor thing.' Mum almost sang the words and I saw Aunt Vanessa's shoulders hunch and tighten. 'Do you get to visit her much? Is she on a lot of meds these days?'

'She is, Flic. And I do visit her, at least once a week, if not more.'

'Could you not, you know, have her taken out of there and at home with you?'

'We did try, Flic, don't you remember, but it didn't work out,' Vanessa said, a strain in her voice.

'Oh yes, that's right, she went totally nuts at Digby, nearly took his eye out. No, it's better for her in there isn't it, where she can be looked after properly.'

Mum picked up Dad's paper and began scanning the page. Such a casual act, and in total contrast to the serious tone of the conversation she had just had with my aunt, who was now looking unsettled. Her hands were shaking as she looked for something to do with them, in the end she ended up wringing one hand with the other.

'I'll get us some coffee.' Wallace approached the counter.

'No, you sit down, please,' Jolie said, smiling at Wallace. 'I will bring you whatever you want.'

I watched as Wallace devoured a plate of bacon and eggs and my aunt merely picked at some white bread and nibbled a single rasher.

My cousins didn't wake in time and were handed the rucksack with bread, cheese and water and told to begin walking. Scarlett and Franny would take the car with my mum and dad and Vanessa. Wallace had been instructed to walk slowly behind us elder ones, as we protested that the lake was far too close to ever want to be in a car. My parents were not walkers, never had been and despite my sisters' protests to come with us, my parents insisted they stay in the car and all I could think was that soon they too would have children who they would insist sit in a car instead of taking the ten minute walk. But actually, what I truly hoped was that none of us ever had children. We had already managed to stop the family name going on just by us being three girls. This was quite an achievement alone. And something that vexed my father on a regular basis. Franny was meant to have been a boy. That was why there was a bigger gap between Franny and Scarlett. Despite our angelic looks, despite how much everyone commented how lucky my parents were to have us, to have been given this beautiful gift of girls, my father remained immodest around the praise he received, which came regularly. But still, Franny was not the boy he had wanted and needed and there would be no more children, and of course, this was only one more reason for him to despise my mum for her failings. As though she alone were solely responsible for the act of nature.

I walked in silence with my cousins, they were barely awake and whilst they knew they would have fun once we were there, they would not emit any of that excitement at this juncture of the day's activities.

When we arrived at the lake Cormac sat down and started eating the bread and cheese.

'Hey, don't eat it all,' Faren said.

'Didn't you see how much Jolie packed in the other bags? There's enough food to last us a week,' I said as I down next to my cousin, who was inhaling bread as though he hadn't eaten in a week.

'Slow down, Hungry Horace,' I muttered under my breath, which he heard and grinned at me. He slowed down anyway.

'Who's up for a swim?' Faren asked. 'I'm going for a swim.'

Cormac and I looked over towards the pier. There were three girls setting themselves up with towels, we clocked them and then looked at Faren who was making his way casually but coolly over to the water, just within spitting distance of them. Then we looked at one another and laughed.

'That is so funny. He has no shame.'

'None.' Cormac put the baguette back in the bag and took out some water and took a huge gulp. He handed it to me and I drank.

'They are taking their sweet ass time.' Cormac liked swearing whenever he wasn't near Aunt Vanessa. It didn't really suit him but I didn't ever mention it. It made him feel good so I just let him get on with it.

After a few minutes the car arrived carrying my dad, mum, my sisters and Aunt Vanessa. There was a lot of commotion getting everything out, but Franny had the right idea and was over to us in a minute, a bucket and spade in her hand.

Our parents set up close to us but gave us a bit of breathing space.

'This is such an awesome spot, right?' Cormac said.

'Right.' I was suddenly distracted by Wallace. He was staring at me.

I shifted and looked at Cormac in case he had noticed. There had been too many incidents that I wanted to mention, and I was keen to talk to Cormac about my opinion of Wallace. But there were too many other elements that rattled around in my head that I would need to say to Cormac in order for any of it to make any sense. And I wasn't ready. Not yet. Maybe not ever.

Scarlett sat down next to us, so she was as far away from the adults as she could be. I sensed that she was still stewing from our father's harsh words over breakfast. I wanted to be there for her. Because I had been in her place, I had experienced what she was going through. I had once been of interest to my father, then I had been cast aside for Scarlett. Now I didn't even get negative attention. I wasn't even worth casting a look at. I couldn't even rile him up as I had tried to do in the study before the cricket game. I was essentially redundant.

I tried to catch Scarlett's eye, I wanted her to confide in me, to tell me what she had wanted to say, but I didn't feel this was the right time. Besides, she was intensely digging a hole with a stick. Still so young in her ways, to pick up a spade would show her vulnerability, her childish side. She did not want to be noticed. But she needed someone. To her, I was just her annoying big sister, and she wasn't going to look to me for anything.

'What do you want to do after college?' I asked Cormac to

distract myself from my sister's frantic hands in my peripheral vision.

'Dunno, engineering probably.' Cormac pushed his hands into the sand.

'Is that because of your dad?'

It was the first time any of us had mentioned Rob. I wasn't sure what the adults spoke about in the evening but certainly none of us had heard them speaking about him around us. It was as though he had just disappeared from our lives, and in his place was Wallace. I wanted to be the one to speak of Uncle Rob, I wanted to be Cormac's therapist. I could help him I was sure of it.

'What do you want to do? When you *grow up*?' Cormac added the last words, almost taking the mickey out of himself.

'I want to act,' I said.

Cormac pulled his mouth down in a sort of impressed way.

'I've been thinking about it for a while now. There's a school. I can go to. It's boarding. I can stay there.'

'Great. Sounds ideal.'

I let out a sigh.

'I just want to be able to forget who I am, pretend to be someone else. Anyone else. You know you can do that when you're an actor? You can be a thousand different people and then you never need to know who you really are.'

'Sounds like you have it all worked out.' Cormac pushed his hands through the sand.

I glanced to my right, so my parents were in my peripheral vision.

'Oh, come on, Cormac, you know what I'm talking about. Don't you ever wish you could just stop being you for like a day?'

Cormac shook his head. 'Can't say I have ever thought like that, but then you are something else aren't you, Rey?'

'What does that mean?' I said, trying not to sound pissed off.

'There is no one like you anyway. So you know, you shouldn't worry about being you. You're fine as you are.'

I squirmed in the sand a little and cleared my throat. I knew this was a kind comment, a compliment even, but what was I supposed to do with it. I never knew what to do with compliments, they felt so alien to me.

'I don't really think about much. It's been tough for my mum. We've all been distracted.'

'I know,' I said too quickly. I picked up some sand and let it trickle through my fingers. 'But aside from Uncle Rob, you know—'

'Dying? You can say the word. I've been having this therapy and they encourage us to use words like "death" and "dying". To say it as it is and not use words to confuse the situation like "passed away" or "gone". More for Faren, like. 'Cos he's the young one.' Cormac added that final part as though I might judge him for taking therapy.

'No, right, I get it.'

He nodded firmly.

'Okay, but there's Wallace now, and your mum, she seems okay, but it's hard for her like you say and, well, just look at my folks.'

Cormac turned his head as if he felt he physically needed to look at them. As we looked over, my dad was leaning against the car on his mobile phone, my mum was bustling around next to my aunt trying to reorganise the picnic area.

'You know, I met some guys the other day in town.'

I looked at him.

'I remember them from when we were here a few years ago. I thought they seemed cool, but they would never have looked twice at me, they were older than me then. But this time, they started chatting to me. They're French but they speak good English. They know some good spots for hanging out. Partying.'

Cormac glanced at me and then back at his feet.

'So when's the next party?'

'In a few days. They told me about a great spot.'

'Yes?' I said quickly.

'It's not far from here.'

I looked at my cousin, who was now so tall and strong. Almost a man.

I nodded. 'Yes.'

'They said they will bring all the alcohol and all the stuff. We just need to, you know, show up.'

'Oh, I can show up. I am a very good show-er up-er,' I said and Cormac laughed.

'Great, so I'll tell them we're in. We'll just make them all think we're in bed and just sneak off?'

'Absolutely. Sounds great.'

So far, I had felt nothing but worry and panic, the ever-growing sense that since Uncle Rob wasn't here, this holiday was going to be a trial for me. But for the first time since we had arrived, butterflies fluttered in my tummy. *Finally,* I thought. Something awesome was about to happen.

26

NOW

The first glass of red wine went down too easily again. And before the dessert had arrived I had told Dexter that my flat had been broken into.

'That is horrible. I am sorry that happened to you. Do you have someone who can take care of things for you?'

'I do,' I slurred. Tiredness and red wine was a lethal combination for me. One glass would suffice.

'Well, we have the first sea scene tomorrow, so that should hopefully bring a bit of distraction for you.'

'Tomorrow?' I hoped I had heard him wrong. I suddenly wanted, no needed, more alcohol in me. But that wouldn't help. 'Why did they tell you and not me?' I tried to steady my voice but it came out shaky. I hoped Dexter would think it was purely tiredness.

'I think they thought you knew. I'm sorry if that message didn't get to you. Nothing like a bit of the North Sea on your skin first thing in the morning to wake you up.'

Oh, God. I was dying inside. I was actually dying inside and I hoped that Dexter couldn't tell and see into my soul but he was looking at me with concern and so I pushed the glass of red wine away.

'I think I've had enough for tonight. Thank you for dining with me again. Maybe next time we should join the others.' Dexter looked across at the table in the corner with some of the crew.

'Yes, we've been a bit antisocial,' I agreed.

'But it's good for us to get to know one another, right?' Dexter asked.

I eyed Dexter suddenly feeling as though I wasn't sure if I was supposed to interpret that in another way, was he someone I could trust? I wasn't sure any more. The letter, the paps, the feature, now my flat had been broken into and trashed and here was a stranger asking to get to know me better when last night he had dismissed me. I wasn't sure if that was for the purpose of the film or for something else.

'I need a swim.' I pushed my chair back.

'Is that wise?' Dexter went to stand. I noted Em at the bar also stood up.

'I'm fine.' I touched his shoulder as I passed. 'I had one glass. I need the practice for tomorrow.' I let out a laugh that was supposed to be light and jovial but came out hard and fast like a gunshot. Dexter said no more, and I made my way to the pool. I turned and looked at Em who was already following me along the corridor.

'I need to be alone,' I said.

She nodded and held back.

I'd had the foresight to put on a swimming costume after I showered. I'd had a feeling I would need a swim and knowing the pool was there, and considering how well I had been doing, I knew I needed to keep it up. I'd had a very small portion of the main course and a little fruit so I knew I was safe to swim without giving myself a sore stomach.

I slid my clothes off and stepped into the cool blue. How fortunate we were to have this, I thought, as a way of getting me into the water and feeling positive.

Where have you been? The voices came to me and I recognised them as the Smith family.

I haven't forgotten you.

I was so glad as I slipped into the pool that I had the company of the three children mother and father from the Camden pool. It was the one thing I was glad I had brought with me.

I took the first stroke and their story came back to me.

The drink seemed to be the answer for the mother. For a while it had been food that she had turned to, but only a short while. Sweets and desserts, there were always plenty of them in the house. Their housekeeper bought them in abundance and every meal was at least two courses. Yet when they were entertaining it was at least four. And those desserts went down too easily. The mother knew she had to retain her figure and so one of them had to go. At first, she found a simple regurgitation was all she needed, but that brought her out in a sweat, and the smell was unbearable. So it was a choice, in the end alcohol won. It gave her a longer hit than sugar ever did anyway and she could balance it out with a workout the next day to get rid of the calories.

It was also a comfort to her when the nights were lonely. The father would often work very late, but there had been less staying away at the weekends, now the eldest girls were a little bigger and no longer babies, the father liked to come home and wanted to be with his children. There would be conversations at the dinner table, a brandy for the father whilst the nanny put the children to bed and then took herself home for the evening. The mother would watch as the father left his chair, took himself upstairs to be with one of his girls. Then the mother would look at the drinks cabinet and she would find the hardest strongest alcohol she could lay her hands on and she would drink until she were numb.

There was a splash and I looked behind me; Dexter had just

jumped into the pool. I wasn't sure if he was in swimming trunks, boxers or naked. He swam up to me, his beard dripping with water.

'I couldn't have you in here all alone even with just one wine in your system. I need you in one piece tomorrow, Levine.' He was right up next to me as I approached the shallow end. I stood up.

'Ah, you came prepared then?' He pointed to my costume.

'Are you naked?' I asked.

'Underwear. Couldn't be bothered to head back to my room.' He laughed. 'And this is probably a bad idea for the sea swim tomorrow, this is about ten degrees warmer than the water we'll be in in the morning.'

'I know,' I said.

Dexter lay on his back and floated.

'You know not everyone can do this,' he said. 'It takes a real amount of trust to let the water just hold you. Did you know the saltier the water the easier it is to float. That's why it's best to learn to swim in the sea. It really holds you up, embraces you, like a big wet cuddle.' He laughed and broke his balance, landed on his feet and looked at me. I stared back at him hard.

'You okay?' he asked.

I was thinking, hearing the words he had just said about the ocean, how it could hold you and embrace you and make you feel so safe. That was how I had felt so many times, that was why I returned to the water as a child, that was why even when it had hurt me, almost drowned me, and there was that continued threat that it could continue to hurt me, I had gone back. It was still the place I longed to be, the only place I knew I could find solace, albeit with chaos. I didn't realise I was crying until Dexter was pushing his way through the water to get to me, already muttering soothing words and I wasn't exactly sure why I had been able to just burst into tears in the middle of a swimming pool with my co-star but I think it something was shifting inside me. I could see the faces of the three girls, smiling but now their faces seemed like inane grins, laughing at me, and the perfect complexion of the mother and father now seemed greyer. Their skin no longer so flawless.

The Smith family had brought me so much comfort, but suddenly I felt as though a hole had cracked open and was about to suck me down into the earth's core.

'I...' I went to speak to say something to Dexter, as though I suddenly had all the answers, but the words were a hurricane in my mouth.

Instead, all I could think of was the sea, of the waves and how they could cradle me, yet hurt me. I thought how I would ride to the sea alone as a child and long for it, yet fear its vastness and capabilities at the same time.

It was supposed to protect me, yet sometimes it could only hurt me.

27

NOW

I pulled away from Dexter and tried to look away.

'I feel silly,' I muttered.

'Don't. This thing we do, it's hard, and I know you have a lot going on. The stuff they are writing about you, that you were the last person to see your sister before she disappeared. It must be really hard for you.'

'Thanks, I just really want to be here and do my job and not have to think about all that, but your words about the sea... I have a strong affinity for it – when I was growing up, I was drawn to it and I spent a lot of time in there. That's all.' I hurried my words out, tried to act as though these conversations were normal and natural for me.

'So you're match fit for tomorrow. That's why they picked you.'

'I haven't been near the sea since the night my sister went missing,' I said and waited for Dexter's reaction. The muddle of words I had been fighting with earlier, were now coming out and it seemed I no longer had any control.

'Okay.' He walked to the edge of the pool and leaned on the side with his legs kicking outwards. 'So not so match fit.'

I shook my head. 'Nope.'

'Ah, well then. How are you intending to deal with this?'

I gripped the side of the pool and let my legs kick out behind me.

'By pretending I'm not me.'

Dexter laughed.

'That's what we do right?' I continued. 'I've been pretending for years. In fact, I can pretty much remember the day I began. It was sort of like an out-of-body experience. I put myself somewhere else and imagined I was someone else, far away from where I was...' I had been looking away in the distance as I had been speaking, I had gone back in time, I was there at the moment in my life, my mother walking past my room, tears on my cheeks. Her glancing at me but never coming to me. I looked at Dexter, and cleared my throat, pulled my lips into a tight smile.

'Anyway, that's my story. How about you?' I kicked my legs, the temperature was cooling around me.

'I was the class clown, my parents put me into drama school to help me expel some of that silliness, I ended up getting a part in *How to Build a Boy* and that sky-rocketed my career.'

'I haven't seen that, I should check it out.'

'You should,' Dexter said. 'You know I asked about the whole security thing and why I wasn't gifted one.'

I laughed.

'It wasn't a gift. More a necessity they felt they needed.'

'I know but I was speaking to Layla and she doesn't seem to know anything about a hired security. It must have come from your agency.'

I thought about Sylvie in her box office at the top of her house. It was just her. Then I thought about Layla and how flappy she had been when she arrived with her two phones and constant scrolling.

She didn't seem on top of her game. I let it drop. I was too tired to care.

'Should we?' I pointed to the sauna.

'We absolutely should.'

Dexter jumped out first. I pulled myself out to sitting and Dexter held out his hand.

'I think we're going to make a very good team you and I, Levine.'

'I hope so,' I said.

Dexter put his arm around me and took me into the sauna where it was warm.

* * *

I was just about to go into my room when Em's door opened.

'Okay?' she asked.

'Yes, I had a swim. I'm going to go to bed.'

'Sure,' she said and closed her door. I fell into bed. Dexter had walked me back to my room and I had not felt any desire to get him inside with me. He was turning out to be a decent human and maybe getting to know him this way was the best for both of us and for the sake of the film. I took my phone and looked at the shot I had screen-grabbed of the face of the woman outside my flat. I would send it Tammy to send to the police tomorrow.

Just before I dropped off, I sent a message to Sylvie. There had been a missed call from her earlier, probably to check up on me and I hadn't yet responded.

All good here. The big swim tomorrow. Give me a call in the morning. Just wondering if you knew much about this security who is here for me. Her name is Em. I don't have the company she works for. Anyway, she's like my shadow. Can't shake her off. *laughing emoji*

The phone slipped from my hand onto the bed and I closed my eyes.

* * *

I dreamt.

I was in the water, fighting to get out, trying to reach the shore. I could see Franny, I was dipping beneath the waves, she was there, she wasn't, she was there.

Then she was gone.

I woke up fighting for air in my lungs. It was midnight. Exactly midnight. I tried not to think too hard about the implications of that. I wasn't in a horror movie, I would be fine.

But my heart was pounding against my ribcage, like a wild animal trying to break free. I sat up and took three long, deep breaths to slow it and that was when I knew I wouldn't be falling straight back asleep again.

I pulled on a thick cardigan and walked to the door. I paused for a moment, and wondered if walking about the house at this time of night was going to be a good idea. I was not easily spooked but the idea of walking around a huge mansion in the remote part of the Highlands gave me chills.

But I was fuelled with anxiety, due to do the sea swim tomorrow and the initial tiredness had worn off. Now my brain was in fight or flight mode, but there was no way of telling it that I wasn't in danger.

The corridor outside my room was cold and my ears were only picking up a low humming sound somewhere far off.

I took a step and the floorboard creaked loudly. I hadn't really noticed it in the day but at midnight it sounded like a foghorn. I winced and carried on along the corridor, the floor beneath me emitting short sharp creaks.

Downstairs, I went along another corridor until I found my way into the kitchen. It smelled like lemon detergent. There were a few items defrosting on the counter, a pack of bacon, some baguettes. There was a tea towel covering something and I took a peek. Freshly baked scones which smelled delicious. I had hardly eaten anything for dinner. I took a surreptitious look behind me as though I might be caught stealing one. I found a plate and then opened the fridge for some butter. There was a small table with one chair at the side by the wall, it was laden with cookbooks, notepaper with lists in scrawled handwriting and a closed laptop. I found space amongst the chaos and lay my plate down and sliced through the soft crumbly scone with a knife. Then I slathered it with butter. I took one bite and emitted a long groan. It was the softest thing I ever had eaten. But it was missing one vital ingredient. A cup of tea. I scoured the cupboards until I found an industrial-size box of Tetley tea bags. I filled the kettle with water noting how it wasn't filled with limescale like they were back in London and sought out milk and sugar.

Back at my table I sipped the tea and ate, thinking of nothing but what I was doing. Anxiety wouldn't often allow me the privilege of eating. I took the plate and cup to the sink and washed them with detergent, reached for some kitchen towel and dried them. Then I put them back where I had taken them from. I had just closed the kitchen cabinet door when I heard a bang. As though a window had been closed or a door had slammed in the wind. My heckles rose and I thought of the letter which had arrived here for me. It was understandable that someone would go to the trouble of working out exactly where I was and this wasn't exactly Fort Knox, but there were security working the front gate and patrolling the area through the night. We weren't the highest profiles, but the word had spread fast. Now someone knew we were here, it wouldn't have taken long for others to try their luck.

I stepped out of the kitchen and into the corridor. The stairs to my room were to my left, the dining room and front door and hallway to my right. I could see through into the conservatory in front of me where it led out into the garden. The sky was a dark blue and starless. I had already seen how it didn't get dark here in the summer until very late at night and even now, it wasn't totally dark. Just a suggestion of it.

I heard another loud bang and edged my way along the corridor where it opened up into the dining room.

Bang.

This time I jumped. It was closer. I looked to my right and saw a pile of neatly sliced logs next to a fireplace. I stooped to pick one up and clutched it in my right hand. I don't know why I was trying to play the tough girl but I could hear something and I didn't want to go and wake anyone else up. I walked to the door which led out of the dining room and onto a side door. There was a large glass pane that was distorted so I couldn't see straight through it clearly, but I could see something. A moving shadow darting back and forth. As I froze, the shadow became larger, until it was almost filling the entire pane. It was a face and they were looking right at me.

28

CORSICA, JUNE 2008

I was late to meet Cormac because I had been held up helping Vanessa move some things from one of the rooms that didn't get used. She had been considering renting it out as a holiday home during the months of the year when she and the rest of us wouldn't be using it. It made me feel sad and mad all at once, knowing that someone, many people and children would be here when we weren't, enjoying the views, lounging in the drawing room and running freely around the gardens.

'Isn't there another way?' I asked.

Vanessa laughed. 'Oh Rey, you are so much older than you are.' She paused next to the box she was packing. The sweat was dripping from her face. 'So mature. Probably more so than you ever needed to be.' She laid a hand on my cheek. 'You poor thing.' She breathed out. Then suddenly, as if she had been momentarily in a trance, she seemed to snap out of it and looked at me, a slight look of embarrassment on her face and then she turned back to her task at hand.

'I have run out of money, Rey. The upkeep of this place and our new home in Ireland is too much for me. The boys have settled. I can't downsize and sell. They are happy where they are. Another move so soon after losing their father would destroy them. Of course I'm not happy about having to rent this place out, but I can't afford to just keep holidaying here. The old place has to earn its keep.'

She looked at me. 'It will be fine, sweetie. You will still come and visit. Everything will stay the same, I promise.'

Everything will stay the same.

I heard those words echo around my mind as I walked to the beach to meet with Cormac.

'Took your time.' Cormac tried to sound agitated but he was too easy-going for that nonsense.

'I was helping your mother.'

'Fair dos.' Cormac gave his head a firm flick and his hair, which had grown longer on top since the last time I had seen him properly, flew to one side.

'I didn't know you were having financial difficulties?'

Cormac snapped his head back towards me, his expression became crushed. 'Who said that?' There was an air of defensiveness in his voice.

'Well, Vanessa, obviously.'

Cormac's face began to contort ever so slightly. 'Dunno, but s'pose things are difficult, now we don't have a dad.'

I felt a jolt in my chest at the reality of Cormac's words.

'Okay, well, sorry for bringing it up, Vanessa said she was thinking of renting out the place—'

'And why not, it just sits there for half the year not doing anything.'

'It's a good idea,' I said, still feeling pained by the prospect. It was silly really. It wasn't my house, but it was my sanctuary. I had come here each year since I was a baby and I always felt safe. This was the first time I had been here and I didn't feel safe. Uncle Rob created a presence that made everything different. But his death had ended that, I felt fearful. Worried.

That image of Wallace outside Franny's room again was in my mind's eye.

'Right, so what's the plan?' I asked Cormac and we both looked towards the other side of the beach where it curved around out of sight.

'That way,' Cormac said and he set off with speed across the uneven sand. I kept up with him but I was walking twice as fast. He was annoyed by what I had said, I could tell, but he wasn't going to get mad, that wasn't like him. He would hold it all inside and maybe get mad later when no one was looking. All those hormones and deep emotions had to go somewhere.

We arrived at the other end of the beach having not spoken to one another the whole way. It had taken just under fifteen minutes.

Cormac looked at me.

'We meet here.' Cormac pointed to a cave. 'And we don't tell anyone, this is our secret. Okay,' he said without question.

I thought back to the other night; Franny crying, Wallace appearing outside her door. I just wanted to forget that things were not under my control, that I was just a damn child at the end of the day and I had no power. Maybe everything would be okay.

'Yes,' I said. I thought of my sister, of her small hands and features, still so pure, so doll-like. I thought of her all the time. Just for one night, maybe I could not think about her and just be in the moment, live life, feel like a teenager should feel. I deserved that didn't I?

29

NOW

The door swung open and there stood a burly man I recognised as one of the security guards I had seen hauling the paparazzi. I blew out a breath.

'You scared me!' I half whispered.

'Sorry,' he said in a broad Scottish accent. 'Just doing a check.'

'Thanks, I appreciate it.' I felt my body relax.

'Just locking up here, so you okay, everything all right?'

'All fine here. I stole a scone from the kitchen, but don't tell anyone,' I said and he laughed whole-heartedly. I looked at his belly protruding over his trousers and didn't think I had any worries about him ratting on me for my midnight gluttony.

'Oh, don't worry, your secret is safe with me, bairn.'

I wasn't sure what a bairn was but it sounded nice and cosy. I said goodnight and headed back upstairs to my room.

I heard a floorboard creak and as I looked over towards Em's room, I saw a light go off from the crack under her door.

I entered my room and sat on the bed. I was full and satisfied and sure I would be able to sleep now.

I picked up my phone to check the time and I saw that a message had come back from Sylvie.

Rey, I'm not quite sure what you mean about private security? I haven't arranged anything and there was no arrangement with Expanse over this. I'm slightly concerned. Can you call me first thing?

I felt my stomach drop.

What the hell was she saying? Dexter had seemed adamant that Expanse had not arranged for the security and Sylvie, it seemed, was confirming the same.

There was a woman about to go to sleep in the next room who claimed she was here to protect me. But it seemed no one, least of all me, knew who she was or where she came from. I began to shiver from the shock. Who the hell was Em and why was she here?

30

NOW

I tapped lightly on the door at first and then louder. I heard dragged footsteps and then eventually the door opened.

'Rey.' Dexter sounded groggy. His hair was a little wilder than I had seen it earlier and he was wearing striped pyjama bottoms and a blue T-shirt.

'Can I come in?' I didn't stop to wait for an invite. I barged past Dexter and went to the other side of the bed, where I thought I might be safe away from the door.

'What's going on?' He closed the door and came over to me, but not too close.

'Em has not been hired by Expanse or my agent.'

Dexter rubbed the side of his face, just above his beard.

'I thought it was a bit strange,' he said sleepily.

'I know, right, I did too, but I kind of ignored it. I just presumed it was all part of the super service they were offering. My agent told me I would be protected here. I guess she had been referring to Tweedle-dum and Tweedle-dee. What do you suppose I should do?' I heard my voice crack and I felt shaky.

'Sit down for a start,' Dexter said and then went back to the door and locked it. He picked up his phone from the dresser and looked at it. 'I should call the police?'

I sat for a moment then I jerked forward.

'No. don't.'

He looked at me. 'Sure?'

'Not right now.'

The words from the feature were flying through my mind. And then Cormac's warning. *Someone will find out what we did.*

What if this was all a test. What if this was some sort of game. I had been sent here and now I was trapped. I would have to confess all.

'Okay.' Dexter went instead to the corner of the room and came back with two glasses and a bottle of vodka.

'One shot to calm your nerves. You look terrible.' He poured me a glass and I sipped it, flinching at the acrid taste.

'The door is locked. My phone is fully charged with enough reception. I can call the police anytime.'

I nodded. I was still shaking. Dexter pointed to the top of the bed.

'Climb in. There's room enough for four. Unless you need me to take the couch.' He pointed to large but knobbly-looking sofa. I walked around and climbed under the covers. I pulled the duvet up close to my chin. Dexter sat up next to me.

'Do you want to tell me anything?'

'Like what?' I asked, but knowing it was a dumb thing to say.

'Like how come you are receiving threatening letters, why the press is all up in your face and why there is a woman posing as your personal security three doors down!'

I stared ahead. Not wanting to move or speak.

'I don't know, Dexter. I am worried that woman, Em, is here to try and hurt me.'

Dexter let out a noise that meant he was confused. 'It didn't look very much like she was trying to hurt you. And I mean that sincerely. These last few days she has been all over you like a fly. It seems as though she very much wants to protect you. So I'm thinking she is meant to be here, for the right reasons. Maybe someone is out to get you – there was that letter after all – so she might know something about that? Or maybe she is just a bloody loyal fan and has your best interests at heart and just so happened to have trained at MI6.' There was a hint of joviality to Dexter's voice, and I felt my body relax ever so slightly.

'I don't know what I should do,' I whispered.

'Don't worry. There are highly trained killing machines a mere press of a button away.'

Dexter pointed to a small black box on the dresser.

'Is that some sort of panic button?'

'Leads straight to the security at the front gate.' He almost laughed. 'It would be quicker to call the police and wait thirty minutes for them to get out here,' he said.

'I thought you said you didn't have personal security? Why didn't I get a panic button?'

'Because we all presumed you had brought your own security. We all thought Em would be enough. Bloody hell, if she got any closer to you she would be riding on your back.'

'It's not funny, Dexter. It's pretty disturbing. I should probably call the police. But I think I want to confront her first.'

'Now?' Dexter shifted uncomfortably and sounded perturbed.

'No, first thing. I want to ask her outright; I want to hear what she has to say.'

'Are you sure? She's pretty big. I mean, I don't think I could help you out there.'

'No, I'll do it alone.'

'Okay, you're officially nuts.'

'I'll go to her room at dawn and have it out with her. You'll wait here and if I'm not back after ten minutes then call the police.'

'Ten minutes? She could have strangled you and disposed of your body in ten minutes.'

'I don't think she will have. Like you say, I think she is genuine in some weird way. I just don't know how yet.' I lay down. My body had begun to relax from the vodka. 'I just need to sleep. Think about it in a few hours.' I could hear my voice getting sleepier.

I heard Dexter stand up, move the duvet back and slowly climb into bed next to me. It was all I had thought about for weeks, the prospect of the two of us next to one another in bed, but tonight I was just glad I had his company and for those few brief seconds before I fell off the slope into a sleep, I didn't think about the prospect of anything happening between us or being the one to instigate something. As alien as the sensation was to me, I knew I simply felt safe with him next to me.

* * *

I woke up with a start to the sound of soft music playing. I sat up, initially unsure where I was, then I could see blades of light seeping through the curtain. It was dawn, it was Dexter's room I was in, and it was his phone alarm.

Dexter made a slight groan. 'Is it time to go and get our butts kicked?' he muttered and I almost could have laughed. I got up and went to the toilet then I came back in and Dexter was sitting up rubbing his face.

'You need to make it a quick butt kicking though, we're due out of here in an hour.'

I pulled my cardigan tighter around me. 'Okay. Ten minutes.'

'I'll be right here,' Dexter said and walked me to the door and then stood next to it, with his phone in hand. 'Scream if you need me.'

I walked the length of the corridor until I reached my room and Em's room opposite. I looked back at Dexter still standing in the doorway and my heart fluttered at the sight of him there, watching over me.

31

CORSICA, JUNE 2008

My mother had decided that we needed a formal sit-down meal. Cormac and I had found one another and discussed whether getting down to the beach for the party was now still an option. 'Of course it is,' he had said. 'The adults will be busy eating and getting drunk and we can just skip off unnoticed.'

I nodded and just put my faith in him.

Mum had been in the same room but busy chatting with Vanessa. 'We're only here for a few more days. I can't believe it's gone so fast, we'll be going home soon,' she said as she badgered Vanessa and Jolie over the menu. 'We must have scallops. We always have scallops; do you remember, Vanessa?'

'I remember, Flic,' Vanessa said wearily. I noticed she had been this way for a few days now. She should have been basking in the glorious early days of her new relationship with Wallace. But perhaps his change of behaviour had affected hers. Perhaps they weren't such a tight fit after all and all they were was the sum of that meet cute. A story to tell others. Perhaps my aunt was only seeking some kind of company now that Uncle Rob was gone. I had heard my father speaking badly of Wallace on more than one occasion, only to shushed heavily by my mother – one of the few times I had seen him listen to her.

Eventually Vanessa seemed to have been worn down enough to give instructions to Jolie to head to the market to pick up scallops and vegetables and fresh bread and cheeses for a dinner.

Mother told us girls to dress nicely. I found a yellow sundress and white cardigan. Scarlett went for blue and Franny, pink.

We somehow found ourselves together in the hallway as our father passed through.

'Now look at that, all my beautiful girls together.' I couldn't help but look around to see who he might be saying this for, and sure enough Wallace was just coming down the stairs.

'Would you mind, taking a picture of us, Wallace, old chap? Me with my three beautiful girls?'

Wallace took the digital camera from the table in the hallway and we positioned ourselves next to our father; me on one side, Scarlett on the other, and Franny in front, Dad's hand on her shoulders as though he were a sports coach giving an Olympic runner a quick squeeze before they competed. It was stiff and formal. Scarlett smiled too hard as she always did and when we all went our separate ways, I watched my father linger next to Franny, his hands on her shoulders still, a faraway look in his eye. Scarlett had slumped herself into a chair in the hallway.

'Oh, come on,' I said as I headed into the dining room. 'Now is not the time for your antics.'

At the dinner table, I sat down opposite Cormac and we eyed one another briefly, I knew he felt nervous about the evening and that it might not even go ahead but we both had to believe it would. Ever since the opportunity had come, we knew that we couldn't let it pass. We were at an age now where we wanted more than the freedom the villa and the area around it gave us. We were ready for the next phase of adulthood, and this was it: a real party, on a beach, with strangers. And there would be boys. I was excited. I didn't want anything to get in the way.

Everyone sat down and there was enough noise as if there were ninety of us, not nine.

The overhead fan did very little to relieve us of the hot evening air and the candles reflected the sheen of sweat across everyone's faces.

I noticed Scarlett had made it to the table and was looking as though she needed to go back to her bed, not be sitting down to dinner. Could she not pull it together just for one night.

Jolie was rushing around filling everyone's wine glasses and I stood up and took the water jug and followed behind her.

'Thank you,' she whispered.

'No problem,' I whispered back.

My father had been seated next to Franny and Faren at one end and Vanessa, my mother and Scarlett at the other. Cormac and I were slap bang in the middle.

'Hello,' Wallace said. I looked to him as he took the final seat next to me.

'Hi,' I said tightly.

I now wanted so badly to be able to speak with him. But we had managed so far with so little interaction that I was beginning to feel we had some sort of telepathy going on.

'Oh, this is so nice,' my mother said. 'A lovely prelude to our evening out.' She fanned herself with a napkin. I blew air into my forehead. My fingers slipped around my iced-water glass from the condensation. I looked at my father, uncomfortable in the heat but drinking his way through it.

I looked at Cormac, making sure I had heard that right and his face bore the same perplexed expression as mine probably did.

What did my mother mean by their evening out? They hadn't mentioned anything before, and I knew that an evening out would scurry our plans. Jolie would be summoned to babysit us and then there was no way we would be able to just slip away the way we had planned to do with all the adults comatose from alcohol and not noticing if we were here or not.

I gave Cormac a questioning look but he quickly looked down at his plate, not wanting our across the dinner table exchange to arouse suspicion. But as I looked to my left I could see someone was already on to us as Wallace's eyes flicked from one side of the table to the other. He seemed a little jittery too.

I cleared my throat. 'Where are you off to tonight?' I asked to the table, but mainly to my mother.

'We've been invited for drinks up at the Braziers' house,' my mother said with total pride in her voice. I had heard of the Braziers; they were one of the wealthiest families in the area. My mother had mentioned their names so many times due to the one occasion she was in the local supermarket and she found herself in the provisions aisle with Susan Brazier, the wife of Marcus Brazier. It had been a real moment for her, even though no words were exchanged, only a simple smile from each party, but my mother had come back from the supermarket and raved about it to all of us for hours. She still would say, 'Remember that time when Susan Brazier and I were in the supermarket together?' as though they had been shopping like a couple of old girlfriends. I had wished since that day that my mum could make friends with Susan because it was exactly what she needed to boost her confidence and maybe she would find in Susan what she truly needed in a friend, and had never really had to date. But not tonight. Why did it have to be tonight? I needed them all here drunk, not leaving Jolie to keep a beady eye on us. We could no longer just slip off unnoticed. Jolie would take her role as babysitter very seriously this evening and there might not be a chance of us getting to the beach.

'That's, wow, that really something, Mum, well done,' I said with complete seriousness and adoration for my mother's achievement. She swung her head around at me as though I had just shot her with my words.

'I don't need congratulating, Rey, these are people just like us, it's only due to us not being here for the last few years that we haven't been invited sooner.'

I heard Vanessa clear her throat and saw from the corner of my eye Wallace shifting in his seat.

'Anyway, we will all have a lovely time, I am sure. They have just extended their house and refurbished the pool to a now indoor and outdoor pool and spa, with an ice pool! I have heard it is supposed to be wonderful for you. I don't think I'll be trying that, even after a few drinks!' my mum hooted. I even saw my dad raise an eyebrow and a small smile. He would be very pleased they were all now suddenly chums with the Braziers. This would have been exactly what my father was waiting for but would not have expressed it in the same way. Like all his emotions, he chose to keep them close to his chest, he would never wear his heart on his sleeve the way my mother did. Whilst she would declare her affection by screaming, 'I love you, darling!' across a crowded street, Dad's motto was 'love doesn't always have to be shown publicly'.

'So what time are you off?' I asked.

'About nine, straight after dinner. Don't worry, Jolie will be here for you all.'

'Mum, I'm nearly seventeen, we don't need a babysitter,' I whined in a way that sounded as though that was exactly what I needed. Jolie put a plate of scallops and puy lentils in front of me.

'Sorry, Jolie, no offence.'

'None taken, my darling.' She patted my head softly.

'Scarlett, Franny and Faren need sitting and so Jolie will be here so you can all relax. Vanessa and I can enjoy our evening knowing you are all here.'

I felt an eye roll coming on and so I supressed it. Picking up my fork and devouring each scallop in two bites much to my father's distaste as he looked over at me displeasure punctuating his usual neutral expression. He dabbed at his head with a napkin.

We were just heading into the second course when the doorbell trilled loudly from the hallway. Vanessa's chair scraped backwards, and she went to stand.

'I get this.' Jolie was already out of the door yet I saw a look of unease pass between Vanessa and Wallace.

Vanessa didn't touch her food again, she only sipped her wine, twisted her napkin in her hand and a minute later Jolie came back into the dining room.

'There is a lady here to see you, I tell her—'

'It's fine, thank you, Jolie.' Vanessa was up and walking past Jolie before she could finish her sentence.

I took a sip of wine, wincing inside. It was still not palatable to me, but I drank it anyway, because I knew one day I wished to be a seasoned wine-drinker. I had watched my parents drink wine from the moment I could see, it was the fabric of my existence.

It was several minutes until Vanessa returned and all the while I was thinking about how Cormac and I would get out of the villa tonight and down to the beach. From his furrowed brow and dipped head, I was sure that Cormac was thinking exactly the same. I was depending on him and he on me to come up with the perfect solution.

I excused myself to go to the toilet and when I reached the downstairs WC it was occupied.

'Nearly done!' came Jolie's voice. I skipped upstairs. My parents' room was the first bathroom I came to and although I would not normally, I entered and used their en suite.

I washed my hands at the sink, and as I picked up a towel to dry them, my eyes were drawn to a small container of pills. It was not

unusual for me to see an array of pills and potions in my parents'
room, especially on my mother's side. I picked up the container and
read: 'Sleeping tablets – take 1 an hour before bed.'

Without hesitation, I unscrewed the lid, took two tablets, put
them in my dress pocket and headed downstairs.

Jolie was clearing plates, and it was several more minutes until
my aunt returned to her place at the table. To say she was looking
flustered would not be an accurate explanation. She looked as
though she were somewhere else entirely in her mind, even when
Wallace tried to subtly get her attention, she clearly didn't want to
meet his eye.

Mains were served. By this point, my mother had drunk several
glasses of wine, and was having a wild time, clearly excited about
the evening with the Braziers. And who could blame her. It was
something that she craved, to be with people, to share her life, to
laugh and drink. She was always the life of the party, and I was
happy they had finally invited her.

I looked at Cormac a few times, but he would just look away. I
hoped it was because he did not want us to be seen trying to have a
secret conversation at the dinner table, as someone, most likely
Wallace, would pick up on it and then we might draw attention to
ourselves.

I knew by dessert my mother would have left the table, rarely
indulging in the sweets when she was drinking. On my eighth
birthday I went into her bathroom and saw the whole toilet pan
filled with brown and speckled with red. We had just eaten a choco-
late and raspberry cake as part of the celebration dinner, a specific
request that I had given my mother because I once heard her tell
someone that chocolate and raspberry were her favourite sweet
combination. I was always confused as to why she would throw it
up so soon after having just eaten it. Eventually I began to see repe-
tition between her eating a sweet dessert and there being remnants

of it in the toilet pan not long after. Sometimes I would seek it out, just so I could keep the pattern alive in my mind.

By the time the sweet did arrived, a crème brûlée, I was beginning to feel anxious that we wouldn't be able to make it out on time. It was coming up for 9 p.m. By the time the sweet was demolished by most, except me, my sisters were being ushered upstairs by Jolie, much to Scarlett's protests of 'I'm not tired', which could be heard for minutes as she was escorted to her room.

Eventually all the adults left the table, and it was just me and Cormac.

'What will we do?' he hissed.

'It's okay.' I smiled and I held out my hand containing the two sleeping pills. 'I have a plan.'

32

NOW

Em came to the door dressed in her uniform of black jacket and trousers.

'Are we off already?' She looked confused as she assessed my attire of pyjama shorts, vest and cardigan.

'No. But we need to talk.'

I did the same thing I had done with Dexter hours earlier. I pushed my way into her room.

I saw a space similar to mine, perhaps a little smaller. A window, which was ajar, overlooking the lawn which framed the entire house. I was distracted by the neatness. Just one rucksack on the floor. A pair of black trousers folded neatly on a chair. The bed already made, and the curtains pinned back.

Em closed the door behind me, pausing to look at Dexter waiting by the doorway.

'We have ten minutes, then he's calling the police,' I said standing in the centre of the room and folding my arms. Em looked crestfallen and this was a relief. I was prepared for anger, for rage, for anything, actually, but this.

'So, do you want to tell me why you're here?'

Em seemed to drop her security demeanour. Her shoulders hunched; she sat down on the bed.

'I am a professional. I do personal security. That is what I do.'

'Right. But I didn't employ you. Expanse didn't employ you and neither did my agent. So who sent you?'

Em sucked in some air. Then she let out a half laugh.

'You really don't know? Or you do know but you're pretending you don't know. Or maybe, you just don't want to admit that you know.'

I felt a tingle along my back rise to my shoulders and across my chest. The classic 'someone walking over my grave'. This was someone from my past, I had known this the minute Dexter hinted at doubting Em's authenticity.

Em looked at me, in a way that suggested she felt sorry for me.

'I didn't ask to be here. I was sent here. By my father.'

She paused as though I might immediately know who she meant before she finally said, 'Wallace.'

33

NOW

I felt my whole body go tense at the sound of his name. I had known him such a short while. I had known him only then. And never afterwards. It had been so fleeting that I barely remembered what he looked like. Feelings were shooting through me, memories of the villa that summer, but it had been such a blur and a mix of emotions in the end, that I wasn't sure what I was experiencing. But seeing this woman in front of me, little memories of his face were coming back to me. She had similar features. But mainly it was her height and stature. Those were the things I remember about him. How he seemed to take up space, how he owned the room. How he managed to be the same height as my father, if not taller.

'Your father?'

Em nodded. 'He sent me. To protect you. He said, "She deserves to be protected. She needs to be. None of this was her fault."'

I sucked air in as though I couldn't get enough inside my lungs.

'W... why?' I stuttered. 'Why would he do that?'

'Because he knew you, he knew your family.' Then she looked hard at me. 'Because he knew.'

And those three words hit me the hardest. They almost felt physical as though I had been prodded in the chest.

'And I know, obviously. Everything.' She stood up, walked across the room to the chair where her rucksack was perched next to it. She bent down. I edged my way to the door, reaching for the handle ready to grab it and run out. Em turned and stood up and walked back to me. She was holding something in her hands part of it hanging out in her loose grip and I instantly recognised it, the memory of it shooting me with nostalgia like a drug to the vein.

She opened her palm to fully reveal what I already knew was there. A small home-made bracelet, white and green beads spelling out the name.

Scarlett.

34

CORSICA, JUNE 2008

The adults all left for the Braziers' leaving us kids and one adult in charge. Jolie.

She looked shattered from a day tending to our every need and so Cormac helped her clear the table and load the dishwasher and I hand-washed the wine glasses.

'I'm going to make you a drink,' I called out to Jolie who had just flopped into a soft chair in the corner of the kitchen. I looked behind at Cormac who was bringing the last plates through to put in the dishwasher.

'Oh, thank you, Rey, that is so kind of you two to help me. I don't know what I would do without you sometimes. Now, you are all older, it is so nice to have the help.'

'Okay. I will make you a hot chocolate. Now sit tight. And just relax.' I eyed Cormac again who was now closer to me, watching over the proceedings. I looked around at Jolie. She was sitting back in her chair, her eyes closed. Perfect.

I warmed the milk on the stove and scooped in teaspoons of chocolate mixture. I pulled the sleeping tablets from my pocket, looked again at Jolie, her eyes were closed tightly. I pulled out the two sleeping tablets from my pocket and dropped them in the pestle and mortar. I carefully and quietly crushed them with a swift movement and avoiding any banging. I scooped out the crumbs and put them in the chocolate milk. I poured the whole amount into a mug and added a dash of brandy to conceal any bitter taste from the pills.

I turned to go to Jolie, and I paused for a second. I was sure that Cormac was about to say something. He had the look of someone who wanted to speak. Maybe that was the moment he wanted to tell me to stop, this was a mistake and we shouldn't do it. But I moved quickly past him and over to Jolie.

'Here you go,' I said and she opened her eyes.

'Oh, what a good girl you are.' Jolie took the mug from me and took a tentative slurp.

'And brandy too?'

I nodded. I edged away from Jolie and leant against the kitchen counter. I glanced over at Cormac who was looking between me and Jolie, his face was riddled with anxiety, I tried to tell him with eyes to change his expression but it looked as if it were staying for the foreseeable.

'What will you do tomorrow on your day off?' I asked Jolie to ease the atmosphere. If someone walked in here they could slice right through it.

'I will go and see my mother. She has a friend staying. I will make them some pasta.'

'Jolie, you must rest, you cannot always work,' I scolded.

'This is my family. I wish to cook for them.'

Jolie took two large sips of the hot chocolate. I had purposely made it less hot so that she could drink it quickly. Already the wait was killing me – I just didn't have it etched across my face the way Cormac did.

I passed the next few minutes by wiping the surface with a

cloth. Then Jolie was beside me, trying to put her mug in the dishwasher.

'Leave it, Jolie, I'll do that.'

I took it from her, and she walked, unsteadily I noticed, to the door.

'I'll just...' She stopped and rubbed her head. 'I'll just be in my room. Tell Franny and Scarlett I will put them to bed in a moment.'

'Don't worry, I'll get them settled,' I called after her. Jolie raised her hand in thanks and was gone.

I looked at Cormac.

'Jeez, could you have been any more tense?'

Cormac frowned. 'What?'

'Your face the whole time.' I shook my head. 'Never mind. I'm going to put Scarlett and Franny to bed then get changed. It should have worked by then. I'll meet you back here in half an hour.'

I left Cormac looking confused in the kitchen.

Scarlett was already in her pyjamas and had brushed her teeth. 'I'm going to watch a film. Mum said I could watch a film on my laptop.'

'Okay,' I said. 'I'm going to read a book to Franny. I'll see you later.'

Scarlett was already busying herself with loading a DVD into the laptop.

I went to Franny's room and found her tucked up in bed.

'Oh my, someone is keen!'

'Can we do the snail book?'

'Yes. Of course.' I picked up the book Franny had chosen and climbed up into bed with her.

'Where is Jolie?' Franny whispered. It was late for her now, she was tired.

'She's having a lie-down.'

'Okay,' Franny whispered.

'Right, are you ready?'

Franny nodded as eagerly as she could.

I finished the story quite quickly, even though I was taking my time. I relished these moments with Franny. I didn't get to be with her alone very often. When I did get some one-on-one time with her, Mum would suddenly be there, somehow pushing us apart or orchestrating a reason why Franny needed to come away and be with her immediately. I wanted to be close to my little sister, but it always felt impossible when my mother was around.

'You've got your bracelet on?' I lifted Franny's arm. 'Do you want to take it off?'

Then I noticed the name on the bracelet, it was Scarlett's name spelled out with beads.

'You're wearing Scarlett's?'

'Yes, we swapped.'

'That's sweet.'

'Just for one day, then we will swap back tomorrow.'

'Ah. Good plan.'

Franny had closed her eyes and was on the edge of falling asleep. I kissed her cheek and then her nose.

'Goodnight, little lamb.'

'Must you go?' she whispered and her voice tugged at my heart.

'I'll stay a while,' I whispered back.

'Goodnight,' she said in barely a whisper. And I stayed until her breathing changed from shallow to long and deep. Then I got up and crept away.

* * *

I took a little time to get myself ready. I applied some sprays, changed into a new bikini and layered up with a dress and sweat-shirt. I carried my flip-flops and walked downstairs to Jolie's room. I called her name once and heard nothing. I peeked around the door, and she was lying flat on her stomach, her arm stretched out across the bed. I approached her and checked her breath. She was softly snoring.

Back in the kitchen, Cormac seemed a little brighter. He was sipping a stubby beer.

'Coast all clear?'

'Yep. She is sparko.'

'I just hope you didn't give her an overdose.'

'It's two pills, Cormac, she will be fine.'

'Great, then let's get to this party.'

Cormac led the way out of the villa, and I followed.

35

NOW

I took the bracelet from Em's hand and looked at it. It was Scarlett's, the one she had worn when she was in Corsica. She had made it, along with one for each and every one of us.

'Where did you get this?'

'From my father, obviously.'

I looked at Em.

'And where did he get it?'

'From Corsica.'

I made a mind-bending attempt to recall back to the night Franny went missing. My mind was a frenetic collage. I didn't want to try and think of why Em had given this to me claiming it was from her father, Wallace.

'I can't do this right now.' I walked out of the room still holding the bracelet in my hand.

'Don't you want to know?' Em called after me.

Dexter was still at his door. 'You okay?' he asked.

I nodded and ducked into my bedroom and closed the door.

I sat on the bed and ignored the light knock on the door, which I knew was Em. I stripped and put on my swimming suit. I had just

under an hour until we were getting picked up, I needed to think. I
needed to swim.

I was glad that no one followed me to the pool, that they'd had
that foresight to just leave me for a while. Em being here, telling
me she was Wallace's daughter, it was all too much. It was an
overload of memories that were trying to formulate in my mind,
and it wasn't working. They were just muddled and hazy and
messy.

I took to the water and found some comfort in the words that
came at me from the Smith family.

*In the end it was only the drink that the mother could think about. It
helped to numb any feeling, because the feelings she was having she did
not like. When the drink was inside her, she didn't have to be a mother or
a wife. She just existed. She didn't need to have responsibility for anyone.
And she didn't have to think about anything.*

*She drank every night because if she didn't, she would be left with
only her raw feelings. And that was not a good place for her to be. Because
when she was left with them she thought about her daughters and she
was always left with a raw knotted feeling, a pure hopelessness. And
underneath that, a slow burning, raging anger, a fire that started in the
pit of her stomach which she extinguished each evening with the first shot
of liquor.*

*Because without it, she wasn't sure what she could be capable of. She
looked up to the ceiling to where her daughters' bedrooms were, and she
knew it would be something truly heinous.*

I was crying again. When I was swimming I barely noticed it at
first until I got the sore sting in my nose. I stopped swimming and
leaned against the edge of the pool.

The Smith family had distracted me only for a while, but the image of Scarlett's bracelet was back in my mind. Why did Wallace have Scarlett's bracelet?

I hauled myself out of the water and went back to my room to change.

When I was dried and dressed, I knocked on Em's door.

There was no answer. I knocked again and when she didn't come, I pushed the door open. Her room was empty. The bed sheets stripped and piled in a corner, her one bag and spare trousers were gone.

Back in the hallway, Dexter was now outside his room.

'We have to get going.' He looked terrible. As though he had barely slept, which of course, neither of us had.

'Bus is downstairs.'

'Okay.'

'How did that go with Em?'

'She's gone,' I said.

'You what? What did she say? Why was she here?'

'It's complicated, but someone I was on holiday with in the villa the night my sister disappeared sent her. She is his daughter.'

'This is weird. I knew shooting this movie with you was going to be interesting but my God, you've surprised me, Rey. I know you don't want to talk to me about it, and rightly so, so I won't ask. I just hope you're okay, and that you're okay to keep working. I don't think I want anyone else now. I'm used to you.'

I smiled. Dexter had totally surprised me. I had this image in my head of what it was going be like between us, and I had been completely wrong. He was nothing like the way Tammy had portrayed him. He was, as far as I was concerned, a gentleman.

'I'm used to you to,' I said.

'Let's go to work. I'll just grab a jacket.'

He went back into his room, went to his wardrobe and opened it. The weather here required layers and I was wrapped in a thick cardigan. My eyes were drawn to the chest of drawers in Dexter's room, right next to me. There was a small sheet of paper with a telephone number written on it. I leaned in to read the small logo on the top sheet. Noble Aegis Resort and Spa. It was exactly the same notepaper as the note that had arrived in an envelope to me. I felt my body turn cold.

I thought about Dexter all the way to the beach, assessing his behaviour over and over, our moments together in the pool, in bed together last night, the conversations, and the laughs. He had been charming and understanding. What did this mean? Was he really trying to scare me? Did he set up the paps to come and photograph us?

Then there was how quickly Em left after our conversation. Was Dexter instrumental in that as well. My skin flashed with goosebumps. She did leave quickly... She had been sent to a job but then she was gone. Had Dexter wanted her gone?

I looked over at Dexter sitting next to one of the hair designers, laughing and making her laugh in return. He looked over at me and smiled. My expression remained neutral and then his face changed to one of concern.

He mouthed, 'Are you okay?'

I let my mouth form a small smile.

'Fine,' I mouthed back.

Outside, on set, the sea looked grey and cold and so I made my way straight over to get coffee.

The woman at the coffee stand was again staring at me but barely smiling.

'Hi,' I said. I felt anything but positive, but I wasn't going to let this girl take the last inch of what I was forcing out of me.

She pulled a tight-lipped smile and when Dexter arrived next to me, she was all smiles and 'Morning' to him.

I slunk away to the trailer to change into my costume.

I felt sick at the prospect of getting into the water, but I knew I had no choice. We had already begun filming scenes; I was expected to be the face as well as the body in the water from today's scene.

I knew I had to do it. They wanted to get a few shots of me at the edge of the water, with Dexter behind me. I had to strip to my costume. My skin prickled and I felt the cold shoot through to my bones. I started to shiver almost instantly.

I felt a hand on my back, it was warm, but I stumbled when I turned and saw it was Dexter.

'Hey.' His voice sent his usual positive vibes my way. But I wouldn't allow it to penetrate me this time. I looked around to my right and saw the mountain staring down at me. I had been told what I was to do. Just walk into the water and begin to swim, just a few metres out. That was all they needed of me today.

And so I edged away from Dexter and the words of encouragement he continued to fire at me and I thought, *Fuck it; it's now or never.*

The water was so cold it took my breath away. And then in the place of my breath, was an image. An image. His face, the one who was always going to be there. He had been waiting for me, to get back into the sea, he had been coming for me all this time.

I swam but it was rapid and frantic.

I wasn't ready. I was never going to be ready.

I tried a few more controlled strokes, to distract myself, to warm up, to swim away. Yes, I needed to swim away from all of it. From Corsica, from Franny, from my mother and all that she didn't do, and him. My father, and everything he did.

Voices echoed as ripples of waves hit me. I gasped for air now, breathing in but it no longer came naturally. I bobbed up and down, the waves carried me now, the horizon appeared and disappeared, and I began to think back, and I realised that this was always going to happen, this was always going to be the outcome for me. Time was deceptive, I felt I could hide behind it but it was also fluid, never stopping to allow me to come to terms with anything, to seek repentance. I had vowed I would never get back into the water, but I never really had a choice. I had returned to it once more, like I always did.

My focus began to get hazier, and the memories started to pound at me, hitting me hard with every pelt of wave. Franny was there, and Scarlett, Jolie was asleep and then Franny was gone. People were shouting and my mother was screaming, screaming at me. It's all my fault. I did this to us. I did this to us. Voices were louder but I couldn't speak, I couldn't shout, I couldn't ask for help. Just like all those years ago, I felt helpless, powerless to what was happening.

Hands on me, under my arms, I was being lifted and pulled. I landed in a RIB, faces staring at me, talking to me, asking, telling, 'You will be okay, Rey, we've got you now. You're safe.'

But they didn't know, they didn't understand, that keeping me in the water was the only way I knew to be safe.

'I can't,' I said. 'I can't.'

'It's okay, Rey, you're safe.' A man's voice. I didn't recognise it, but those words, you're okay now, didn't ring true. I didn't believe him.

At the shore it was Dexter who was there ready to receive me. I was carried to the trailer and laid down on the day bed.

'Rey.' Dexter leaned over me then he was ushered away whilst a first-aider shone a light in my eye and then a large blanket was wrapped around me, and I was handed a drink which was so hot that I could barely hold it.

My mother was right. I was the one who did this.

36

CORSICA, JUNE 2008

There were lights, someone had set up a small speaker, which was pumping out loud dance music. It could be French, but I liked the beat anyway. Cormac looked around at me and we both grinned at one another.

We arrived next to a group of ten or eleven others, all similar ages and older. I am handed a beer and I start drinking it immediately, finishing almost half in three large gulps. I felt the stress of the last few hours melt away. A guy caught my eye, he was cute, obviously French and clearly wanted to come over and say hi. Cormac moved in with a crowd of lads his age and before long they were all laughing. I looked over and the guy was approaching me.

'Hello,' he said in a beautiful French accent.

He handed me another beer which I drank as quickly as the last and I was pleased with how impressed he seemed by that. We spoke for a while in his broken English, which was awkward but fun and then he pointed to the sea.

I didn't need much persuasion to get into the water. I had been waiting for someone to make the first move because somehow, I felt self-conscious wanting to be the first. I had a buzz from the beer, but I was going to make sure I was careful this time, the waves were a lot calmer. I could feel the presence of my cousin there watching me.

I waded into the water, and I lay back, letting it hold me, the light sensation of the waves as they bobbed me up and down, gently rocking me and lulling me. I felt the presence of the French boy next to me, he was laughing, splashing me at first then falling into a relaxed rhythm with me. Before long I heard the laughter and splashes of others until I looked around and saw there were at least eight of us bobbing around in the waves. I was so relaxed that it took me a moment to realise that something was going on on the shore. I looked to my right and saw that everyone was leaving the water and swimming to the beach. I dropped my feet so I was standing up to my waist. I saw several adults walking along the beach and I recognised two of them as Wallace and Vanessa.

I clambered to the shore, suddenly feeling anything but serene and chilled. I felt sick and hungover. Because I knew that something very bad had happened and it may have something to do with what I had done.

37

NOW

I was transferred back to the house and my shots were cancelled for the day.

I took to my room and asked not to see anyone, not even Dexter, who said he was just next door if I needed anything.

I had told everyone I was okay but really, I was far from that. Images darted at me, flashes of a memory, a face, then they were gone.

I knew I had been scared of the water because it was the last place I had been when Vanessa and Wallace came looking for me. That massive body of water, no matter which part of the world I was in, held *all* my fears and demons. I had avoided the sea for so long because that was where I went to soothe, to heal, to feel and to forget. I thought how all stretches of water were connected somehow and that the atoms from the sea in Corsica had at some point managed to merge with the atoms in the North Sea. It had been carrying the past as it carried me. I was out of the water, but I felt as though I were drowning in my past. History had found me and drenched me through.

I closed my eyes, no longer needing a swimming pool to spur on the story of the Smith family. They had come to me at a time when I was vulnerable and weak, and had begun to tell me their story. And now I knew why. Their family had been my family story all the time.

The mother was at home. They had not been entertaining that evening, it had only been the mother and the father. The father was restless, the mother could see he was. It unnerved her. He kept clearing his throat. She took out a pack of cards and began to deal them, laid them out on the table between them where they were residing in the drawing room.

The father briefly looked over his paper at the game his wife had set up and returned to his reading. Then he put the paper down and stood up and went and poured himself a whisky. The mother swallowed hard, the feeling of a large stone was in her throat. She felt her heart rate begin to rise and a fierce pumping in her chest. The father took the whisky and swallowed in one gulp.

Then he cleared his throat and walked past the table where the mother had set the cards up and headed for the stairs.

The mother turned, the words in her throat were caught behind the stone, and unable to get them free, she was helpless, as much as a victim. But what words would she have said and what power would they have had?

She didn't know at the time, that she had all the power, that she was the mother, that just like the cards she had just held in her hand, she could have dealt the superpower. She laid them carefully on the table and that was that. If only she had had some guts. Some gumption. If only she believed in herself to know that she was all they needed. Her presence. Her arms around them.

But the words stayed where they were, lodged far down in her throat, so when the father took himself upstairs, she stayed where she was and looked up at the ceiling and at the exact moment she heard the creaking of the floorboard, she knew which daughter's room he had gone into. She stood up, went to the bar in the corner, poured a long drink and swal-

lowed it down along with those precious valuable words. She drank more until all she felt was so numb and she could barely feel her own body any more.

Yet all she could hear was her own voice, ringing inside her head telling the father that he was not to go upstairs. He was not to go into one of his daughter's rooms, he was not to touch his own flesh and blood in that way and not any one of the three beautiful babies that they had brought into this world. If only she had found a way to let the words free to own them. Then she would have told him he was sick. He needed help. And that she would stand by him whilst he got that help. Or if he could not be helped then he needed to go far away from them. If only she, the mother had done that.

Later, when she went upstairs to her bed, she walked past the bedroom where she heard soft sobbing. She stopped, a pair of eyes like a startled rabbit were staring back at her. Saying so much, but just like their mother, the eyes were trying to say something that the mouth was unable to. The mother looked away and went towards the husband where he lay sleeping and lay down next to him.

38

CORSICA, JUNE 2008

'Franny is missing,' Cormac said to me when I finally reached the shore. He was there already with a girl.

'What?' My heart was in my mouth. I saw blue flashing lights and there was a police car arriving.

'You need to come back to the villa.' Vanessa put a towel around me. She was calm and so I remained calm. I did not believe it was an emergency the way the police were rounding up all the other people from the party and taking them to police cars. Franny would have just walked off, sleepwalking. She was fine. I had tucked her up in her bed. She was fine.

'Where are they taking them?' I asked.

'To the police station. They all need to be questioned,' Vanessa said.

'But we didn't do anything!' I spoke. 'We were all here, we didn't see Franny?'

'I know,' Vanessa said. 'But I need to you to come back to the villa, you and Cormac. There are police there, they need to ask you some questions.'

'What sort of questions?'

Wallace was walking ahead; he opened the door to back seat in the car. I got in one side and Cormac the other.

'What's happening? What happened to Franny?'

'The police want to ask you those questions,' Vanessa said calmly again and I felt a wave of sickness rise from my stomach and I caught it, pushed it back down.

'Why?'

'Because you were the last to see her.'

There were more blue lights when we got back to the villa. Cormac walked with his head down, I was sure he was ready to confess all that we had drugged Jolie. It was our fault, of course it was, or my fault. Cormac actually had nothing to do with it.

I walked into the villa and my mother launched herself at me. She managed to scratch my face and I felt a searing pain, and when I touched my cheek there was blood on my hand. Wallace had already grabbed hold of her by this point. But she was screaming.

'This was all your fault!'

Wallace took my mother to the other side of the room, but I could still hear her cries, her allegations. She was right, I felt the guilt consume me, it surged through me. It was my fault. I gave Jolie the tablets, she had been asleep. She had not been able to see what had happened, why Franny was no longer here. And I had run off to the beach. I ran upstairs to Franny's room but I was not able to get in; there were men in uniforms in the room, I was told in French to stand back.

I looked into the room next door and Scarlett was sitting on the edge of her bed, my cousin Faren sitting next to her. I looked at Scarlett's wrist where she was playing with a bracelet. It had Franny's name on it.

'Why do you have Franny's bracelet?' I asked accusingly and Faren, despite his young age, fired a look at me. Despite over a week in the French sun, their tanned faces were now pale and drained of all colours.

'We swapped,' Scarlett muttered. And then I remembered seeing Scarlett's bracelet on Franny's wrist when I was reading to her. I edged away and went back downstairs to the room that Jolie used when she stayed over. I could hear loud sobs, an alien version of Jolie's voice, she was talking in both French and English. My father paced the hallway, then he left, came back again, then paced some more.

'I was just asleep, who would do this, who would do this?' she repeated. 'I was just asleep. I am sorry, I am sorry.'

I went back into the kitchen, and I waited. I waited for someone to come and hold me, to take me in their arms and comfort me. To tell me it was all going to be okay.

I waited for my little sister, Franny. But I never saw her again.

39

NOW

'Do you think you will be able to continue filming?' Sylvie asked down the phone. 'Maybe I should fly out and be with you? Do you need some support. Is it all too much, the stories? The news features?'

'I don't need you to fly out,' I said croakily. I had been in my bed the whole day. Expanse were eager to know how I was doing, and Sylvie had been asked to find out. But I was numb. I felt nothing. I'd experienced a tidal wave of fear and emotion and now... nothing.

'They don't want to have to bring someone in again. They are already behind schedule.'

'I know. I am a pain. I am a burden.'

'No, that's not what I am saying. Nor are they. We just need to know, are you up to this, Rey?'

I thought for a moment. I had to keep living. I couldn't remain in limbo all the time, waiting for someone to rescue me, waiting for Franny to come home.

'I will be okay,' I spoke. 'I'll get up tomorrow and I will go to work.'

* * *

I didn't bother to go down for dinner and about nine o'clock there was a knock on my door.

'Come in.'

The door opened slowly and eventually, Dexter came through carrying a tray. He put it on the bed next to me and closed the door. I was too tired to try and edge away from him.

'I brought you a little supper. Some soup and bread.' He pointed to the food proudly as though he had made it himself.

He sat down on the edge of the bed. We both looked at one another.

He pushed his hand into his pocket and pulled out a piece of paper, unfolded it and held it out to me.

'Hey, look.'

I eyed the piece of paper in his hands. There was some scrawled handwriting which read:

Call me tonight.

There was also a telephone number. I looked at the top of the page and saw the familiar logo – Noble Aegis Resort and Spa – that had been on the note I had received warning me to watch my back.

I shook my head. 'What is it, I don't understand?'

'It's that girl from the catering department, the one who didn't like you.' He laughed. I didn't laugh and his face fell serious. 'Well, she gave me her number yesterday and then again today. I'm guessing she likes me. But you know. It's not a good idea to get involved with the production crew.' He shoved the note back in his pocket. It made sense to me, why Dexter had the same paper in his room. For a while I had doubted him, thought he had been trying to play mind games with me. But it had been that little bitch from catering who had somehow landed that envelope outside my room. Some people had issues with celebrities. It had happened before to me and lots of people I knew. People get affected by everything you do or don't do, or they are so affected by the role you play in a movie or series that it triggers so much in them that they feel they need to reach out to you, mostly in a positive way, but sometimes, like this, in a negative way.

'I wouldn't bother calling her back,' I said.

'Oh, it speaks.' Dexter readjusted himself on the bed.

'That paper was the same paper I received that note on. It told me to watch my back. Our caterer girl didn't just not like me, she has some serious issues with me.'

'Oh.' Dexter dropped his head. 'Well, I wasn't going to call her anyway. Blondes aren't my thing.' He laughed. I tried to smile. He cleared his throat. 'But seriously, I'll get onto it.'

'Thank you,' I said.

'So are we back on for tomorrow? Sorry to sound heartless.'

'No. It's fine.' I took the tray and laid it on my lap. 'I'll be back. I just...'

Dexter waited for me to finish.

'You know what happened in Corsica all that time ago. They never found my sister. I was in the water when she... when she went missing and I never forgave myself. I thought I could just get back into the sea and everything would be okay, but it seems the very opposite happened.'

He nodded. 'Sounds like you could do with a bit of R & R.'

'I've had nothing but that, for years.'

Dexter looked down his nose at me like an adult would to a child. 'Come on, Levine. Who are you kidding? Not yourself. I'm not a therapist or a psychologist but I imagine there is a lot of past trauma there that you haven't dealt with. The last few years have been your way of hiding from it all. Partying away your memories.

Maybe you need to just address it all once and for all. Then recover. Rejuvenate. Come back a better person.'

I was silent for a few seconds then I nodded. Because of course he was right. No one had ever told me that I needed therapy before. No one had ever guided me towards something wholesome and healing. But of course I would. Because Dexter's advice was only based on what he thought he knew about me, what he had seen on the surface, a missing sister that I never dealt with. There was a whole childhood of trauma I was carrying.

'Right. Enjoy your meal.'

'Thank you for bringing it,' I said.

Dexter stood up and walked around to my side of the bed. He leant over and kissed me gently on the forehead. 'You're all right you know, Levine.'

Then he let himself out and closed the door gently behind him.

I sighed, leant my head back against the headboard.

My phone had been going all day and I had not replied to any messages. I could still hear them vibrating through. I flipped my phone over and began looking at them.

There was one from Tammy telling me that everything was okay at my flat. Freckles was fine. And the security had arrived.

Security? Oh no... I called Tammy, and she answered after seven or eight rings.

'Hello?' She sounded breathless and there was loud music playing in the background.

'What's going on?' I asked.

'Rey?'

'Yes, obviously it's me, my name came up on your screen I presume.'

'Yes it did, sorry. I'm just in a bar.'

'I can tell. Thank you for sorting everything out. Tell me, who is the security you're referring to?'

'Oh, it's a woman. She said her name was Em. She left me her number. Do you want me to send it to you?' Tammy shouted.

'No, it's fine. I have it.'

I hung up on Tammy and called Em.

'Hello?' she answered.

'It's Rey. Rey Levine.'

'Hello, Rey.'

'Why are you at my house? And why did you leave so suddenly.'

'I'm sorry I felt I was best out of your hair.'

'So why are you there?' I asked.

'Because I need to help you. That was the deal.'

'What deal?' I asked.

'My deal with my dad.'

'Wallace,' I confirmed.

'Yes. The deal was that I protect you over the next few weeks whilst all this stuff is happening to you, the press, the paparazzi. Rey, it was his dying wish.'

40

NOW

In the end it was two whole days of rest I received before we got back to shooting for a further five days. It was hard. But that was what being an actor entailed for me. It was a job unlike any other and sometimes I had to embrace the difficulty of it. I knew I would be heading back to Camden soon and I had booked myself in with a top therapist to begin what could be a long period of counselling.

I was in the water for very short periods and nothing like I had envisioned in the end. Dexter seemed to think they jigged the script around to accommodate me because that was how much they wanted me for the part. We had natural on-screen chemistry apparently. Dexter didn't highlight that it was far too late to get anyone else in for the role now.

The first day I walked through Camden after I got back, I felt a serene sense of calm. The sun was shining, the summer heat was warming my soul, so when my phone buzzed in my pocket I pulled it out without thinking. When I saw my sister's name in my messages I stopped walking. The air suddenly felt a little cooler as I ducked towards a park bench to read her message.

Hey, it's me. I'm sorry I did that article. I wasn't thinking straight.
I wanted to speak to you. Are you free? I'm in London for one
night.

I thought for a moment before I texted back. It had been many years since I had seen Scarlett. I was dubious. There must be more to it. She knew I was back filming again. Did she need money?

But it didn't matter. Scarlett never reached out to me, no matter how much I had tried to be a good sister to her when we were younger.

Sure. I know a place. 7 p.m.

I texted back and then sent her the directions. Then I booked us a table online and began walking home.

I hadn't even realised I was walking past the leisure centre when I almost collided with a body.

'Sorry,' came the familiar northern accent and I looked up into the eyes of Lloyd.

'Oh,' was all I could muster.

'You're back,' he said. He was wearing a light blue polo shirt, it brought out his eyes. He had a tan.

'I am.' We both moved to the side of the street away from passing pedestrians.

'So, how was it?' he asked.

'Cold. Nicer here.'

'Camden missed you.' He smiled shyly and I felt my stomach flip over.

'I missed it too.' I thought back to our last interaction, how at the time I had thought Lloyd had rejected me. The part I had refused to hear was that he had told me he liked me. That was the part I was remembering now as we talked about the town as though we might be talking about our own feelings. It was hard for me to gauge as this was not my forte: relationships, dealing with my real inner feelings.

'I don't suppose we can tempt you back, we have some great deals on right now.'

I laughed and Lloyd laughed as well.

'I—'

'Look—'

We both went to speak at the same time.

And laughed again.

'I'd like to take you out for a drink, Rey. If you have time.'

I breathed out loudly. 'I have loads of time, actually. I'm not due back on set for a few weeks.'

Lloyd nodded. 'That's good. That's great.' He was beaming. 'Could I ask for your number?'

'It's on your system,' I said.

'I know, but that's not right, I'd like to take it from you.'

I took his phone off him, he opened it with his code and then I typed in my number, saved it under 'Rey' and handed it back to him.

'I have to go, I have a dinner thing, but I'd love to see you this week?'

'Me too. Amazing. I'll call, I'll text.' He laughed. 'It was great seeing you, Rey.'

He grabbed my hand just before he walked away and squeezed it. The sensation that had begun in my stomach sent electric jolts all around my body.

* * *

I arrived at the restaurant before Scarlett. I knew the owners and they had put aside a table in the furthest corner at the back and were on the lookout for any paparazzi.

I saw Scarlett walking past the window before she came in through the door. She was in a long white and purple cotton dress, her hair was long and wild, with layers of coloured beads around her neck. She was approached at the door by a waiting staff, I watched their brief interaction before Scarlett was shown to our table. She let out a long sigh and plonked her bag on floor next to her chair, the noise attracted the attention of a neighbouring table. Her chair scraped loudly as she got herself comfortable.

'It's sweltering out there, how can you cope with London in the summer?' she began, as though we had just spoken last week and not several years ago.

'I guess I'm used to it.' I sipped my iced water and pushed a glass towards her. 'How are you, Scarlett?'

'Frazzled.' Her eyes were darting about, not resting on anything for more than a second, and I noted she had barely looked at me yet.

'Can I get you a drink?' I asked, my calmness was illuminating amongst the chaos of my sister.

'Water's fine,' she said, finally seeming to relax as she sipped from the glass.

'Did you want to order food?'

'Yes, I'm absolutely starving, aren't you? You look skinny? All that filming, did they ask you to get that skinny?'

'No. I guess I might have been under a bit of stress recently.' I stared at Scarlett. Although she had already apologised via text, I needed to hear something from her.

'Well, yes.' She put her glass down and managed to eye me for a few seconds.

'What you did, bringing that story up again after all these years.'

'I know,' Scarlett said. 'It was stupid. A journalist approached me, offered me some money and I didn't even think. I needed the money.'

'You could have come to me? Why didn't you come to me?'

'We don't speak do we, I wasn't about to just pick up the phone and ask you for money.'

'So you thought you'd do something to hurt me instead?'

'I didn't know how much it would hurt you, that's why I got my friend to do the break-in. To deflect from the story, make people feel sorry for you.'

'What?' I put my glass down on the table a little too hard.

Scarlett looked at me.

'They didn't take anything!' she said and for a second we were teenagers again.

'That's not the point! You don't just do one thing to fuck up my life and then do another equally fucked-up thing.'

And then in my mind I thought – *unless you are fucked up*.

'I've known Becca for an age. She did it as a favour.'

'Some favour,' I said. 'Jesus, Scarlett,' I said a little louder this time. 'Why would you think I'd be cool with this?'

''Cos you were always cool with everything. You always held your shit together, no matter what.'

If only she could have seen my life behind the scenes these last few years. I was doing the very opposite of holding my shit together.

'But the thing is...' Scarlett took a long drink of her water. 'There were some things in the article that I said that were true.'

I took a deep breath, not knowing where this was going or if I was ready to hear it.

She dropped her voice to a whisper. 'I know what happened to Franny that night, Rey. That is why I said what I said; I didn't think anyone would believe me, but I'm tired of holding it all in.'

My fingers clenched tighter around my glass and I wished it was wine.

'I know what happened to Franny. I saw them take her and I am almost certain she is still alive.'

41

CORSICA, JUNE 2008

Scarlett watched her sister from the window as she and her cousin Cormac disappeared down the driveway. No one thought she knew much but she had heard them talking about the beach party. She was jealous, she wished that she was old enough to go off and do things like that. But everyone still saw her as the annoying middle child who still needed looking after.

She couldn't sleep so she walked around the house, found a snack in the pantry and went into the craft room to finish a project she had been working on earlier.

With the house being so quiet – there was no sign of Jolie either – Scarlett became quickly absorbed in her task and an hour or two quickly passed.

She heard the front door open and raced to her bedroom where she tucked herself under her sheets. She heard footsteps and the door to her bedroom opened. The usual dread and fear consumed her as she prepared for what might happen. But the door closed as quickly as it had opened. Scarlett let a few minutes pass and then she crept from her bed. She heard whispered voices and so she stood at the top of the stairs and waited until she saw three figures gathered in the hallway.

The smallest was Franny, half asleep and rubbing her eyes, the other two were her Aunt Vanessa and Wallace. The front door opened, and a lady stood there, a woman that Scarlett had never seen before, she was wearing a shawl around her head, even though it was warm outside. Scarlett watched as the lady took Franny in her arms. Vanessa followed her out. Wallace closed the door.

Scarlett ran to the window at the top of the landing where she could see out into the driveway, she could see the woman holding Franny and Vanessa walking alongside her. They disappeared out of sight. Scarlett saw a flash of headlights and the sound of a car driving away. Then she watched as Vanessa walked back up the driveway. This time she was alone.

42

NOW

'That was the last time I saw her.' Scarlett's voice was hollow and airy.

'Wallace and Vanessa?' I hissed.

'Wallace and Vanessa,' she echoed.

'They took her,' I said to myself, trying to work it out, to piece it all together.

'I was terrified to go back to Corsica after Uncle Rob died,' I said.

Scarlett looked at me with intrigue.

I nodded as though egging myself on as I allowed more memories to come back.

'You probably wouldn't remember, but his presence at the villa... he was our safety net, Scarlett. When Uncle Rob was there, our father... he stayed away from us.'

Scarlett looked down at her drink. This was hard for both of us, it was the first time we had ever discussed what had happened to us as children.

'When he died, we didn't go back to that place for years. And then when we did, I was terrified that the only bloody respite we got from our father's filthy wandering hands was gone as well.' It felt uncomfortable yet good at the same time to let some of this out.

'I... thought about it a lot but I never knew if it had happened to you too,' Scarlett said huskily.

'Of course it did! You think you were his first victim? It was me, then you and then it was going to be Franny. I was pretty sure up until that point he had not been anywhere near her. As far as I knew, she was still safe. But without Uncle Rob there on holiday, I knew she wouldn't be.'

'But what was it about Uncle Rob?' Scarlett asked. 'What made Dad stay away?'

'He had been in the police force. His very presence always made our father uncomfortable. You wouldn't have seen it, you were too young at the time. And there was something else, just his very being, the type of person he was, it was as if he cast a huge safety net over all of us. I longed to be there all the time. I never wanted to leave. When he died, I knew that holiday would mean Franny was next.

'But then there was Wallace. And he scared me at first. I wasn't sure what him being there meant. And then one night, Franny had a nightmare.' I looked out of the window as I saw the images playing back at me as though they were happening right now.

'I went to her room, and there was Wallace. It took me a moment to figure it out. When I saw our father outside his room and I realised he was awake too, I realised that Wallace had, I don't know, intercepted or something. That Dad had been on the way to Franny. He was Uncle Rob's replacement. He saved Franny.'

'That night and the final night,' Scarlett said.

'They took her away,' I said to Scarlett. 'To save her?'

Tears were falling down Scarlett's cheeks. And then in the same way the sea had reminded me I had been hiding from the trauma of my childhood, my father's abuse, my mother's neglect, I had managed to recollect our final summer there in Corsica. Our last time together as a family. And I saw myself in Scarlett then, the loss she had endured. It wasn't just mine. Franny was Scarlett's little sister too. We had lost our little sister, but we had also lost ourselves and one another too.

43

NOW

I opened the door to the cafe and there was Em sitting with a tall glass of something pink and frothy in front of her.

'I didn't think this was your sort of place,' I said as I sat down in front of her and eyed her milkshake, 'and that this drink was not your sort of thing.'

'Very much my place. You shouldn't judge someone by how they look. Deep down I'm just a girl like you. I came to do a professional job because that was what I promised to do and when I promise something I do it. Properly.'

I sat down opposite Em, turning up for our meeting as I had promised I would when she texted me to ask. It had been a pretty emotional night last night with Scarlett, so when Em told me she had something for me from Wallace, I figured it was time for the tsunami. Just let all the trauma and feelings spill from me.

'Okay. Well, thank you. And I'm sorry to hear about your father.'

'Thank you.'

'I take it you were close.'

'We were.'

'I don't remember him mentioning you.'

'My father suffered with depression. All through my childhood. Right up until the day he died. But his main goal in life was to help people. When he met Vanessa, she told him everything about her life, about you three girls. About her fears and frustrations. It took everything out of my father to step in and replace your uncle for that holiday in Corsica. I don't feel shocked to hear I was never spoken about. All I know is that we were close. And you knew him for all of what? Two weeks?'

'I'd say less than that.'

'Right.' Em opened the rucksack next to her and pulled out a white envelope. She handed it to me. 'This is from him. It explains why he asked me to come and look out for you.'

She jerked the letter towards me, and I took it.

'You don't need to open it now and you don't need to talk about it with me.'

Em slurped her milkshake, put a note on the table and then stood up.

'I've set up a new video doorbell at your flat, I'll send you the instructions to set it up on your phone.'

I frowned; I was confused. None of what Em was doing made sense.

'No, please wait,' I said and Em slumped back into the chair opposite me.

Then I ripped open the letter.

Dear Rey,

I know this may seem strange that I am writing to you fifteen years after the last time we saw one another, but it is time for you to know the truth. To know what happened that night when Franny went missing. I trust you will keep this information to yourself once you have read this. Dispose of it even. No one should read this, no one should know. But I know you are good at keeping things quiet, at not telling people things even when they are important.

Your Aunt Vanessa was more like you than you ever knew. She and her sister went through the same thing that you did when you were little. She didn't ever know for certain that her brother Digby, your father, would walk the same path as their father, but abuse can run in the family. And your father picked up the same traits as your grandfather. You never met him I know. He died before you and your sisters were born. When I met Vanessa, she confided in me and after some observations, many in fact, and a few drunken half confessions from your mother to your aunt, it became obvious to me that Digby had unfortunately strayed down the same path as his father.

We both knew that you and Scarlett were older now, you were almost a woman and Scarlett was becoming one. It was Franny who we feared for. And who your mother feared for.

It was she who orchestrated the whole thing. Getting your father to leave the villa that night by practically inviting herself to the Braziers' party. She was not a natural party animal. It took your mother all her strength just to get up in the morning sometimes, partying with millionaires was not on her agenda. But she knew your father would be thrilled to attend. He had been wanting to associate himself with the Braziers for years. There was no way he was ever going to miss that party. Vanessa and I returned home first. I was going to distract Jolie whilst Vanessa took Franny from her bed. She trusted Vanessa more than anything. She was the one she would go to without any questions. All the time. It was easy for Vanessa to carry her from her bed and take her to the lady we had organised to look after her for a while.

But when we got back, we discovered Jolie was asleep. We tried to rouse her to see if she might wake, but she did not. So it *was an easier task than we had anticipated. Franny was taken from her bed by your aunt to the lady we had agreed would look after her for a while.*

Your mother had planned to stay in Corsica and wait for Franny. It was supposed to be a few months, a year tops. But we never saw her again. No one has seen or heard from her in fifteen years.

We believe she is still alive. But without any solid proof we cannot say for sure.

Your mother did not blame you for Franny going missing that night, despite how that may have come across to you. She had many frustrations and anger, and the main one was your beauty and the beauty of your two sisters. If you three hadn't been such a sight to behold, she believes your father would never have been interested in you. Removing Franny was the last resort and the only way to break the chain of abuse. We think we saved her in the end.

As you read this letter, I am no longer of this earth. But I wanted to say that I enjoyed the time I spent with you. I always knew you would make something of yourself. I have watched all your movies. I was proud to say that I knew you. Your aunt was also proud. We talked of you often. She was so fond of you. She misses you dearly. But she feels the weight of guilt for what happened to Franny. The plan failed in a way, the lady we left her with obviously got scared and took Franny further away for her own protection. Your Aunt Vanessa knew the lady just about enough to know that she was a good woman. She had cared for many children before Franny but had not been able to have her own children. We think and hope and pray that her life was good.

I am telling you this now so I can go to my grave knowing that I have told you the truth and all I can do is hope that you will forgive me for my sins. I am sorry that you were robbed of a life

*of knowing your sister, but I hope you can understand that as
adults we made the right choice at the time for her own welfare
and safety. Your father was well respected in the world of busi-
ness. He had enough money to put it where he needed to, and
with your mother's depression and drinking, he would have used
that to have you all taken away from her. She never found the
strength to rescue either you or Scarlett, but she did make the
right decision in the end.*

*There is not much else for me to say to you other than I wish
you the best and I hope you live a happy and healthy life.*

*Your aunt misses you dearly and hopes one day you might
find it in your heart to visit her.*

Much love,

Wallace

I folded the letter and placed it front of me. I felt the familiar
sadness engulf me. But this time, the sadness for everyone. For
Vanessa, for Wallace, even my mother, who had been in on it all the
time.

'I need some air.' I stood and Em followed.

'Why did you come?' I asked Em. 'I was so horrible to you,' I
said as we walked together back to my flat.

'I told you, I made a promise to my dad. It doesn't matter what
you said or how you said it to me. My dad liked you a lot. He saw so
much in you. So much potential.'

I thought of all the times Wallace had looked at me, the way he
had been there to scold me after my foolish drunken behaviour at
the beach. He had been looking out for me the whole time.

'What's next for you?' I asked Em.

'I have a job in Ireland.'

'Will you see Vanessa?' I asked.

'Yes,' Em answered.

I felt a pang, a pine for my aunt. I had so many questions. So much I wanted to ask her. But I couldn't do that over the phone.

'You should go and see her. She would like it if you did.'

I knew she was right and I decided to keep the idea in my mind. I had been thinking a lot more about Franny but in a different way, in an alive way. Something that I had not been able to do before. Some of the guilt had gone, I no longer believed I was to blame for what happened to her. I was also coming to terms with it being the best solution. I only hoped that she was safe and well somewhere and, like Wallace had said in his letter to me, she'd had a good life.

First, I needed to complete a film. Then I would consider what I needed to do, to complete the puzzle and lay all the demons and ghosts to rest.

Em saw me back to my flat and we said our goodbyes.

'So I'll mention you'll be in touch then?' Em asked, and was that a smile I detected on her face?

I nodded. 'Yes, tell my aunt she will be hearing from me.'

Em nodded, waved and was gone.

My phone pinged as I put the key in the door. I looked at the message. It was from Dexter.

Hope you're good, Levine. Looking forward to getting back to work with you in a few weeks.

I found that I was smiling. Because I had finally begun to understand what a platonic relationship with a man felt like and it felt good.

I bashed out a reply.

I'm getting there. Looking forward too x

I opened the door and Freckle was crying out a loud meow.

Tammy's cleaners and organisers had done a magnificent job on the house, it was even better than it had been. I was now able to find things I hadn't seen for years.

I picked Freckle up and took her to the sofa. I lay down and closed my eyes. Usually when I tried to rest, my mind was flooded with images of my past, none of them in any kind of order or correlation and never making much sense to me.

But this time, I saw Franny and before long I was asleep and she was in my dream. She was no longer on the horizon, dipping in and out of sight, she was no longer a constant worry in the back of my mind, she was running. She was free. And she was happy.

44

NOW

I waited in the foyer of the leisure centre. It was gone 10 p.m.

'Why did you want to meet here?' I asked Lloyd.

Lloyd went over to the door and locked it from the top downwards.

'Oh, should I be scared?' I asked playfully.

'Nothing to be scared of.'

He took me by the hand and led me through the turnstile and into the changing rooms.

'So, we're swimming? I don't have my costume?'

'You don't need a costume! You know they do nude swimming here once a week? They close off the pool to everyone and only the nudey swimmers are allowed in.'

I laughed loudly it echoed around us.

'I don't believe it.'

'Believe it,' Lloyd said and started walking round the corner to the pool edge. I followed then he turned.

'You forget I've seen all of you already, Rey,' he said casually, as he began removing his clothes. 'Cameras are on the blink. Never did get that technician out this week. Damn it,' he said, now naked. He turned and looked and me and jumped into the pool.

I looked up at the cameras, still a part of my mind wondering if this was a trap, if someone was trying to frame me again, and I would find a naked picture of myself online tomorrow morning. But part of the therapy I had just begun was that I would need to start trusting again. People, situations. Have a little faith.

I still wasn't at hurling myself into water stage, so I whipped off my clothes, sat down on the edge of the pool and slipped in gently.

Lloyd was halfway across the pool. He spun round at looked at me.

'Okay?' he called.

I nodded and waited at the edge, treading water a little.

Lloyd swam back towards me and when he was right next to me, he put his arms around my waist and gently pushed against me so my body was leaning against the side of the pool and he was pressing against me, then he leaned down and pressed his lips against mine.

My body melted at the essence of him, his scent, his taste. Then he was off again, swimming and I could hear his laughter echoing around the empty pool. I pushed my feet against the side of the pool and swam out to the centre to join him.

ACKNOWLEDGEMENTS

Writing a book is a turbulent task. You start off full of creativity and hope for how the novel will turn out and then you must endure a whole roller coaster of emotions to get to the end. I'm always thrilled when I finish a book but then I can't wait to get cracking on the next one. I am mostly alone for the majority of the process and it is only towards the end when I hand the baton over to the team at Boldwood to create their magic that I feel as though I am part of the process. I'm now in my fifth year with Boldwood Books, and *Her Last Summer* is my tenth book. I feel incredibly lucky and honoured to have been able to write professionally for half a decade and to have produced this many books to date.

The usual suspects to thank are, of course, the whole team at Boldwood (which just keeps growing) specifically Emily my editor, Amanda and Nia for all the all the hard work you do to keep us writers in work!

I always like to thank my kids because they are one of the reasons I do this. I love writing, but I keep pushing myself every year to do better for them. So thank you, Savannah, Bodhi and Huxley. You're the best. Thanks especially to my wee man Huxley for coming up with Dexter's surname. You plucked that one out of your brain pretty swiftly son! You star.

Finally, thank you lovely readers for picking up another one of my books, or this may even be your first, either way, thanks for the support.

ABOUT THE AUTHOR

Nina Manning studied psychology and was a restaurant-owner and private chef (including to members of the royal family). She is the founder and co-host of Sniffing The Pages, a book review podcast.

Sign up to Nina Manning's mailing list here for news, competitions and updates on future books.

Visit Nina's website: https://www.ninamanningauthor.com/

Follow Nina on social media:

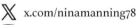 x.com/ninamanning78

instagram.com/ninamanning_author

facebook.com/ninamanningauthor1

bookbub.com/authors/nina-manning

ALSO BY NINA MANNING

Psychological Thrillers

The Daughter In Law

The Guilty Wife

The House Mate

The Bridesmaid

Queen Bee

The Waitress

The Beach House

Her Last Summer

Women's Fiction

The 3am Shattered Mums' Club

The 6pm Frazzled Mums' Club

THE

Murder

LIST

THE MURDER LIST IS A NEWSLETTER DEDICATED TO SPINE-CHILLING FICTION AND GRIPPING PAGE-TURNERS!

SIGN UP TO MAKE SURE YOU'RE ON OUR HIT LIST FOR EXCLUSIVE DEALS, AUTHOR CONTENT, AND COMPETITIONS.

SIGN UP TO OUR NEWSLETTER

BIT.LY/THEMURDERLISTNEWS

Boldwood

Boldwood Books is an award-winning fiction publishing company seeking out the best stories from around the world.

Find out more at www.boldwoodbooks.com

Join our reader community for brilliant books, competitions and offers!

Follow us
@BoldwoodBooks
@TheBoldBookClub

Sign up to our weekly deals newsletter

https://bit.ly/BoldwoodBNewsletter

Printed in Great Britain
by Amazon

42600728R00155